BITTERSWEET SERENITY

SHAWN,
ENJOY IN GOOD
HEALTH & SPIRIT.

LOUETTA
ONEY

BITTERSWEET SERENITY

By

Louetta Oney

1stBooks-rev.03/28/00

About the Book

There's a therapy clinic called SERENITY, yet it's anything but serene. SERENITY is the creation and obsession of Dr. Martin Braddock, a scientist who enlists unorthodox methods for treating phobias. He claims to be the "Guardian of Hope" and the "Messenger of Enlightenment" but in reality, Dr. Braddock has succeeded only in twisting the simple truths of innocent victims, and enforcing emotional terrorism.

Bittersweet Serenity, an 80,000 word mystery, commences with Krystyna Kramer-Braddock, desperate to erase her connection with the maverick scientist she once married. Nevertheless, Krystyna's demands for a divorce have resulted only in a volatile series of denials from her estranged husband. Then, quite unexpectedly, Dr. Martin Braddock is agreeable to the divorce and suspiciously eager to declare a truce. The ill-fated truce sends Krystyna traveling to a remote mountainside where she discovers sadistic experiments choreographed by the scientist, and aided by an evil cohort decidedly cut from the same ebony cloth.

It comes as no surprise that what Dr. Braddock cannot lure, finesse, or manipulate, he'll seize outright using the abundant resources available to him; family money that sometimes also serves as a backbone, and much worse, a soul.

The bottom line, Krystyna has good reason to be afraid.

Regardless, Krystyna Kramer-Braddock is forced to confront the scientist as well as the shadowed side of SERENITY.

* * * * *

Bittersweet Serenity was a winner in the North American Fiction Writers Awards of 1999.

CHAPTER ONE

The weather scarred road sign read: WHISPERING FALLS sixteen miles. Krystyna Kramer-Braddock clenched the wheel of her Jeep Cherokee, the washboard country road spiraling a narrow pathway deeper into the evergreen carpeted mountains. Her dreaded destination was a remote hideaway, and knowing all too well the owner, undoubtedly worthy of coveting the darkest of secrets.

Krystyna had been summoned to this isolated place by a solitary telephone call; a truce had been declared, at long last.

A multitude of misgivings persecuted her thoughts, reminding Krystyna that three long years had passed since she and her estranged husband, Martin Braddock, had seen one another. And now, he had contacted her, ultimately ready and agreeable to the divorce he previously took great pleasure denying her. Suspicious, Krystyna found the age-old issue of faith and trust at stake once again, made more difficult yet because she held neither for this unconventional man; a man she had not loved, but nevertheless married at a vulnerable time.

In the beginning Martin had been incredibly charismatic, Krystyna strongly attracted to the lust-for-life sparkle in his emerald eyes. It was much later when she came to see for herself the smoldering madness lying in wait.

On many an occasion Krystyna held profound reservations for Martin's unorthodox way of thinking and his deceptive scientific projects, and on most of these occasions verbally expressed her skepticism to him. However, Krystyna had learned, early on, when to stand up to Martin, and more importantly, when to back away to a neutral corner.

Over time Martin steadfastly reaffirmed for Krystyna that his professional dedication and lifetime works of wonders would one day bring him immense rewards and recognition from the scientific community, thereby proving Krystyna, and all the other disbelievers, wrong, once again.

And all this, Krystyna thought, from a highly educated man with an impressive degree in behavioral sciences.

Another battered road sign caught her immediate attention: WHISPERING FALLS five miles. Needing to compose her thoughts before going further, Krystyna pulled into a combination cafe and gas station, and seated in a cracked red vinyl booth, she ordered a sandwich.

Martin had known all along that Krystyna psychologically needed a divorce; a divorce he vehemently battled against, erecting emotional roadblocks of guilt for her. No, was his answer, time and again. He didn't have a specific reason because he simply didn't need one. And, he certainly did not need a divorce.

Consequently, Krystyna had become a problem, one Martin regarded as an unpleasant thorn in his side, keeping always in mind that thorns in his side were never tolerated. Extracted slowly perhaps, painfully slow, then buried deep and unceremoniously.

Krystyna, on the other hand, harbored an insatiable need to put to rest her failed marriage, and with a divorce decree signed and sealed, she could then reclaim her life for her very own. A life free of Martin. Free of his evil. The well-being of her future depended on whether Martin had expressed the entire truth to her, or whether he had lured her to him under the guise of another calculated deception. Knowing Martin as she did, Krystyna had come prepared to demand her rights if need be, and she would not back down from Martin this final round.

Peering out the window of the cafe, Krystyna noted a slate blue stationwagon pull before the gas pumps outside. A man in dirty overalls, one red plaid shirtsleeve rolled up, the other sleeve loose and dangling free, leaped quickly from the driver's side and began pumping gas into his vehicle. His eyes darted side to side, and back over his shoulder in the direction he had just traveled.

Paying for her sandwich, Krystyna walked outside, the damp autumn chill evident in the early afternoon half-light. As she crossed over to her Jeep, Krystyna now paid greater attention to the man in the overalls, and to his wife and two young children seated in the back seat amid mountains of wrinkled clothing and household goods.

Throwing the passenger door open, the woman ran to the back of the stationwagon where ropes had been carelessly thrown over and across an untidy heap of personal belongings atop the vehicle. The haphazard mound of chairs, overfilled boxes, and bulging suitcases leaned precariously close to one edge; the woman took no time to set things straight.

Instead, she called out to her husband. "Please hurry."

"I know, I know!" The man responded, his eyes darting about as before.

One of the two children in the back seat began to cry.

"Hush now, we'll be gone soon." The woman called out, her frantic fingers zipping and unzipping her corduroy jacket, the repetitious motions unheeded, buried in a dark oblivion.

The whimpering child asked, "Are we ever coming back to WHISPERING FALLS, mommy?"

Terror froze for an instant on the woman's face. She looked back to her husband as she whispered. "No, never."

As the man in the overalls finished pumping the gas, he stared for a long moment at his wife; a bleak half-smile surfaced. "So much for serenity!" He said, shrugging his shoulders.

Nodding in agreement the woman absentmindedly withdrew some money from her coat pocket and ran inside to pay for the gasoline.

His attention directed elsewhere, the man in the overalls failed to hear Krystyna approach him. The man whirled around to face her, the color drawn from his grimacing features.

"Excuse me. I noticed that you came from the east." Krystyna said. "By any chance are you from WHISPERING FALLS?"

A long moment passed as the man carefully chose his words. "Maybe. Why do you ask?"

"I'm meeting someone there and I wondered if perhaps you knew of him. His name is Dr. Martin Braddock."

The gas cap fell from the man's hand, scrambling brazenly across the rain-splattered blacktop. He stepped and bent over to retrieve it, fingers shaking, his movements erratic. The woman returned then, a puzzled and apprehensive expression touched her brow when she saw Krystyna standing beside her husband. Wordlessly, the woman motioned for them to leave, impatience burning in her eyes. The man hurriedly reclaimed his seat behind the wheel of the stationwagon.

Undaunted, Krystyna questioned the man once more, stepping over to his vehicle. "Do you know of Martin Braddock?"

A muffled squeal slipped innocently from the woman's rigid lips, white knuckled fingers grasping the man's arm, silently pleading.

The man answered Krystyna as he patted his wife's hand to comfort her, his tone somber and bloodless. "Everyone in WHISPERING FALLS knows of Dr. Martin Braddock."

He paused, stealing a glance at his wide-eyed children in the back seat. When he turned back to Krystyna, desperation lined his haggard features. "I'm sorry, but I don't have time to talk. If you're headed up to WHISPERING FALLS I suggest you pass right on through. Better yet, if you want to keep what ever peace you have in your heart, then turn around here and head for home, where ever that might be!"

The slate blue stationwagon quickly pulled away from the gas pumps, and as it did so, Krystyna read a florescent pink bumper sticker plastered against the cracked chrome: SWEET SERENITY - WHISPERING FALLS.

An alarming thought emerged in Krystyna's mind, an intimate insight reminiscent of years gone past. Recaptured in this instant and given new life, this thought became saturated with an old and familiar reality, a cold clear-cut truth never to be forgotten; Martin, are you playing God, again?

CHAPTER TWO

More determined than ever, Krystyna drove the final few miles to her destination. Along the way she noted another car and two pickup trucks overloaded with household goods, traveling down the mountainside as an exodus of terror driven individuals seemingly continued.

Several homes could be seen here and there amid the lush Pacific Northwest countryside. Numerous FOR SALE signs had been staked in once meticulously cared for lawns; lawns now weed ridden and overtaken by neglect. Windows and doorways were boarded up securely with sheets of plywood on a dozen or more homes. Only a few remaining houses appeared to be occupied by their owners; smoke lingered from a chimney, a soft light peered through a laced curtain, yet no one could be seen wandering about, nor tilling the fields, or tending the farm animals.

Krystyna abruptly pulled over to the graveled edge of the road when a large billboard sign caught her eye, and momentarily caught her off guard. Stunned, her foot firmly on the brake, hands gripping the steering wheel fiercely, the florescent pink advertisement forced a flood of apprehensions to the surface.

The words crawled a cold dance across her skin as she read the sign.

EXPECT A MIRACLE AT "SERENITY"
CELEBRATE LIFE IN PERFECT BALANCE!
LEARN TO LOVE YOURSELF AGAIN!
DISCOVER INNER PEACE!
CONTACT DR. MARTIN BRADDOCK
GUARDIAN OF HOPE, MESSENGER OF
ENLIGHTENMENT
212 HILLSIDE DRIVE, WHISPERING FALLS,
WASHINGTON
1-503-332-6163.

There was little to question now, Krystyna thought. Martin was stirring the cauldron pot once again, perhaps with a different recipe of sacrilegious ingredients, yet nevertheless with the same obsession in mind. Only the haunted faces of the innocent victims had undoubtedly been changed; fresh blood, both vulnerable and enticing to the wrong person.

Swearing furiously at Martin under her breath, Krystyna vowed not to get involved. She did not dare allow herself to think beyond that! She had come for her divorce, nothing more, and certainly nothing less!

Following the signs to WHISPERING FALLS, Population 191, Krystyna made a final turn onto Alder Street. A myriad of small businesses was situated side by side, undoubtedly at one time offering the small township a surprising array of retailers and merchandise. There was an old-time atmosphere in the quaint clapboard siding of the Victorian buildings, and antique country elegance now tarnished with the passage of time. Upon closer inspection, elaborate details of woodwork, once painted and maintained regularly, now faded into the background in embarrassment, their skins cracked and peeling.

Most of the small establishments along the main street hailed signs that read: CLOSED FOR BUSINESS or FOR SALE BY OWNER. Krystyna noted that a restaurant and Laundromat seemed deserted, an eerie darkness veiled behind leaded glass windows. A daycare center also appeared long since abandoned. A single car was parked outside the only grocery store.

Two elderly women, bundled up against the cold, shuffled down the lonely street, their feet sending flurries of fallen leaves up into the air, the sound crisp as it cut through the passive stillness.

For a town of nearly two hundred residents, it was more a ghost town.

Spotting a public phonebooth, grateful to have found one, Krystyna dialed the telephone number and held her breath expectantly. When Martin answered on the sixth ring, Krystyna was impatiently twisting a lock of her long chestnut brown hair between her fingers.

"Martin, it's Krystyna."

"I'm glad you've arrived safely, Krystyna. It's good to hear your voice. No trouble finding WHISPERING FALLS?"

Agitated with his small talk, Krystyna attempted to curtain her anger. "No Martin, I had no trouble. But, as you already know, I'm anxious to get this over and done with. When and where can we meet and finalize the details?"

Martin chuckled; his laugh both familiar and strangely comfortable to Krystyna. "That's certainly direct and to the point, as usual, Krystyna. However, I'm afraid I can't get away until six, possibly seven o'clock tonight."

Krystyna's slender fingers wound more tightly in her chestnut curls; long tendrils now nearly completely freed from their braid. "I had hoped we could come to an agreement, Martin, sign the documents this afternoon, and I would be on my way home by dark."

"Some things take time, Krystyna. You should know that by now."

She knew all too well! Hadn't it been Martin who dragged his feet where the divorce was concerned? Taking a deep breath, Krystyna refused to let Martin think he had taken the edge off her courage and resolve.

"All right." She said.

"I might also suggest that you postpone your departure until morning, Krystyna. I'm sure you've just discovered the roads up here can be quite treacherous, even in the best of conditions. You may as well give some thought to staying in one of my guest rooms."

Outraged at Martin's suggestion, Krystyna was nevertheless well aware of his games, both personal and professional, and furthermore, she knew the rules by which he played. Just the same, those very rules scared her to death, simply because there weren't any rules.

"I think it best I stay in town." Krystyna stated. "That is, *if* I decide to spend the night."

"As you wish, my dear Krystyna, but I have a strong feeling you'll change your mind."

She could easily envision his shrewd smile in this moment and it troubled her. Quickly, she ended the conversation after Martin gave her directions to his home. They would dine together at seven o'clock that Tuesday evening. Checking the time, Krystyna saw that it was a quarter till three; several hours remained before she would come face to face with Martin. The very thought did little to warm her spirit.

Indeed, Krystyna certainly did not welcome a long drive down the dark mountainside at night, and with great reluctance, elected to find a room to rent for the one evening. Unfortunately, she couldn't remember seeing a motel or a hotel on her short tour of the town. Hoping to locate one listed in the local telephone book, Krystyna soon found there was no phone book in the booth.

Frustrated, Krystyna pulled the turquoise ribbon from her hair and absentmindedly tossed it into her purse as she left the phonebooth.

Minutes later she entered the only grocery store and toured the meager establishment, silently acknowledging there were no other shoppers meandering down the narrow aisles. Krystyna approached an aproned young woman, a grocery checker, claiming her place at the one cash register and checkout stand at the front of the store.

"Can I help you?" The young grocery checker asked with a sweet smile.

"Yes, I hope you can." Krystyna began. "I'm looking for a motel or a hotel where I can rent a room for tonight."

The young woman's attention was quickly drawn over Krystyna's shoulder; she leaned heavily to one side, squinting her eyes as she sought to make out something in the distance.

Shrugging her shoulders, the young woman turned back to Krystyna. "You won't find anything of that sort around these parts."

"Perhaps a boarding house?" Krystyna asked.

8

"No . . ." The young woman stopped, her eyes again drawn to a distant aisleway.

Turning around, Krystyna wondered what so held the young woman's attention. She saw nothing, no shoppers, no movement, she heard only the faint drone of the refrigeration units.

"I knew it!" The grocery checker shrieked, suddenly pointing with her finger. "I saw him."

"Who?" Krystyna asked, confused. There was nothing there.

"He's slimy, one of the worst yet!" The woman's youthful face contorted into a grimace. She quickly reached for a densely bristled broom, one that had been adapted with an unusually long handle. "Got to get him, no matter what."

The grocery checker gripped the extended handle of the broom as if it were a bayonet and the battlefield lay directly before her. "You stay here."

She instructed Krystyna. "I'll kill him!"

"Who are you going to kill, for God's sake?" Krystyna said, placing a hand to the woman's shoulder. "There's no one there."

Confusion settled over the woman's sour expression. "I have to do it. He's there! I saw him . . . well, part of him. Maybe it was a long hairy leg. Then again, maybe it was just his tail . . ."

Krystyna studied the grocery checker for a long moment. "Why do you have to kill him?"

"It's part of the . . . therapy at SERENITY. The doctor's diagnosis was entomophobia, the intense fear of . . ." She paused, her eyes cast suddenly to the floor. "You don't understand. I don't want to do this awful thing. It takes my all just getting close enough to kill him."

"Look," Krystyna said, folding her arms impatiently before her. "I'm only a stranger here and I don't know you, don't understand the circumstances. But, I will not stand aside and let you kill someone."

The young woman's eyes went wild. "It's not someone, it's some . . . thing!" She grabbed the long handled broom with both hands. "I can't waste time. I've got to kill it, kill the thing that I fear most . . ."

"Show me this . . . thing."

"This way, then." The grocery clerk said, withdrawing an aerosol can from her smock, tucking it under one arm. "They're very sneaky, those little critters. Bite right into the perishables, they do. Nasty creatures . . ."

Krystyna looked at the young frightened woman. "Are you about to do battle with a bug?"

"I've got to kill it, kill the thing that I fear most. That's how to get rid of the fear; face the fear and figuratively eat your enemy."

"I suppose you've been told that?"

"Yes," the young woman answered, stopping suddenly as her eyes caught sight of a black smudge creeping across the cracked linoleum. "I see you, you filthy insect!" A loud thwack sounded as she hammered the broom across the floor.

A series of shivers descended on the frightened young grocery checker as she stooped to examine closely the underside of the broom. "The slimy remnants of the creature!" She looked as though she would faint, her lips curling into a scowl, eyes rolling back, one trembling hand grasping the broom handle.

"Are you all right?" Krystyna asked.

"I will be . . . I need a moment."

"What you need, young lady, is a second opinion!" Krystyna said.

The young grocery checker shrieked again. "I knew it. Another one!" She grasped her broom and was scurrying down the aisleway. "I'll get every one of you, you filthy creatures, and I'll not rest until I do. I'm going to kill the thing I fear most, I'm going to kill . . ."

Stunned at the woman's behavior, Krystyna suddenly felt very drained. The truth, staring her right in the eyes, was a dangerous thing. The truth, Krystyna wondered, was this Martin's truth? She hesitated even to speculate on the answer.

Krystyna moved toward the front doors. Just as she reached them she spotted a bulletin board, quickly scanning the numerous business cards, advertisements for liquidation sales, and the miscellaneous odds and ends posted there. A tattered homemade flyer entitled, ROOMS FOR RENT, caught her attention. Krystyna pulled the flyer from the bulletin board and walked outside under the increasingly dark sky.

No less bewildered by the young grocery checker's strange behavior, Krystyna pushed this from her mind as she drove around the small town, memorizing details, deciphering street names, and finally located the address on the flyer advertising a room for rent.

She got out of the Jeep, before her an immense log house. In the background the shadowed sun touched down on the horizon; a final death-defying effort, only to be lost moments later as darkness reclaimed the sky. A sudden, biting chill crept over Krystyna's slight frame as she climbed the stout planked stairs of the house, the roughly hewn railing prickly beneath her fingertips. She knocked heavily on the timbered door.

An older woman stood in the doorway; her long black hair liberally streaked with gray, her still handsome face lined with time, and brown, even for November. The woman's mahogany eyes peered out at Krystyna with undiluted suspicion. "Yes?"

"Hello, I'm Krystyna Kramer. I'm from Seattle and I've come to WHISPERING FALLS to meet with . . . someone. I understand you have a room for rent?"

"Perhaps." The older woman hesitated, surveying the young woman before her, studying the depths of Krystyna's pearl gray eyes. "How long would you be staying, Ms. Kramer?"

Krystyna relaxed just a bit and gave the woman a sincere smile. "Just for tonight. I plan on leaving first thing tomorrow morning."

"Why don't you come in from the cold and we'll have a cup of coffee and talk the matter over?" The woman offered.

Stepping across the threshold, Krystyna was not quite prepared for the simple yet exquisite beauty of the log structure. An immense stone fireplace provided a golden glow against the

11

backdrop of a staggering display of posts and beams rising high above to the vaulted ceilings. Overstuffed chairs in a rainbow of colors were arranged before the hearth. Warm blanket throws were tossed over a pair of upholstered loveseats, and richly woven area rugs covered most of the polished oak floors.

"Please have a seat. I'll pour us some coffee." The older woman stated as she retreated, moments later returning with two china cups.

"Black?"

"Yes, that's fine. Thank you."

Claiming a seat nearest Krystyna, the woman introduced herself. "My name is Orenda Reed. There hasn't been an occasion for anyone to rent a room from me in quite some time. We don't have many tourists in these parts any more. The isolation, I would guess." She paused, sipping her coffee. "However, you're welcome to stay the night, if you wish."

"That's very kind of you."

"Many years ago when my husband, Evan, was still alive, we rented out all four of the cabins. Hunters and fishermen would reserve the cabins months in advance. The hot springs at the far edge of our land were favorites for the newlyweds. But then . . . WHISPERING FALLS was much different in those days."

Krystyna leaned forward. "I couldn't help but notice many of the residents have moved away. Perhaps the economy?"

Orenda Reed laughed, a strong hint of sarcasm in her tone. "No, I'm afraid that has nothing to do with it. Our town prospered from the early days on. Life was good here. Neighbors were more than friends, more like family. Everyone pulled together. Everyone cared. It's just not the same now."

"Can you tell me why?" Krystyna asked, not entirely certain she wanted to hear the answer.

Orenda's mahogany brown eyes sparkled in the firelight. "My grandmother was a Native American medicine woman, and it has been said that I inherited much of her wisdom. It does me little good now! I have no answer for your question. Something is wrong here, very wrong; I can only say that much."

Reaching out to pat Krystyna's hand gently, Orenda smiled. "Don't let it worry you, Ms. Kramer. You'll be long gone from here by the time anyone has figured it out."

"I expect so." Krystyna said.

Orenda called out to someone in another part of the house. "Samuel, come here if you would."

A moment later a young man of about twenty appeared at Orenda's side. He wore faded blue jeans and a green sweater, and it wasn't until Krystyna gazed into his eyes that she instantly recognized that look . . . that terror, that same haunting desperation she associated with Martin's patients.

"Ms. Kramer is spending the night with us, Samuel. I want you to straighten up the first cabin, bring in a good supply of wood, and start a warm fire for her."

Samuel's glassy eyes widened, his fingers busy pulling at a loose thread of yarn at the collar of his green sweater. "I don't have to . . . you know . . ."

"Don't fret so, Samuel. You'll be fine." Orenda said, and rising from her chair she spoke again to the young frightened man. "Here, I'll help you down the stairs."

Krystyna watched from a nearby window as the two walked out the front door, the young man's eyes screwed tightly closed, one arm wrapped firmly around Orenda's waist, his other arm flung across his eyes, blinding his sight with double certainty. Orenda assisted the young man down the front stairs, a single step at a time, pausing on each step, whispering words of comfort in his ear, providing him reassurance that he would not fall, he would not come crashing down; the earth would not open up and swallow him. She wouldn't let it.

At the bottom of the steps, Samuel hugged Orenda closely to him, a smile of deep appreciation on his pale, thin, quivering lips.

Recognizing the awkwardness of the moment, Krystyna remained silent as Orenda rejoined her.

Sipping the last of her coffee, Orenda tried to explain. "That was Samuel, my youngest son. He has an affliction, I guess you might call it. He's desperately afraid of heights. A simple flight of stairs will cause him to lose his sense of balance. You might imagine he's taken a great many nasty spills as a result. Samuel is not backward as some may expect. No, not that, by any means. He's been . . . hurt, deeply hurt in a small corner of his mind. The poor boy has horrifying nightmares; he falls down the face of a cliff, he spins over the railing of a bridge, or tumbles head first off the roof of a skyscraper, even though he's never seen a skyscraper, much less been in one."

"I wouldn't think that possible, in that event." Krystyna stated, an alarm sounding off in the deep recesses of her mind.

Orenda stared at Krystyna for a long serious moment. "Neither would I."

"Have you taken Samuel to a doctor?" Krystyna faltered. "Please, forgive me. I certainly don't mean to pry."

"I know. I can see the goodness in your heart." Orenda smiled once again. "Another cup of coffee, Krystyna?"

"Yes, please."

As the conversation took a decided turn to other topics, Krystyna soon realized her question had not been answered; it had been clearly evaded. That alone made Krystyna wonder all the more.

Some time later Orenda escorted Krystyna to the rear of the property where four small log cabins were situated near a thicket of fir and pine trees. The first cabin's door had been left slightly ajar, and when they entered Samuel was tending a blazing fire in the fireplace.

He stood up abruptly as a capricious grin crept over his boyish features. "Welcome to the Reed Ranch."

"Thank you for the welcome and the warm fire, Samuel." Krystyna extended her hand. "I'm Krystyna Kramer."

Nodding, Samuel looked pleased with himself. Orenda stepped over to him. "Shall we go back to the house now?"

Samuel nodded once again.

Reaching for her purse, Krystyna opened her wallet. "I'm happy to pay you what ever the charge."

"We'll discuss that over breakfast." Orenda said. "Just come over to the house when you're hungry."

"I will, thank you again. I'll be leaving for a few hours to meet my . . . friend for dinner, so don't be alarmed if you hear my car pull in later."

Orenda Reed studied Krystyna carefully. "Go with caution on these dark country roads. Goodnight."

"Goodnight to you both." Krystyna said, closing the door of the cabin.

She sat for a few minutes before the fire thinking, contemplating, trying to unravel some of the bizarre behaviors she witnessed in this town, and at the same time attempting, without success, to clear her mind for the all important dinner engagement with Martin.

Later, after changing into the only extra set of clothes she'd brought with her, Krystyna was soon back on the road, following the directions Martin had given her earlier on the phone. As the Reed Ranch was on the southern most reaches of WHISPERING FALLS, Krystyna found it necessary to return to Alder Street, passing through the business section, what there was of it, and finally onto another less traveled road taking her further east.

She had not scouted this area before, and it was by far the most remote, and neatly sectioned off by vast acres of emerald, forested land.

Certain she was going in the right direction, Krystyna's headlights flashed on another florescent pink sign: SERENITY . . . NEXT LEFT.

Krystyna swore again under her breath, the sign evoking a natural outburst.

This was the place, she decided, and after cresting a small incline, Krystyna had her first look at SERENITY.

Floodlights scanned the perimeter of the property and afforded Krystyna a good view of the expansive white stone building. The structure was encircled by a tall, high-tech security fence and there was an impressive manned security gate at the entrance. Sophisticated outdoor lighting served to enhance the immaculate landscaping, which included a front courtyard, ornate water fountain, and meticulously maintained flowerbeds. Elaborate details of architecture were to be found in the multi-faceted angles of the roofline. Lights shone brightly in contrast against the ebony night sky from dozens and dozens of intricately designed windows.

Adjacent to the structure a large asphalt parking lot was filled with fifteen or twenty cars, and even at this time of evening, the bustle of activity inside the building was very apparent.

SERENITY stood stately against the country skyline; incongruous, an out-of-place work of art, a showpiece better placed in the heart of any large city.

Why here, of all places? Krystyna wondered.

Continuing another mile along the graveled drive, a second white structure had been built, nearly as large as SERENITY, also inconsistent with its surroundings, and unmistakably Martin's home. Krystyna drove nearer the house and parked the Jeep Cherokee a short distance from the four-car garage, sitting for a long quiet moment, staring at the house, thinking.

Due to his wealthy upbringing, Martin was accustomed to living with the finer things in life; antiques from every corner of the world, an impressive collection of rare art pieces, luxurious and elaborate furnishings done in rich velvets, silks and brocades.

Nevertheless, Krystyna would never have thought Martin capable of creating this white monstrosity of a house. Clearly, art deco dominated the decorating theme, just as with SERENITY, and again she remarked at how very inappropriate and unsuitable it was here amid the plain and simple creature comforts of country life. Apparently, Martin had again taken nonconformity a bit too far!

Krystyna rang the elaborate doorbell; a chime sounded in the distance, a repugnant imitation of a once familiar tune.

Martin opened the door, emerald eyes glistening, an enormous smile on his handsome face. He reached out and took Krystyna's hand, gently guiding her into the foyer. Their touch was both familiar and well seasoned to him, instantly exorcising memories he would have thought long dead.

"Krystyna, how wonderful to see you again."

"And you, Martin." Krystyna said softly, trying to read what ever it was that just danced in his eyes.

Martin led Krystyna down a flight of marbled steps to a sunken living room decorated with an ocean of white leather furniture, glass tables and chromed light fixtures; all ultramodern and sleek styled. Pouring two glasses of red wine from the mirrored bar, Martin politely insisted Krystyna sit with him and talk before they dined.

Feeling she had little choice in the matter, Krystyna agreed, only after she came to realize Martin was just as nervous about their meeting as she was herself. He twirled the one end of his blonde well-trimmed mustache, his only nervous habit, as he explained more about the designing and construction of the house and of SERENITY. Clearly, he was very proud of his efforts.

However, Krystyna refused to compliment him where she believed no compliment was due. Martin's taste had certainly undergone a dramatic change these past few years. Without asking, Krystyna knew that her favorite pieces, Martin's exquisite trio of European leather folding screens, would not be found here in this modernistic decor. Also missing were the pair of teal velvet overstuffed chairs, perfect for sinking down into and reading a good book in total sublime comfort. Gone, all gone.

In the midst of their small talk Martin reached for Krystyna's hand, a stab of remorse riveting through him when he least expected it. "You've changed little, Krystyna. Your eyes are still the same delicate shade of smoky gray."

Withdrawing her hand, Krystyna gave Martin a disapproving smile, her words frost-covered. "I appreciate the compliment Martin, but I've come here to discuss other things, as you well know."

"Ah yes, the divorce."

Footsteps resounded in the distance, drawing closer, descending the marbled steps, halting at the entrance to the living room.

Martin turned toward the sound, twisting one end of his mustache. "We were just discussing the divorce. It's definitely time you joined us."

Krystyna turned around. A tall attractive blonde woman dressed in white flowing silk slowly approached her.

"Let me introduce myself." The woman said to Krystyna. "I'm Stephanie Roberts. The next and *last* Mrs. Martin Braddock."

CHAPTER THREE

Krystyna made a valiant effort to cover her welcomed surprise. "I'm very glad to meet you, Stephanie."

Glancing back to Martin, she added. "I suppose congratulations are in order."

"Yes, I would expect they are." Martin answered, reluctance in his voice. "I'm sorry that you had to find out this way, Krystyna, but Stephanie and I have set a date for our wedding to take place just as soon as the divorce is final."

A profound sense of relief flooded over Krystyna. Her divorce would no longer be an unattainable goal, but rather a long awaited reality. Thank heavens, Krystyna thought, my life and association with the maverick scientist will truly come to an end, and soon!

"I'm sincerely pleased for you both." Krystyna found herself saying, her thoughts spinning wildly.

"I do hope you mean that." Stephanie stated firmly. "I would not take kindly to any further delay in our plans. Quite naturally, Martin has explained about your forestalling the divorce time and again . . ."

"Wait a minute. That's not true." Hearing this ludicrous accusation, Krystyna's anger flared.

"Let's forget all about that and put it behind us." Martin suggested, offering Krystyna a smug yet intimidating smile. "Don't you think that's best for everyone concerned?"

Krystyna met his piercing stare with equal force. "Maybe you are right, Martin. I'll promise not to play dirty, but only if you don't. How's that for compromises?"

"That will have to do." Martin said with some hesitancy.

Stephanie turned to Martin, tracing the line of his jaw with a slender finger, cupping his chin in her hand; a portrait of unspoken intimacy. "I'll have that glass of wine now."

Krystyna watched Stephanie as she gracefully seated herself in a white leather chair, an enormous diamond engagement ring glittering in the soft light. A contrived smile lined Stephanie's full red lips as she waited patiently for Martin to leave the room.

Moments later, Stephanie began. "There are a few things I thought I would bring to your attention. There's no need for pretense here. The battle is over. I wanted to assure you Martin is quite ready to give you an equitable share of his holdings, both here in the States and abroad. I can further assure you that you will lack for nothing the rest of your natural life."

"I'm sorry, Stephanie, but you've incorrectly assumed that I'm holding out for a larger share of Martin's money. You've got it all wrong. I'm not the least bit interest in him or his vast fortune!"

In the breadth of the stale silence that followed, Stephanie thought it prudent, nevertheless, to establish her own position, and to remove any lingering questions remaining in Krystyna's thoughts.

"All right, Krystyna. That subject having been brought out into the open, I've a few things to share with you. You must realize that Martin has a new life now, and other than his work, I am the single most important part in that life. Martin and I are a team; I'm his computer wizard and his right arm. We've worked together for three years, side by side, long exhausting hours of research, even longer weary months of trials and errors. But, we've accomplished a great many things together and it's Martin who credits me with his success."

Pausing, Stephanie leaned toward Krystyna to place greater emphasis on her words; silken words smothered in venom. "You see, Krystyna, unlike you, I believe in Martin, I believe in what he believes. I, too, can see an exciting and prosperous future through his eyes. And there is no place for you in Martin's future."

"Believe me, I'm praying for that day." Undaunted, Krystyna offered Stephanie a shrewd smile of her own. "He's all yours, Stephanie. I only hope you see the man behind the mask before . . ."

"Before what, Krystyna? I've seen who he really is."

"Perhaps you would do well to remember that I know everything there is to know about Martin."

"But your information is a bit out of date, wouldn't you say?"

"Not necessarily, Stephanie. The basics are all there. Some things never change. For instance, I know when to hit Martin and precisely where it would do the most damage."

"If that were the case, Krystyna, you would have done so before now."

"Maybe not. I haven't felt pushed into a corner until today."

Gathering her thoughts, Stephanie rose to a standing position. There was a hint of something far more sinister and menacing when she stared into Krystyna's eyes once again. "Just remember, I'm the glue that holds Martin together, and these days . . ."

At that moment Martin chose to return, a devil-may-care smile flickering across his handsome face.

Although hungry earlier in the evening, Krystyna now toyed with the food on her plate as she listened to Stephanie boast of Martin's so-called scientific successes, one after bloody one. For the most part, the techniques Stephanie led Krystyna to believe were innovative and breakthrough discoveries, were little more than rehashes of Martin's earliest failures.

Each and every failure had undoubtedly cost someone somewhere a very dear price; a slice of their figurative heat, a piece of a golden memory, a portion of their revered childhood, or worse . . . a slender thread of a chance for a stable future of any kind. All in the name of scientific progress, all in the name of doing something wonderfully good for mankind, all in the name of Martin wants the golden ring all for himself; the honorary awards, the recognition by his peers, the prestige.

And Krystyna knew that Martin would let nothing stand in his way, absolutely nothing.

In the early days, Martin had been overconfident when he combined electromagnetic therapy with traditional hypnosis for the treatment of those poor unfortunates experiencing multiple personality disorders and schizophrenia. Eleven patients and nearly two years later, his theories failed miserably and with disastrous results. Two of these patients still lived a lonely existence in padded cells, locked away in asylums for the remainder of their days, incoherent, unreachable. And the others . . . the other nine men and women had committed suicide. Krystyna cringed inwardly at the dark memory of this event.

Martin had exhausted another two years on developing and experimenting with an avant-garde synthetic drug; a drug he dogmatically claimed would arrest all addictions of the human psyche. Only three volunteers died this time.

Experiment after experiment, small successes of little importance interwoven among the devastating out-and-out failures; too many for Krystyna to forget, or forgive.

The topic of discussion, however, skirted around Martin's latest novel idea, SERENITY. This caused great concern for Krystyna. Solely because Martin had chosen an isolated location for his most recent endeavor, lead Krystyna to believe that he had something very serious and secretive to hide. It seemed reasonable for her to assume he had gone undercover to wreak havoc once again, without drawing undue attention to himself, and undoubtedly without the approval, or knowledge, of the BOES, the Board of Ethic Sciences.

With his arrogant and defiant attitude, Martin would never have approached the board members for their consent, cooperation, and professional support. And more importantly, with Martin's monetary resources, he need never beg for financial backing to fund his numerous experiments, old and new alike.

Martin had the world in his hands, and Krystyna shivered at the mere thought.

Martin seemingly read Krystyna's mind. "I'm surprised at you, Krystyna. You've been here nearly two hours and you've not asked about SERENITY."

"Perhaps, you'd rather I didn't know." Krystyna answered thoughtfully.

Martin leaned back in his chair, assessing Krystyna's comment. "Quite the opposite. I'd love to share my crowning accomplishment with you and . . ."

The ringing of the telephone interrupted Martin's sentence. He reached to a nearby buffet for the phone and carried on a short conversation with the caller.

Martin's expression became troubled and uneasy as he turned back to Krystyna. "That was Michael Overby, my attorney here in WHISPERING FALLS. He's drawn up the necessary papers for our divorce. He was due in another half-hour to oversee and witness the signing of the divorce documents. But, I'm afraid he's been unexpectedly called out of town on personal business."

Not another delay, Krystyna thought. Will this nightmare never end? "Let's sign the papers anyway and you can have your attorney look them over tomorrow after I've gone."

"I'm afraid I can't do that, Krystyna. Michael Overby has the divorce papers with him, and he'll not be returning quite so soon."

Stephanie leaned forward, her own eagerness and impatience for the deed to be done boldly displayed in the coolness of her blue eyes and her rigid posture.

Krystyna tried very hard not to scream her words. "Just *when* is your attorney returning to WHISPERING FALLS?"

Martin was slow to answer. "Monday morning."

The words echoed over and over in Krystyna's mind; Monday morning, Monday morning. And this was only Tuesday. Monday was a full six days away!

"I can't possibly stay until then, Martin."

"You must." Stephanie said, her tone emphatic. "The divorce papers must be signed on Monday."

"Stephanie," Krystyna snapped back, "I'll not have you dictate to me what I should, or shouldn't do!"

Martin was quick to intervene. "As we each have something to gain from this, I'm sure we can all get along reasonably well until Monday. Again, I offer the guest room to you, Krystyna."

Raising an eyebrow, Stephanie pouted from behind her wineglass.

"That won't be necessary." Krystyna said angrily. She was nothing less than furious with the postponement. "I've made arrangements in town."

"Perhaps it's best this way, Krystyna." Martin said. "We'll have more time to discuss the details of the divorce. And, I'll also have a chance to introduce you to SERENITY."

Martin quickly proposed a toast. "To Monday."

He was the only one smiling.

CHAPTER FOUR

Krystyna noted it was after nine o'clock by the time she left Martin's house. She was quite shaken with the delay in her plans, and desperately needed some time alone to think it over. As she drove past SERENITY five or six cars were still in the parking lot; lights shone from a dozen or more windows. Business must be good! Krystyna thought bitterly.

Minutes later she found the Reed Ranch without difficulty and quietly let herself into the first cabin; a welcoming oasis in the midst of an emotional wasteland. Samuel had evidently tended the fire once again as it glowed, radiating warmth and light. Krystyna disrobed, wrapping a warm quilt around her body, snuggling into an old rocking chair before the hearth.

She let her thoughts take their own course, weaving and winding as they may. Beyond fatigue, Krystyna was emotionally exhausted, a strong sense of disappointment heavy on her shoulders. She had waited three long years for her divorce, certainly a few more days should be easy by comparison, difficult as they could easily prove to be.

However, Krystyna would never trust Martin's actions or his words. Had he lied to her again? Perhaps not this time around, Krystyna thought. Apparently, he needed the divorce just as Krystyna needed it; he had a new wife waiting in the wings. Same need, different reasons.

Krystyna fell asleep before the warmth of the fire.

When Krystyna awoke she was ravenous. She quickly showered and dressed, braided her long chestnut brown hair, and knocked on Orenda Reed's door. "Good morning, Orenda."

"Good morning. Come in, I've just made an enormous stack of pancakes." Orenda said, gesturing for Krystyna to follow her into the kitchen.

A carafe of coffee sat on a round oak table placed beneath a windowed wall in a cozy alcove. The large kitchen was surrounded with authentic butcher-block countertops and numerous oak cupboards. In spite of the modern appliances to be seen scattered about the room, Orenda preferred preparing her meals on the antique wood-cooking stove.

A platter of plate-sized pancakes was set on the table. "I hope you're hungry, Krystyna."

Pouring coffee for both of them, Krystyna smiled. "That I am."

Orenda took off her apron and sat down at the table. "Did you sleep well?"

"Yes, as a matter of fact, I did. Surprisingly well, considering I fell asleep in the rocker."

"You must have been exhausted after your dinner last night."

Krystyna immediately stiffened in the chair. "Yes. Orenda, I found out last night that I need to stay here in WHISPERING FALLS until Monday. Would you consider renting the cabin to me for that time?"

"I don't have a problem with that." Orenda studied Krystyna, instinctively sensing her misgivings. "However, you don't seem very happy about staying the few extra days."

Pouring maple syrup on her pancakes, Krystyna sought to find the right words. "There has been an unexpected but unavoidable delay in my plans."

"Business?"

"Personal business that needs to be finalized, once and for all."

Orenda smiled knowingly. "Business of that sort usually means a man is involved."

"Yes, a man. I don't know quite how to explain."

"That's all right, Krystyna, I understand. If you feel the need to talk to someone, I'll be here."

"Thanks, Orenda." Krystyna concentrated on the pancakes in front of her. "I thought I would go into town today. I'll be needing some more clothes and a few necessities."

"A few merchants are still open for business. Chances are you may find what you need. Try to keep yourself busy, Krystyna, and maybe the days will go by more quickly for you."

"That's just what I'll do. Do you need anything from town?"

"Indeed, I do." Orenda said. "I've ordered a book and it should be in by now. Would you mind picking it up for me?"

"I'd be glad to. Where at?"

"There's a bookstore called BOOKENDS ETC.; it's on Alder Street. You can't miss it."

"I'll browse around while I'm there. Orenda, you're very welcome to come along with me, if you like."

"Thank you, but no. I don't like going into town much these days. Much too depressing. I avoid it if I can."

Pouring a second cup of coffee, Krystyna relaxed after her breakfast, chatting comfortably with Orenda, fast becoming good friends, trying to make the day a good one.

Driving along Alder Street Krystyna soon realized she would have no difficulty finding a parking place; only two other cars were parked out front of the numerous shops. Her first stop was a clothing store for women, the exterior of the building clean and well kept, in solid contrast to the deterioration only steps away.

The owner, Virginia Pedersen, introduced herself to Krystyna the moment she walked through the doors. The middle-aged woman was at Krystyna's heels the entire time, following behind Krystyna as she straightened shelves, realigned hangers, buttoned buttons, zipping zippers. Virginia Pedersen wore white gloves as she worked, and at the first sign of dust or grime smears on her white gloves, a fresh clean pair replaced the soiled ones instantly.

While trying on several outfits, Krystyna remarked to herself that the woman must be a clean-freak, obsessed with dust and dirt.

Krystyna finally purchased a pair of jeans, two sweaters, a pair of woolen slacks, slippers and nightgown. All the while, Virginia incessantly dabbed her cleaning rags into a bottle of disinfectant and wiped up behind Krystyna each and every spot Krystyna would happen to touch or brush up against. She vacuumed the carpeting where Krystyna had walked. She wiped down the mirrors in the changing rooms Krystyna had used.

Virginia offered no excuses for her compulsive behavior, unable and unwilling to explain her preoccupation with cleanliness. To Virginia it remained much like a fragmented picture, a twisted picture that she had unerringly become, and something she failed to understand herself.

Virginia merely resumed smiling happily as she dusted and cleaned, disinfectant in white gloved hands, vacuumed some more, wiped the mirror down again for good measure, and came back to realigning the hangers on the racks for the umpteenth time.

As Krystyna paid for her items with a credit card, she noticed a large sign on the wall: NO CASH ACCEPTED - CURRENCY CARRIES GERMS.

Virginia Pedersen fastidiously folded and wrapped Krystyna's purchases, offering an apology of sorts. "You must excuse the mess today. I've only had a few hours to clean. Ordinarily, my shop would be spotless, but I've been so busy straightening up my house . . . surely you understand?"

"Yes, of course." Krystyna said hesitantly.

Virginia Pedersen smiled warmly. "And do come in again. I appreciate the fact that you chose to use your credit card. I hate to handle money! The germs and the dirt, you know!"

Krystyna reached for the door and Virginia Pedersen was ready with her rags of disinfectant, wiping away any fingerprints even before Krystyna was out of sight.

Locking her packages in the Jeep, Krystyna spotted BOOKENDS ETC., and next to the bookstore was FAIRCHILD'S HARDWARE. She decided to browse through the hardware store first and as she drew closer, Krystyna read a sign posted on the front door: WE NEVER CLOSE. A small bell chimed as she crossed the threshold of the establishment.

Apparently the only shopper, Krystyna wandered down several aisles before a young man breathlessly came out of a back room carrying a tall stack of boxes.

Peeking around the boxes, the young man smiled. "Good day to you. William Fairchild Junior here." He said, placing the boxes aside. "What can I help you with?"

"Nothing actually. I just wanted to browse a bit."

"Browse all you want. Come back anytime. We stay open all day, and all night. Seven days a week, fifty-two weeks a year. Open all holidays, Thanksgiving and Christmas alike. Wouldn't want to miss any customers."

"Do you really have a need to stay open such hours?" Krystyna had to ask out of curiosity.

"Well . . . yes. Have to be prepared, my father always said. He's William Fairchild Senior. Give the customers the time to browse, give the customers the time to buy. That's our motto. Wouldn't want to be closed if someone should be needing something important. No, I sure wouldn't want to miss any customers."

"I see." Krystyna whispered as she skirted out the door, bewildered and more than just a little bit frightened at witnessing yet another person with a bizarre behavioral trait. Was the entire town afflicted? Krystyna wondered.

Taking a moment to compose herself, Krystyna stood outside BOOKENDS ETC. peering through the windows, but not seeing, only feeling an enormous black cloud of apprehension; the weight of the cloud beginning to drag her down. She dared not form her suspicions into words, not just yet. She'd let them sit and smolder a while longer.

Upon entering BOOKENDS ETC., Krystyna was pleased to find one other shopper scanning the multitude of bookshelves. Somehow this was comforting. She was also excited to find a tremendous selection of books of all kinds, as well as a fantastic collection of bookends and bookmarkers. Krystyna lost track of time as she flipped open one book and then another, reading several passages, becoming engrossed in the literature that she so loved. The other shopper left the bookstore without Krystyna noticing.

Suddenly an abrasive sound grated across the hardwood floors, the sound halting directly behind Krystyna. "Excuse me."

Krystyna flinched, turning around quickly. "Oh, you frightened me."

"I'm sorry." The older gentleman said. "Most folks can hear me coming a mile away with this bum leg of mine." He rapped his knuckles along his right thigh; a wooden leg.

"I'm Garrett Chambers. I own BOOKENDS ETC. Anything in particular you're looking for?"

Very wary now of anyone, Krystyna eyed Garrett Chambers with great scrutiny. "Not for myself but I am here to pick up a book on order for Orenda Reed."

Garrett Chambers nodded his head, his curly gray hair framing his friendly face. "Yes, Orenda's book arrived yesterday."

The gentleman walked back to his large desk, the right leg held stiff, dragging somewhat across the floor. Rummaging through a pile of books he withdrew one and handed it to Krystyna. His soft blue eyes questioned Krystyna in silence.

Feeling it necessary to explain, Krystyna continued. "I'm renting one of the cabins at the Reed Ranch for a few days, and as I understand, Orenda doesn't come to town much; I felt it was the least I could do."

"That's very kind of you, Miss . . ."

"Krystyna Kramer."

"You're not from around here, are you?" Garrett Chambers asked, already knowing the answer.

"No, actually I live near Seattle."

Claiming the oak chair behind the desk, Garrett Chambers looked quite relieved to be off his feet. "You'll have to excuse me. I still have pain in this old leg of mine. Of course, the leg has been gone since the second World War, but the pain is still there."

He eyed her closely. "Phantom pain they call it."

Krystyna thought she should pay for the book and leave as soon as possible. Conversation with Mr. Chambers was beginning to sound much like the rest of the town. "How much for the book, Mr. Chambers, and I'll be on my way."

"Not to worry. Orenda has an account here. I'll bill her."

"All right then. Thank you very much." Krystyna turned to leave.

"Miss Kramer, I wonder if I might have a few moments of your time?"

Alarmed, Krystyna felt a sliver of panic cut into her. Before she could say no, Garrett Chambers started talking.

"I realize, Ms. Kramer, that I may appear nearly as odd as the rest of the folks, but I assure you that I'm just the old me, nothing bizarre, nothing obsessive or compulsive about me, except maybe that I like to read a lot of books."

"However," he continued, "you take young William Fairchild next door. He's another story. His young wife complained to no end about William's lazy ways. He'd shuffle into work, slouch around for a couple of hours, and call it a day. Old man Fairchild paid him well even if he didn't lift a finger. But, young Fairchild's wife didn't respect a man who didn't earn his wages. So, William Fairchild got help! He's now a human dynamo, a workaholic, a ball of fire every waking moment of his tortured life. His young wife ended up leaving him because she never saw him anymore."

"Why are you telling me all this?"

Garrett Chambers smiled gently as he ignored Krystyna's question. "Virginia Pedersen, the owner of the women's clothing store across the street, was once the worst housekeeper you could ever imagine. Her bridge club refused to play cards at her home for all the clutter and the dirt. Virginia dressed like a slob, lived like a slob and was even married to a slob. So, Virginia Pedersen got help! Now, she's a perfectionist, a stickler for cleanliness, a nitpicker if I ever saw one."

Cautiously, Krystyna questioned Mr. Chambers. "I've just met both of them. How could you know that?"

31

"I admit I was watching you from the windows."

Leaning toward Krystyna, Garrett's soft blue eyes were clear and deadly serious. "There are many more to tell of."

Krystyna took a step toward Garrett Chambers. "What of the young woman at the grocery store?"

"Annalee Smith. Sweet thing, but never could control her fear of insects. So, Annalee Smith got help! She seemed to overcome her fear of critters . . . for a while. Then, well, she became obsessed with bugs, compelled to kill as many as she could."

"Why are you telling me all this?" Krystyna asked for the second time.

"Straight and simple, you're a friend of Orenda Reed; any friend of hers is a friend of mine. I believe in forewarning . . ."

The front door of the shop opened, footsteps announced another shopper. "I'll be right with you," Garrett Chambers called out to the shopper.

Rising from his chair, Garrett walked to the far side of the shop, his right leg dragging stiffly, and pulled a single book from a shelf, handing it over to Krystyna. "Interesting title; my gift to you. Perhaps we'll talk again, and please, by all means, say hello to Orenda for me."

Garrett Chambers absentmindedly massaged his wooden leg as he slowly approached the shopper.

Both books under her arm, Krystyna left the bookstore and went to the Jeep. Once seated she looked at the cover of the book Garrett Chambers had given her. It was entitled: THE ILLUSION OF SERENITY.

CHAPTER FIVE

A wave of fear swept over Krystyna as she held the book, THE ILLUSION OF SERENITY, in her trembling hands. Yes, she thought, Garrett Chamber's suspicions paralleled her own.

Indeed, a morbid mockery of peace and serenity had infiltrated WHISPERING FALLS, leading its people down a garden path, when in reality, a bloodstained detour down a darkened alleyway carried more truth.

If Krystyna allowed herself to think about all these things she knew she would be eternally sorry. It all pointed to Martin. It smelled of him. It had to be his creation, and so what did that make these people, Krystyna wondered? His puppets? His monsters?

And, what did that make Martin? She trembled at the implication.

Scanning the contents of the book, Krystyna noted it was written by a colleague who had once been good friends with Martin. The scientific journal clearly defined the criteria of approved standards and codes of ethics used by governed experimental institutions. The author listed nationwide research laboratories that upheld high quality programs, both proven successful and reliably trustworthy. The author gave multiple suggestions for treatment, and multiple names of qualified physicians who treated their patients in a controlled, safe environment.

The entire book was a warning on how *not* to become a human guinea pig.

Closing the book, Krystyna sighed wearily. Was it possible, she wondered, that a large majority of the residents from WHISPERING FALLS had fallen for Martin's extravagant promises, optimistically placing their confidence and trust in him and his treatment of phobias? She was well aware of how incredibly convincing he could be, an excellent salesman when the situation called for it; selling potatoes to the potato farmer. But, only *if* and *when* it suited Martin's purposes.

Krystyna also realized that something must have gone terribly wrong, even by Martin's unconventional standards. But what?

Making a promise to herself, Krystyna vowed that she would have her divorce, signed, sealed and delivered on Monday. She would move heaven and earth if need be to accomplish this feat. Nothing must stand in her way.

Yet, in the interim she would be well advised to learn a bit more regarding Martin's most recent activities and of SERENITY. Even Garrett Chambers was about to mention something about being forewarned. It certainty would not hurt to keep herself armed with all the information she could gain on Martin. Krystyna also realized it very likely Martin would employ any number of low-down tactics to stall the divorce, if only for sadistic reasons buried deep in his methodical mind. After all, he'd gotten quite good at it these past three years.

Accepting that Martin could throw a curve when it was least expected, Krystyna drove straight to the library.

Not only was the library open, but a young woman sitting at the information desk proved to be very helpful. In a matter of minutes, Krystyna ascertained that a great many articles had been written about Martin and SERENITY in, THE WHISPERING FALLS COURIER, the local newspaper. The young librarian set about to locate specific copies of the newspaper and as Krystyna waited for her return, she wandered around the empty library making a place for herself at a long walnut table.

The librarian returned with numerous boxes of newspapers, each box stamped in date order. Krystyna thanked the young woman and set about to determine the approximate date of Martin's arrival in WHISPERING FALLS.

The local newspaper was published once weekly and each edition was merely three or four pages at best. Quickly scanning these weekly editions, Krystyna located the first article nearly eighteen months previous. This article was a formal welcome to Dr. Martin Braddock and his associate, Ms. Stephanie Roberts.

34

Clearly, Krystyna could assume they had been living here at least a year and a half.

The next article went on to explain about Dr. Braddock's world renown scientific work, expounding on his impressive credentials and background, to which Krystyna's anger flamed at the counterfeit exaggerations. Next, came an inflated acknowledgment by the town council for Dr. Braddock's very generous financial contributions made to several worthy causes, including the food bank, daycare center, and the fire department, only to mention a few. In addition, Martin was praised for donating his precious time lecturing to the senior citizens and a few other smaller organizations.

With the construction of SERENITY, and of course Martin's spacious home, a great many jobs had been created for the people of the town, many supplies required from the local retailers. Numerous others had been retained to provide a royal welcome to all those flocking to SERENITY. Another feather in Martin's cap.

Martin had presented himself to the town as a good guy, and they evidently ate it up, every last drop. Thoroughly disgusted, Krystyna knew Martin's true motives were not entirely for the good of the people. This was merely a repeat performance where he had again exploited his vast knowledge of human behavior, emotionally seducing and captivating his rapt audience. Quite the propmaster, this Pied Piper of WHISPERING FALLS!

Next, Krystyna found another news item dated nearly a year ago, complete with photograph, announcing the grand opening of SERENITY; the white monstrosity nothing more than a hell-bound hideaway. And it was here that Martin, the self-proclaimed Guardian of Hope, Messenger of Enlightenment, offered to treat phobias of any kind. He had been quoted with saying that each and every person was touched with some disorder or another, and most assuredly everyone needed to deal with those behavioral patterns with a tailor-made treatment designed for each unique individual.

She leaned back in the chair, her instincts screaming, an eruption of emotions nearly overwhelming and suffocating. Krystyna fought back tears of repulsion as the young librarian approached her.

"I'm sorry to interrupt you, but there's a gentleman here who also wishes to look over those older issues of the local newspaper. Would you be willing to share the boxes with him?"

"I suppose that would be all right." Krystyna answered, not entirely happy about the situation. "But I'm not nearly through, however."

"Hello." A tall dark haired man whispered as he sat down across the table from Krystyna. "I promise not to get in your way."

Krystyna eyed him cautiously before moving a single box of newspapers over to the stranger's side of the table. "Here, I'm done with this box."

The dark haired man accepted the box wordlessly and began shuffling through the contents, his chocolate brown eyes catching a glimpse of Krystyna from time to time.

Returning to the articles, Krystyna read countless statements declaring the phenomenal success of Martin's work at SERENITY. First-hand reports by dozens and dozens of community members related their heartfelt appreciation to Martin for alleviating profound stresses in their lives due to any number of psychoneurotic behaviors. As a result, Martin had been placed upon their collective pedestal, a devout following of believers keeping his dream alive for him.

Engrossed in the material, Krystyna failed to note that the dark haired man left the table, only to return minutes later with several thick volumes under his arm. Thumbing through the books, he glanced up at her, a calculated sparkle in his mysterious chocolate brown eyes.

Agitated by the man's presence, Krystyna nevertheless concentrated on the newspaper's portrayal of a town nurtured and rescued by a solitary stranger in their moment of greatest need. There was no mention of a silent yet deadly force at work;

to the contrary, each graphic account emphasized the golden promises to be found under the roof of SERENITY.

Then, something had happened, events spiraling downward.

A smattering of reports told of several prominent, and not so prominent, community figures who suddenly moved away from the area. The reasons given for their leaving, purely chance, decidedly circumstantial, either involving job transfers, or family related. However, the many weekly editions failed to explain why some families had hastened away in a matter of hours, often overnight, and more often without apparent provocation or forethought. Krystyna wondered why these actions had not come under greater question.

Also, it occurred to Krystyna that over the last six months of newspaper articles, a transparent downplay and whitewash of significant events had taken place. A suicide, the first in decades to take place in WHISPERING FALLS, had taken the life of a distraught young woman. Family members had feverishly urged the woman to resume her treatments with Dr. Braddock at once, but the young troubled woman had refused.

Over time, arguments and heated debates developed between neighbor and neighbor, family member versus family member, some steadfastly favoring Dr. Braddock's treatments, and others vowing these very treatments had ruined their lives, doing much more harm than good. The town, it now appeared, was in a state of chaotic upheaval; those who believed, and those who did not.

Nearly three months ago the editor of the one-man newspaper operation had written a final accounting, claiming it to be his last edition. THE WHISPERING FALLS COURIER was closing its pages forever. The voice of the town had now fallen silent. The editor had abruptly decided to move to Pennsylvania.

Krystyna sighed out loud, gathering the last bundle of newspapers back into their box. "Here you are," she said to the dark haired man seated opposite her. "I've finished with the newspapers."

The man was slow to respond, his eyes glued to one of the books before him, dozens of newspapers randomly scattered across his side of the table, pages turned down to mark his place.

Reaching for her purse, Krystyna shrugged her shoulders and was about to rise from the table when the dark haired man finally spoke to her. "Did you find what you were looking for, Krystyna?"

Stunned that the man knew her first name, Krystyna met his meaningful gaze across the table. "Krystyna?" She repeated, unconvinced she had heard the man correctly.

The man slid the opened book before him across the table so that Krystyna could see for herself what had captured the man's attention. Cautiously, Krystyna looked down at the book. It was a WHO'S WHO of scientists and their esteemed group, the page turned to an accounting of Dr. Martin Braddock. A sketchy biographical history of Martin's professional life took up the space of a few paragraphs, and along with this was a photograph taken many years ago while Martin and Krystyna were still living together as husband and wife. The caption beneath the photograph read: Dr. Martin Braddock and his wife, Krystyna, attended the seventh annual fund-raiser for the BOARD OF ETHIC SCIENCES.

Indignant and outraged, Krystyna nearly shouted at the dark haired man. "Have you been spying on me? Looking over my shoulder?"

A gentle smile softened his ruggedly handsome face. "Seems to me we've been digging up information on the *same* man with the *same* shovel."

Why had she not really looked at this man before now? Had she been so focused on the newspaper articles that she'd forgotten an important lesson Martin long ago imposed on her? Never take your eyes off the other fellow.

Krystyna took in a long deep breath, exhaling just as slowly. "I'm afraid you have me confused with someone else."

She waited for the man's response and it came in the form of golden glitter dancing in the chocolate brown of his eyes, and a mischievous grin lifting one corner of his mouth. His whispered words were cool and confident. "I think not."

The dark haired man rose from his chair, slowly leaned across the table, bringing his tall form closer to Krystyna, clearing enjoying the stare-down. "And no, I was not looking over your shoulder. To be quite honest with you, I was very surprised someone else had a need to dredge up information on the infamous Dr. Martin Braddock. Perhaps, you can tell me exactly why you're doing just that?"

Placing a hand on his chest, pushing him firmly away from her, Krystyna also rose from her chair. "I'm going now. Please, leave me alone in peace."

"You're obviously in the right town for that." The dark haired man whispered gently.

Her fingers suddenly ice cold, Krystyna looked hard at the dark stranger. "I wouldn't know. I don't live here."

"That doesn't mean you aren't a cohort in Braddock's crime. After all, you're a Braddock by name."

Pulling her purse strap up over her shoulder, Krystyna gave the mysterious stranger a faint smile. "Good-bye."

Golden threads sparkled in the man's eyes as he murmured softly. "Not good-bye, Krystyna, by any means. We'll meet again, and much sooner than you know."

Krystyna walked to the front doors of the library before she turned, stealing a glance in the dark haired man's direction. The stranger was standing there, tall and lithe, a roguish grin curving at one corner of his mouth.

CHAPTER SIX

Checking her rear view mirror to make certain she wasn't followed by the dark haired stranger, Krystyna returned to the Reed Ranch. She stopped at the main house just long enough to give Orenda her book, agreeing to return for dinner.

Once again, Krystyna found that Samuel had built a warm fire for her and after she put her purchases away, she showered and dressed in one of her new sweaters and slacks, arriving for dinner half an hour early.

"At least let me help you set the table." Krystyna suggested to Orenda.

"That would be fine." Orenda agreed as she stirred a copper pot on the wood cooking stove, the kitchen warm and cheerful, the aroma of delectables dusting the air.

"Over there you'll find the dishes." Orenda said, pointing a finger. "We'll need a table setting for four as both by sons will be joining us tonight."

Locating the silverware and glasses, Krystyna continued. "By the way, Garrett Chambers says hello."

Stopping her motions at the stove, a faint smile covered Orenda's features. She was very pleased that he had sent his regards. "Garrett is a good friend. What did you think of his bookstore?"

"He has a fantastic selection of books. It would take days just to read all the titles."

"Believe it or not, Garrett has read most of them."

"He mentioned his passion for reading." Krystyna remembered him saying, among other things.

"Orenda, Garrett Chambers also spoke of others from the town who have had dramatic changes in their behaviors. I met several myself."

Turning around to face her, Orenda's deep mahogany brown eyes were instantly touched with fear. "This is very true. My dear Samuel is not the only one, of that I'm certain."

A shuffling sound rustled into the kitchen. "Did you call for me?" Samuel asked his mother.

Orenda smiled gently at her youngest son, running her fingers like a comb through his dark blonde hair. "Yes, it's nearly time for dinner. Please put a pitcher of water and one of milk on the table for us."

Samuel nodded to Krystyna as he poured the milk. "Hi, Krystyna. I thought you were only staying with us for a night."

"Well, my plans have changed a bit, Samuel. I'll be staying through part of Monday."

"Maybe you'd like to go horseback riding before you leave?" Samuel asked enthusiastically. Then, a vacant film of terror covered his face, his words edged with pain. "I don't ride anymore myself. I'm afraid of heights, you know."

"Yes, I know. But . . . you could teach me to ride. I'm certain you could. I'd enjoy that very much. Do you have many horses here on the ranch?"

"Only two now. And yes, I could teach you, but from ground level." Samuel stated, a delicate smile resurfacing.

Orenda was busy placing serving dishes heaped with delicious mounds of food on the table. "It's time to eat everyone."

As they dished up their food Krystyna noted that the fourth chair at the table remained empty. Moments later, footsteps sounded on the back steps, pausing outside the kitchen and then entering, the hardwood floors creaking under the weight. A large shadow emerged into the brightly lit kitchen.

Orenda smiled gently, looking from the shadow and then over to Krystyna. "My first born son, Logan."

Krystyna turned around in her chair, disbelief sending wave after wave of shock drilling through her. The salad fork fell from her hand, clattering sharply onto her plate.

"I believe we've met already." The dark haired stranger whispered softly. "Good evening, Krystyna."

Logan Reed grinned devilishly as he seated himself beside Krystyna, tossing her a conspiratorial glance.

Exceedingly curious about the exchange between her eldest son and Krystyna, Orenda kept any questions to herself for the moment, allowing her senses to savor what they could.

"Mother, another fine meal you've prepared for us." Logan said, and to Samuel he added. "Were you able to mend that section of fence today?"

"Much of it. I plan on finishing it tomorrow." Samuel answered.

Krystyna was at a loss for words. How on earth had this situation, all of a sudden, become so very complicated? The dark haired stranger intentionally brushed her arm with his sleeve as he dished salad greens upon his plate, clearly enjoying his role of agitator. But, Krystyna knew the worst of it was yet to come. Krystyna's past would soon catch up with her, and certainly with Logan as the catalyst. She was desperately seeking time to think this through when Logan forced the issue out into the open.

"Mother, I do believe that Krystyna has something to tell you." Logan said evenly to Orenda. "I believe she has lied to you about her identity."

Astonished at Logan's blunt as a brick attitude, Krystyna realized she must do what she could to make amends. "Orenda, please hear me out. My name is Krystyna Kramer . . . Braddock." Pausing, Krystyna was met with Orenda's piercing mahogany eyes; a flash of anger smoldered there.

Krystyna continued. "Perhaps, I've not told you the entire truth, but I've not come to your home under false pretenses as Logan would have you think. I omitted telling you my last name simply because I would rather not have anyone associate me with Martin Braddock in any way. However, truth be told, he is my husband."

"Your husband?" Orenda asked, clearly astonished.

Krystyna could see Logan's mouth curve slightly at the corner, a muscle in his jaw flexing. "Yes. We've been married for nearly nine years, and legally separated for the last three. Over the years I've begged Martin for a divorce, I've tried reasoning with him, pleading for his compassion, all to no avail.

No, has been his answer a thousand times, and for selfish reasons, I assure you. The marriage, if ever it was one to begin with, has been long over. However, Martin could never cope with failure on any level; that was always one of his biggest problems. His inability to deal with failure has made him a desperate man. But, recently, out of the blue, I received word through my attorney that Martin was ready and willing to sign the final decree. That's precisely why I'm here, to get my divorce, take back my life, and rid myself of that maniac."

"I see." Orenda said quietly. "And why isn't your attorney handling this for you?"

"Actually," Krystyna faltered, a little guilt ridden. "I'm here against my attorney's express wishes. But, there was simply no other way. Martin had insisted that I come to him alone, face to face, on his ground. That was his one irrefutable condition. I had to come. What choice did I have?"

Logan had remained silent, listening to Krystyna and wondering if indeed her words were truthful. He turned to her now. "I'll ask you again as I did earlier today in the library. Did you find what you were looking for?"

Krystyna immediately stiffened in her chair. "No . . . not entirely."

"Perhaps you've come to join forces with your . . . estranged husband." Logan suggested, his tone of voice silky smooth. "Perhaps a piece of the action?"

"That is an out and out insult, Logan Reed! How dare you judge me, you don't even know me. You're an elusive stranger I happened to meet in the library."

Golden glitters flashed in Logan's brown eyes. "You, Krystyna Kramer-Braddock, are infinitely more mysterious, your actions questionable. I'll also point out that it is you who is the stranger here, not I."

No tears threatened to spill down Krystyna's face now. She was absolutely livid, a ball of frantic anger hot in the pit of her stomach. "You are absolutely right."

Turning back to Orenda, Krystyna quickly stated. "I'm so very, very sorry for intruding upon your home like this. I think it best I leave right away."

Standing, Krystyna glanced over to Samuel. "We'll have to cancel that riding lesson, I'm sorry."

Krystyna turned to move away from the table. "If you'll excuse me now."

Logan quickly reached out and touched Krystyna's arm. "No, I think you should stay. Perhaps I've been too hasty."

"Caustic and rude is more like it." Krystyna countered.

"I'm sorry. Please sit down. Mother's dinner is getting cold." Logan said. He knew this situation was far from over; it was no use denying it.

"Let's finish our meal together, Krystyna." Orenda calmly suggested. "After dinner we'll talk at length."

Her legs threatening to buckle under her, a whirlwind of thoughts spinning violently, Krystyna slowly sat back down in her chair. "Agreed." She whispered.

"Here, Krystyna." Samuel said in an effort to smooth out the rough moment. "Try my mother's casserole. You'll love it."

Throughout the remainder of dinner there were long moments of unbearable silence for Krystyna. In her increasingly feeble attempts to free herself from Martin, and Martin's ghost that followed her wherever she went, like a slime covered second skin, she had never felt so alone, so tired, or so guilty. A malignant guilt that did not belong to her. She had unjustly inherited it, shouldering the weight of it for years. Nine long years.

And all because Krystyna had a conscience and Martin did not.

The table cleared, dishes done, Orenda and Krystyna seated themselves before the fireplace, a carafe of coffee on the hand-carved table at their side. Logan preferred to stand at the hearth, an imposing figure resting one arm comfortably on the oak mantle, his eyes focused on Krystyna. Samuel nervously paced back and forth.

Orenda spoke to her youngest son. "Samuel, I can see you're not very comfortable with this. Let's hear what's on your mind."

After brushing a dark blonde lock of hair from his eyes, Samuel started to fidget with a button at his sleeve. "I'm afraid where this conversation will go. We'll talk about SERENITY sooner or later, and I'm not sure that I want to. Not yet, anyway."

"I know, you've told me nothing about the treatments." Orenda said quietly. "But, you must understand we would never force you into a discussion you weren't agreeable to. Please Samuel, I only want to help you, and I don't know how. What is it that frightens you so?"

Samuel's face paled in terror. "Right now, I'm afraid to know what was done to me. I'm not ready to know. I'm not sure I'll ever be ready."

Samuel's words sliced through Krystyna's heart.

"I respect your honesty, Samuel, and I also respect your feelings." Orenda said. "If you would rather not talk about it now, that's perfectly fine."

Braiding her long dark hair with nimble fingers, Orenda offered her youngest son a warm smile. "However, the time will come one day, my son, and I know you'll be strong."

Samuel looked down at his feet. "I think I'll go to my room now. Goodnight everyone."

From his position at the hearth, Logan watched his young brother retreat, Samuel's profound emotional pain and suffering suddenly all too real, a tangible ache instantly welling up in his own heart. This was the reason their mother had called Logan home to WHISPERING FALLS just a few days before Krystyna had arrived; to discover what evil had been done to Samuel and to find a way to help him.

And now, Logan thought, we have a Braddock under our roof.

Turning to Krystyna, Logan began. "I'm glad that Samuel will be spared much of this conversation. He's been hurt quite enough, don't you think?"

An instant replay of Orenda helping Samuel down the flight of steps reminded Krystyna of the tender fragility of the human psyche. "Yes." She answered softly.

Logan continued to stare at Krystyna, his cool languid poise irritatingly arrogant. "I'm going to ask you some questions. I'm expecting honest answers."

The roaring flames hissed and spit against a momentary silence.

"I want to know if you ever played a part, however small, in Braddock's scientific schemes?"

"No, never." Krystyna answered simply.

"But, you are his wife. Surely, he would have shared his dream of SERENITY with you, above all people?"

"I've not shared his dreams for many years, if ever I did. Need I remind you, once again, that I am his wife in name only, and that particular status is about to change."

"So you've said." Logan whispered. "How can we know you are to be trusted?"

A slow burning anger was rekindled in Krystyna's heart. "I have nothing concrete to show you, no proof ready to pull out of my bag, only my word."

Logan raised his voice an octave. "You've already lied to my mother. So, just how good is your word?"

Remaining still in her chair, Orenda listened from her heart for Krystyna's answer, at the same time intensely aware of Logan's body language.

"I've explained that already." Krystyna said. "Apparently you don't believe much of anything I've said. You've assumed I can't be trusted, assumed I have hidden motives. You're wrong about me, very wrong. You've condemned me for someone else's crime."

Infuriated, Krystyna sought to calm the frenzied fury inside her; nothing seemed to help. "You're acting as though I've personally betrayed your family!"

47

"Now we're getting right down to it! Betrayal!" Logan growled. "That's exactly what's been done to Samuel and all the others in this town. They're victims of a fraudulent delusion. Can you deny what you've seen with your own eyes?"

"No, of course not." Krystyna's next words slipped from her soul. "And it makes me want to run fast and far away, like all the others."

"I think you know a great deal more than you're willing to tell." Logan suggested angrily.

"And if I do?" Krystyna asked bitterly.

"You could help Samuel. You could help all the others." Logan's baited words were sharp-edged and crisp. "Or, you could get your divorce decree signed, and run away like a coward."

A searing eruption of anger tore through Krystyna as she rushed from her chair to stand before Logan, her gray eyes transformed into frosted panes of cold marble. "I'll say this only once, Logan Reed. I've not betrayed any of you here. If anything, I am the one person who could probably help you. Who better than I, Dr. Martin Braddock's wife?"

Logan stood perfectly still, his words halted before he could speak them, Krystyna quickly placing a single finger to his lips. "No, Logan. You listen to me. You really listen. If you want to help Samuel and the others, you'll need me. I can get inside where no one else can. Now, there's a mouthful of truth for you. Chew on that for a while."

Krystyna's pearl gray eyes commanded respect as she continued. "Here's the deal. I'm not leaving WHISPERING FALLS without my divorce. That, I assure you, will be finalized on Monday. You've got my full cooperation and help until then, and only then. That's it. That's all. Take it or leave it!"

CHAPTER SEVEN

"I'll take it." Logan whispered, only now seeing the firelight weaving burnt embers of scarlet throughout Krystyna's chestnut brown hair.

Krystyna turned to Orenda. "Could I use you phone? There are two calls I'd like to make right here and now."

Orenda gestured to a small oak desk, an unspoken question on her lips. Her eyes followed Krystyna as she retrieved the phone, pulling the long extension cord back to her chair.

Krystyna raised her gray eyes to Logan for a meaningful breathless moment before dialing the number.

"Hello, Martin. It's Krystyna."

Nodding, she listened to Martin. "Yes, I'm well aware that I didn't leave you a number where you could reach me. That was quite intentional, Martin. However, I'm calling you now. I've decided to take you up on that offer for a personal tour of SERENITY."

Krystyna smiled gently. "I'll be bringing a friend along with me, I'm sure you won't mind. His name is Logan Reed."

A roguish grin pulled at one corner of Logan's mouth.

"Tomorrow evening would be fine." Krystyna answered. "Eight o'clock."

There was another pause as Krystyna listened to Martin. "A late dinner?" Krystyna hesitated, drawn to the mischievous flash of gold in Logan's eyes. "Perhaps. I'll see you tomorrow then."

Replacing the telephone, Krystyna hoped neither Logan or Orenda would notice how badly her hands were shaking. Inside her, the eye of the storm wreaked emotional havoc, thundering fear straight into her heart, and she closed her eyes tightly against the overwhelming pressure.

Orenda rose from her chair, stepping from the room, returning with several glasses, a small bowl of ice, and an unopened bottle of Scotch. With a quiet grace she poured ice and Scotch into the three glasses, placing one in Krystyna's clenched fingers.

Orenda took a long sip from her own glass before she spoke to Krystyna. "I believe your words to be the truth, Krystyna, and I must listen to my instincts telling me to trust in you."

"I'll do my best, Orenda. I promise you that." Krystyna said.

"Well, where do we start?" Orenda asked.

Logan looked over to Krystyna, gesturing for her to be the first to offer a suggestion. She settled back against the overstuffed chair, taking a sip of her drink. "Much of what I found in the library was useful, yes, but there are many gaps to be filled in. Let's go back to Martin's arrival in WHISPERING FALLS. Orenda, you've been here. Perhaps, you should first tell us what you know, what you've seen for yourself."

Closing her eyes for a moment, Orenda breathed a long sigh. Memories swarmed in her mind, vivid pictures from the past congealing together, pathetically real.

"Quite naturally," Orenda began, "Dr. Martin Braddock was the talk of the town. Most people were flattered to find that a prominent scientist had chosen WHISPERING FALLS for his home. At that point there was no talk of SERENITY, we knew nothing about this until much later. Dr. Braddock went about doing good deeds, hired anyone who needed a job, purchased large quantities of supplies from our merchants. Needless to say, he had a profound impact on the local economy; WHISPERING FALLS literally thrived. It was also well known that he made sizable financial contributions to many community concerns. His generosity seemed to mesmerize everyone, save a handful."

"You didn't trust him from the beginning, did you Orenda?" Krystyna asked.

"No, I did not." Orenda reached over the arm of her chair, fingers digging into a bag, withdrawing small pieces of suede, a few beads, feathers, and several twigs of willow reed.

Absorbed in deep thought, Orenda placed the items on her lap as she worked her fingers over the willow reed, continuing to speak. "Garrett Chambers never cared for Martin Braddock either. Unfortunately, a precious few gave a second thought to Braddock's motives."

"When did SERENITY come into play?" Logan asked his mother.

"Braddock was probably here for at least a year before we first learned of it. He made a formal announcement that he would be willing to treat anyone with an emotional stress, a festering hatred in their heart, any phobia that had been allowed to escalate, any quirk of human nature. He was very convincing when he explained that any of these maladies left untreated would lead to a life of trouble and despair. And, not surprisingly, he claimed to have all the cures neatly tucked away at SERENITY."

Orenda paused, her fingers wrapping and weaving small bits of suede together with the willow reeds into a circular pattern. "SERENITY was built and WHISPERING FALLS no longer existed. Those first treated made remarkable progress after only a few months. Those with fears, lost them. Those overburdened with stress, were freed at last. Those who harbored hatred in their hearts, suddenly bent over backward with kindness to their former enemies. An unsuspecting cloud of euphoria hovered over as people cleaned up their lives, and literally cleaned up the town. It was, in all truth, a magical metamorphosis."

Krystyna frowned. "Orenda, you make it sound as though Martin single-handedly saved people from themselves."

Stopping her motions, Orenda held her fingers still a moment. "He did, for a while. Then . . . it all changed. They changed. Some of the people started to relapse, old bad habits resurrected, but this time a hundred fold worse than before they enlisted Braddock's help. Something had backfired along the way."

Logan swirled the ice in his glass, deep in thought. "Were you aware, Mother, of anything significant occurring at that same time?"

"No," Orenda answered. "And I've given this a great deal of thought. It's been close to my heart."

Finishing her drink, Krystyna formed another question. "Was it around this time frame that people from the town started to question Martin about his techniques, and they began to leave WHISPERING FALLS, not knowing what else to do?"

"Yes. There were also those who refused, for one reason or another, to undergo the treatments, and therefore objectively witnessed the drastic changes in behavior of their friends and loved ones nearest them. Some were frightened to live where evil had touched the souls of so many. Others ran like hell-fire, vowing never to return."

"Mother, how many residents are here now in Whispering Falls?"

Her agile fingers worked the beads around the suede circle of willow reed. "Less than forty-five or fifty, I'm told."

Logan groaned. "Why didn't you call me home long ago?"

Orenda stared at her first born son, a penetrating sadness in her face. "I didn't know that Samuel had gone to SERENITY until last week. He kept it from me for as long as he could. His fear of heights had been erased, only to return, intensified, magnified into some large beast that could not be denied. Then came the nightmares. Samuel finally confessed."

"And he refuses to explain how this treatment was conducted?" Logan demanded.

"You heard him earlier. He won't discuss it. I'm not certain that he knows himself."

Logan poured more Scotch in his glass, frustration rustling through his veins, an arrogant curve lifting one corner of his full lips. "Krystyna, tell us, if you will, why Martin has suddenly decided to give you the divorce. Why now, with everything falling down around him?"

"He plans on marrying his associate, Stephanie Roberts."

Sparkles of gold glistened in Logan's intense brown eyes. "He's taking a new wife. That's very interesting."

He gestured to Krystyna with the upraised bottle of Scotch. She declined another drink for the moment. He continued to stare at her. "Krystyna, I have a confession to make. Mother told me she had taken in a guest, a young woman from the

Seattle area, driving a white Jeep Cherokee. Yesterday, I was conducting a small investigation of my own, coming up with nothing, finally hoping to unearth a few clues from what sources I could use at the library. I saw your car parked out front, and I saw you. With everyone else leaving town, the only person still receiving visitors from outside was Braddock. I realized you were here to see him. Until I found your picture in that book, I had no idea who you were. Perhaps my tactics were a bit underhanded, and for that I apologize."

"Apology accepted." Krystyna whispered her words.

Logan continued, his tone somber. "There are a number of unpleasant and very personal questions to ask you. You know Braddock better than anyone else and . . ."

"This is going to get ugly, isn't it?" Krystyna asked, a cold numbing sensation blowing fiercely around her.

Logan's words were soft, patient. "Yes. I won't lie to you. Tomorrow night will be extremely informative, I've no doubt. But, until we know with certainty what it is we're up against, we'll be kept entirely in the dark. It's up to you to enlighten us."

An icy fear wrapped around Krystyna. "If I can manage some time alone with Martin, he may share his secrets with me, if only to boast."

Rubbing her cold hands together, Krystyna stared into the blazing fire. "He always did. He enjoyed torturing me with the grisly details of what he had done to his subjects. I thought it sadistic of him, enjoying the shock-value of those gruesome, immoral truths. He won't have changed."

For the first time, Orenda and Logan witnessed true fear on Krystyna's face. They looked to one another in silent confirmation, Logan feeling a protective urge swell in his heart, Orenda sensing the exquisite pain the young woman before them had suffered. Orenda's fingers worked the beads and feathers in her lap, the pace now quickened.

Continuing to stare into the flames, Krystyna shared another thought. "If Martin does not confide in me, then we must find his notes. They'll tell all."

Logan thought that an excellent idea. "Yes, but wouldn't that information be accessible only by computer?"

"Of course, but he always hand-wrote the original notes, and he always kept them. They retained some disgusting measure of sentimentality for Martin."

"Then perhaps we can find them." Logan said.

"We may have to." Krystyna sadly conceded.

"How has Braddock handled the question of legalities in the past?" Logan asked.

A coldness crept into the somber gray of Krystyna's eyes as she related to both of them the darker side of Martin's dubious past, detailing his scientific mishaps and failures, and the ensuing investigations. "Martin has always carefully chosen his subjects, preferring to label them volunteers; innocent victims who were given no choice but to sign a waiver which would ultimately release Martin from all legal liabilities. On the few occasions when that wasn't quite enough to keep the authorities off Martin's back, he called in his trio of unscrupulous, yet highly effective legal consultants. With their help, and Martin's great wealth, he manipulated escape clauses and invented persuasive loopholes. It's in Martin's nature to cover all his bases, and he has, time and again, risen to the occasion, coming out of a precarious situation totally unscathed."

"He envisions himself invincible?" Orenda questioned.

"Yes, indeed. Driven by his compulsive dream, allowing nothing to stand in his way, Martin has already beaten the odds. He's merely proven to himself that he is powerful, where others are powerless."

A wrinkle curved at one corner of Logan's mouth, his words edged in sarcasm. "It's most unwise for any man to refuse responsibility for his actions; a fall from grace certainly inevitable when it's due him."

"Let's hope so." Krystyna agreed. "I'd like nothing more than to help push Martin from his imaginary throne."

Suddenly, Krystyna recognized a raging hatred in her heart for Martin and its ferocious intensity startled her. Gone was the pity she had once held for him. Gone were the thousand excuses

Martin had given her. Also gone were the empty lies she wrestled with in the dark lonely depths of her conscience.

In this instant Krystyna wondered if Martin's evil had touched her in a way she could not have before known. Could she now hate, as well?

Did Martin's madness touch everyone?

Orenda perceptively caught the expression of contempt on Krystyna's face. "Don't destroy yourself with hatred, Krystyna. Martin Braddock isn't worth it."

"You're absolutely right." Krystyna said. "He isn't."

"Now," Krystyna continued, reaching into her bag for the book that Garrett Chambers had given her. "For that second call . . ."

CHAPTER EIGHT

"I think we may have a possible solution." Krystyna said, raising the book for all to see.

All eyes gazed at the blue-bound book entitled, THE ILLUSION OF SERENITY, written by Jonathan McCabe.

"Garrett Chambers," Krystyna explained, "gave this book to me earlier today, I expect his own way of trying to warn me of the dangers here in WHISPERING FALLS. Coincidentally, this book was written by a former colleague of Martin, the author a well-respected member of a committee which strictly governs scientific experimentation. The BOES, or Board of Ethic Sciences, would very much appreciate hearing about Martin's recent activities. We need to tell them."

"But," Orenda questioned, "will they listen?"

"I believe so." Krystyna answered. "They always had a need to know where Martin was concerned. I remember how closely the board members watched over him in years gone by. He's led them astray, that's all, convinced them he's not treating patients, or perhaps is currently undergoing research. The BOES must be made aware that the people from WHISPERING FALLS need their help; the ongoing process of undoing Martin's evil. They've tried to pick up the pieces before, they'll undoubtedly do it again, tracing down all those treated at SERENITY, ensuring everyone has a good chance at recovery."

Krystyna leaned to one side, reaching again for the phone. She dialed information. "Yes, I need the number for Jonathan McCabe, Los Angeles."

Still clutching the book in one hand, Krystyna dialed the author, the respected board member, but more importantly, someone else who knew Martin Braddock both inside and out.

Tense moments passed while Krystyna waited for someone to pick up on the line. Finally, Jonathan McCabe's familiar voice broke through. Krystyna met Logan's eyes as she began the conversation. "It's been a long time, Jonathan. This is Krystyna . . . Braddock. I hope you and Tina have been well."

She listened to the voice on the other end. "Frankly, I never thought we'd have an occasion to speak again either but then . . . you once told me not to hesitate should Martin become . . . lethal."

Krystyna cleared her throat. "I believe that time has come."

She paused, listening for several minutes.

"No, I've just arrived. I don't have specifics yet." Krystyna answered.

She then repeated three of Jonathan McCabe's questions out loud as she answered them. "Witnesses . . . I'm not sure."

"Accomplices? I . . . don't know."

"Survivors? Yes."

"I don't know that either." Krystyna said, hopelessness creeping into her voice.

Then, Krystyna's eyes widened. "Martin resigned from the membership four years ago?"

"I see. So, you'd been led to believe Martin was conducting mundane research in Europe?" Krystyna then paused, explaining what she could about Martin's secreted activities. A lengthy discussion followed.

Jonathan McCabe was not humored in the least at Krystyna's suggestion that Martin used the name of SERENITY from Jonathan's book. He had explained that he found it quite disgusting, tacky even.

A moment later, Krystyna answered. "I see. Yes, I understand. Expect to hear from me within a few days. Good-bye Jonathan, and thank you."

Logan and Orenda were patiently waiting for Krystyna to explain the outcome of the phone call. "I'm afraid it's not all good news." Krystyna said. "Before any board member can investigate, they must have something concrete to go on. We just don't have that to provide them."

"Not yet," Logan said. "But we will."

An intense silence hovered over the room as Orenda stared for a long moment at Krystyna. "I have to wonder why you married this man, Martin Braddock? Did he steal your heart?"

Pulling her eyes from the fire, Krystyna gently smiled. "No man has ever stolen my heart, and certainly never Martin. I was young and naive enough to think that because he needed me, he also loved me. Although he was charming, intelligent and handsome, I never loved the man. I fell in love with his tremendous potential, I fell in love with his dream of truly helping mankind. But, there were a million clues, as I look back on it now, that should have warned me about Martin."

Krystyna looked from Orenda over to Logan, and back to Orenda again. "You have to understand that every scientist walks the line, that fine line. Every scientist wants to be the one with the discovery of a lifetime; it gets in their blood and eats away at them. They are extremists who believe they are doing the right thing. However, their work is never progressing fast enough, not nearly fast enough, and something's got to give. To that end, a large percentage of scientists experiment on themselves and have for centuries; it's nothing new by any measure. Beyond that, some choose a despicable shortcut and experiment on their fellow man, guinea pig style."

Pausing, Krystyna shook her head back and forth in disgust. "They rationalize their actions by acknowledging the government has conducted secretive experiments on human beings, and gotten away with it, so why not private citizens?"

Krystyna held her glass out to Logan. "I watched the battle go on inside Martin, tearing him apart; which way do I go? But, in the end, it was his final choice. He made his own decisions. I lost all respect for him then."

"Did Braddock ever experiment on himself?" Logan asked.

"I . . . I'm not entirely sure." Krystyna hesitated, her heart in her eyes. "You've not asked me if I have any children. Well, I don't, I'm sorry to say. Martin would not hear of it. He panicked once or twice when he thought I may have been pregnant, making me promise to keep taking my pills. I've always wondered if he had run an experiment on himself,

59

perhaps taking an empirical drug, knowing it would have dire effects on an unborn fetus. Surprising isn't it; the hint of a conscience just when you're so sure there couldn't possibly be one?"

Logan forced himself to turn away from the raw agony of pain mirrored in Krystyna's pale gray eyes. It bothered him too much. Over his shoulder he asked, "Did Braddock ever abuse you physically or use you as a subject?"

She took her time to answer. "No, but he threatened to when he first learned I intended on divorcing him. I waited until things cooled down a bit before I left. We kept in contact through our respective attorneys; that has been our only method of communication. I'd lost track of him."

"And he of you?" Logan asked.

"I would expect so. I settled into a suburb of Seattle, opened up a small bakery, kept to myself, never dreaming that Martin was also in Washington State. It was more reasonable to assume he would have stayed in Los Angeles, nearer his contacts, nearer the action. Martin seemed to disappear, taking his dark secrets with him. What better place for a hideaway than in the vast mountains of the Pacific Northwest?"

"What better enticement than the promise of serenity?" Logan said, the roguish grin barely visible.

"Another question for you, Krystyna." Logan continued, his mood sobering immediately. "I want to know what it is that Martin holds over your head so very effectively?"

"What do you mean?" Krystyna asked, unprepared for Logan's blunt twist.

"As I understand it, after certain waiting periods have been met, and there are no children from the marriage to be considered, contested divorces are commonly granted by a judge. This being the case, you could have obtained your divorce from Braddock long ago. Yet, you declined to do so. That alone leads me to believe he must be holding something over you."

Logan stared at Krystyna. "It would help to know what that is."

Krystyna's ivory complexion paled by several shades. The old painful story would have to be told again. And just in the retelling, emotional scars, once healed, would open anew, bleeding brisk tears of fresh grief.

Slowly crossing her arms in front of her in a subconscious pose to stave off the enemy, Krystyna answered. "You're very perceptive, Logan. I would have thought Martin's intimidation over me was better masked than that. How careless of me."

Logan reached an arm out to Krystyna. She quickly withdrew from his touch, avoiding his eyes. "I'm forever indebted to Martin, strange as that may sound."

Krystyna's small hands now pulled into a tight ball, her back straight and rigid. "Nearly ten years ago my mother and father were involved in a multiple car accident on the California interstate. Mother was killed instantly. Father was critically injured, comatose and paralyzed from the neck down, finally awakening from the coma in a hospital nearly a month later. I spent long hours each day visiting my father, and nearly every one of those days, Martin and I passed each other in the hallways of the hospital. At that time, Martin was teaching a psychology class in the new wing of the hospital. Our relationship was very casual in the beginning, dinners in the hospital cafeteria, long discussions about my father's condition, Martin offering words of wisdom and a shoulder to lean upon. Martin learned that I was faced with a difficult decision. Father's physical condition had steadily improved to the point where he would soon be released to a private care facility, receiving around-the-clock nursing which he would require for the remainder of his life. Regardless, I could not bear to see him placed with strangers; no family around him. You must understand that father had not dealt well with losing mother. He felt lost without her, and now he needed me, his only child, more than ever. I wanted to care for him myself. However, the medical expenses for full-time nursing care were far beyond my financial capabilities. Martin stepped in with an offer to move father and myself into his large estate house, willing to provide a nursing staff complete with physical therapist, any necessary equipment, anything at all that we might need."

Krystyna paused, bringing her eyes to the ceiling and then down again. "It was a very tempting offer. An offer I eventually accepted."

Tears stung at Krystyna's eyes. "Martin and I were married shortly after father and I moved into the house. It seemed the thing to do. Martin saw to it that father had the very best of care, taking a genuine liking to one another. I treasured the time I had with father. Time I would not have had otherwise. Father helped to keep me sane throughout those years of madness. After Martin and I separated, a very generous check was forwarded each month through my attorney; Martin's way of ensuring that my father would continue receiving the special care he needed. At the end of each month, again with the help of my attorney, I returned every dollar that was not spent on father's care. Then, last summer, father passed away, his last days peaceful. I'll always be indebted to Martin for his financial help. I could never have done it alone."

Turning to Logan, Krystyna's words were a soft whisper. "Perhaps, I've allowed Martin to hold this over my head, giving him a bit of leverage, not pushing for the divorce quite like I could. But then, there is a dark side of Martin that I would rather not force to the surface; an anger I would rather not take issue with. I've declined my legal rights to part of his wealth, insisting that financially he's done more than enough already for both my father and myself, and I've had the good sense to bide my time carefully. But, all my efforts have gone into becoming free of Martin, not just for today, but for all my tomorrows."

"Now I understand, Krystyna. I'm sorry this has been so painful for you. Truly I am." Logan said, a lump in his throat preventing him from saying more.

"My son," Orenda spoke softly. "Tomorrow we'll take Krystyna to see the FALLS. Perhaps they will soothe her wounded spirit."

Krystyna watched Logan unconsciously pull back his broad shoulders. "If you feel the need, mother, we will."

Orenda turned again to Krystyna, her fingers finally at rest, gently holding the circular object she had woven in her lap. "I'll explain about the FALLS to you later. For now, I've grown very tired. We all need our rest. But, I wanted to give this to you before you went to sleep tonight." She held the object out to Krystyna.

A plate-sized circle had been curved and bent from the willow reeds, the bits and pieces of suede crisscrossing and meshing together, woven into a network of threads with an intentional opening in the center. Various beads and feathers had been tied with longer strips of suede from the bottom of the reed circle.

The object had a simple beauty to it, Krystyna thought. "Thank you very much, Orenda. But, I'm afraid I don't know what it represents."

"It's a Native American dreamcatcher." Orenda said. "Actually, it's a charm, given from a mother to her children to keep them safe at night. Suspended above your bed, it will allow the good dreams to pass through the woven circle, yet it will trap the bad dreams before they can hurt you."

Deeply touched by the gift, Krystyna suddenly thought of Samuel. What about his nightmares?

"Did you make one for Samuel?" Krystyna asked.

That soul-deep sadness crept over Orenda's face again. "No . . . not one. I made dozens."

CHAPTER NINE

"Now, I'll say goodnight to you both." Orenda said. "Tomorrow is yet another day."

Logan watched his mother leave the room, acutely aware of the delicate vulnerability hidden in her words, his heart aching for the answers she so desperately sought.

"Well, I believe I'll return to my cabin." Krystyna said, the dreamcatcher in her hands.

"I'll walk with you."

"That's really not necessary, Logan."

"Yes, it is." He said, unwilling to explain.

Retrieving her jacket from a coat rack near the front door, Krystyna walked out onto the dimly lit porch, a heavy mantle of clouds embracing the sky, the dark night further blanketed in a thick misty fog. Krystyna instantly froze in place as she heard a low-pitched threatening growl vibrating across the porch; a snarling animal was hidden in the obscure shadows.

Closing the door behind him, Logan whispered, "Taima, come here."

Emerging from the darkness, a very large wolf-like dog cautiously approached, long white fangs exposed, the animal's eyes fixed firmly on Krystyna.

"You have no reason to fear Taima." Logan assured Krystyna. "She's actually quite tame."

"But . . . she is a wolf . . . an animal from the forest!"

"Yes indeed. Her Native American name means Wild Thunder. It suits her well. A few years ago there was a tremendous Chinook wind, thunderbolts blazing across the mountainside, and on this night, Taima was born, her mother dying shortly after giving her life. True to her name, Taima can run like the very wind that accompanied this great storm. And, I admit there is something wild yet exceedingly wise about her. Taima is infinitely dedicated to me and my every wish, and she has yet to decide if you are a threat."

"I don't care for dogs. Never have." Krystyna stated flatly, taking a cautious step back.

The wolf-dog growled suspiciously at Krystyna.

"Taima can smell your fear." Logan whispered. "Reach your hand out to her."

With great reluctance, Krystyna extended her hand, palm side up. Taima's eyes seemed to glow in the darkness as she moved slowly toward Krystyna. The massive dog sniffed at her fingers, down to her feet, then along her jacket, encircling Krystyna, returning to face her once again.

"Logan, I don't think she . . . likes me."

"Lean down." Logan instructed. "Look Taima straight in the eyes. Let her see your soul."

Very slowly Krystyna knelt down, peering into the wolf's penetrating eyes. Taima looked long and deep at Krystyna, a critical assessment in the process. Drawing inches closer, Taima sniffed at Krystyna's hair, smelled her breath, and finally placed one strong paw over Krystyna's shoulder, holding this position for several long moments. To Krystyna's amazement the dog pulled away, casting a sideways glance at Logan, a solitary grunt sending a secretive communication to her master.

Logan's smile was faint in the murky darkness. "You have won Taima's approval."

Standing again, Krystyna felt somewhat relieved yet still frightened by the wolf-dog, even more confused about Logan. "That's more than I can say about her master."

Logan decided not to respond to Krystyna's remark. Now was not the time.

Snapping his fingers once, Logan called out to Taima. "Home, now."

They descended the steps together and began the quarter-mile walk to the cabins, the crisp crunch of gravel beneath their feet, Taima leading the way.

Feeling the damp cold air, Krystyna buttoned her coat. "How did you ever find Taima?"

"I was cutting firewood earlier that day. A storm rolled in quickly, and I was about to leave the woods when I heard a cougar and another animal fighting to the bitter end. Following their war cries, I soon found them, a female wolf and a male cougar, locked in the heat of battle. But, I was too late. Before I could manage to scare the cougar away, he had mortally wounded the wolf. She lay where the cougar had nearly finished her off, laboring to breathe her next breath, laboring to give life to the small pup inside her. The mother lay very still when I approached her, too weak even to raise her head and growl. But, her eyes never left mine. I talked to her, tried to comfort her, told her of the beautiful pup she was about to have. Somehow there was an understanding between us, man and animal, both aware she was about to die, and both aware she had no choice but to trust me to care for her pup in her place."

Krystyna was enormously touched by the story, and even more moved by the tender emotions Logan expressed, and the fact that he had shared this openly with her.

Pointing to Taima twenty feet ahead of them, Logan continued. "You need only to watch Taima to understand her. Her secrets lie in her body language. She watches, she listens, she waits for my command."

"I've never known that emotional connection with an animal." Krystyna said, slowing her pace, stepping over to the first cabin's door. "Well, thank you for walking me to my cabin."

"I would have come this way, regardless." Logan said.

A question formed on Krystyna's face.

"I always stay in the last cabin, nearest the hot springs." He explained, Taima at his side. "Goodnight, Krystyna."

"Goodnight. Krystyna said.

The wolf-dog lurched forward and licked Krystyna's fingers quickly, pulling back to her original position in one smooth graceful motion.

"Goodnight to you, Taima." Krystyna said softly, closing the door behind her.

Krystyna stood in place, her back to the closed door, listening to Logan and Taima's footsteps on the graveled path leading away from her cabin. Closing her eyes, Krystyna could feel the enormous tensions from the day beginning to ease their tenacious hold on her. She let out a long breath.

In her fingers the dreamcatcher quickly reminded her of the living nightmare in which she had now become involved. Stepping into the bedroom, Krystyna hastily removed a picture hanging on the wall above the bed, and replaced it with the dreamcatcher, the smooth beads and iridescent feathers catching the light of a nearby lamp.

The events of the day flashed back into crystal clarity. A single thought ended the deluge, a singular haunting thought taking precedence over the rest. Earlier in the evening, Krystyna had expressed her fervent wish to obtain her divorce, ensuring and enabling her to reclaim her life for her own. And now, the others touched by Martin's madness desperately needed to take back their lives as well.

Krystyna was not the only seeker of peace and serenity.

After breakfast the next morning, Logan suggested they take Krystyna to the FALLS. Samuel declined, vivid pictures in his mind of the towering rocky cliffs above the FALLS, the smooth descent of the water, crashing down and down . . . from high above. No, Samuel could not go. He couldn't bear the thought.

Logan drove, Orenda sitting nearest the window with Krystyna in the middle and Taima in the bed of the truck. The back roads were rough, the logging roads more difficult yet, winding their way deeper into the mountains. At these altitudes the misty fog had disappeared, however, somber ashen clouds hovered in vast drifts in the threatening sky above.

Krystyna was deep in thought when Orenda started to explain the fundamental significance of the FALLS. "My Native American grandmother, a medicine woman, told me of the FALLS when I was still a young child, the story handed down from generation to generation. Perhaps a little embellishment, shall we say, was added here and there, but the truth of the FALLS will speak to those who take the time to listen and believe. Long ago a young Native American woman was traveling on horseback, accompanied by her grandfather, taking a little known pathway through these mountains. The grandfather was taking the woman to meet the man who would become her husband. There was joy and happiness in their hearts, but as the journey became treacherous, the weather taking a nasty turn, the grandfather suddenly became gravely ill. A high fever overcame him as he sat upon his horse, only to fall to the ground, his heart stopping in an instant."

"The young woman was then alone?" Krystyna asked.

"Yes. And it was unfortunate the young woman set about to bury her grandfather according to the custom of that day; two full days of praying at his grave side, chanting the songs of mourning, whispering to the heavens. Her delay cost her dearly. She had no way of knowing another full-blown storm would soon have the mountains in their icy clutch. Snow fell in huge drifts, covering any traces of the little used pathway, and without an exact bearing on her location, the young woman became hopelessly lost."

Rolling the window down, breathing in the clean sweet air from outside, Orenda continued. "Her horse faltered in his steps, the icy banks of snow camouflaging a small crevasse, but the woman jumped from the horse just before it tumbled over and down the slope, the animal dying in a crumpled broken heap. The woman still had her grandfather's horse to ride, but this horse merely led her in circles, again and again returning to the waterfalls. Weak from hunger and the extreme cold, the brave woman wept and prayed she would find her way out of the mountains. Attempting a final valiant effort, now beyond exhaustion, the horse once again brought the young woman back to the FALLS. She saw the futility of her situation, again praying, only this time she received an answer. The voice of her grandfather spoke to her through the rushing waters of the FALLS. He told her she was doomed to be lost forever in the mountains; the best she could hope for was to die a quick death. Before she could lose her courage, the woman flung herself over the rocky cliffs at the top of the FALLS, the boulders below her deathbed. It is said that the spirit of the young Native American woman speaks great words of wisdom through the surging wall of water, the FALLS forming and whispering her words. It is said that her spirit guides those who are lost in the mountains, or, those who are lost in life."

Orenda smiled at Krystyna. "I've yet to hear her voice, but I must try nevertheless. For Samuel."

"I understand." Krystyna said. And now she also knew why the town was named WHISPERING FALLS.

"We're nearly there." Orenda said.

Logan, who had been silent and somber the entire drive, pulled the truck off the logging road and into a small clearing flanked by great expanses of trees. Running his eyes across the terrain, Logan had to admire the celestial beauty of the mountains. They made him feel vulnerable next to their vastness, yet they made him feel alive, in tune with the earth of his ancestors.

Beyond the small clearing lay a trail over irregular ground, making walking difficult through the dense forest. Taima, however, looked very much at ease, a quiet joy in her lighthearted step, coming home to the woods of her blood family. Meager threads of daylight could be seen through the midnight-emerald umbrella of the tree branches overhead. Fallen trees were scattered along the floor of the forest. Dead and discarded limbs, some with their massive network of roots pulled up from the ground, became a black vortex of serpent-shaped arms reaching out to them from the darkness.

They continued along the trail, the onrush of water splashing against rocks in the distance, drawing them nearer. The dense forest thinned out, larger shafts of daylight, though pale, provided more light. An immense opening could be seen at the edge of the trees, and beyond this rose a towering wall of solid rock, seemingly touching the sky.

It was explained to Krystyna that this approach to the FALLS was a bit more work, but preferable to the tourist outlook at the top of the cliffs. When Krystyna stepped onto the rocky banks of the waterway, a slight welcoming spray misted her face. A lush expanse of brilliant green framed the picturesque masterpiece of nature, the rushing waterfall serene, soothing and inviting. A sensation of genuine peace flowed through Krystyna as she drank in the sight.

Orenda cast a knowing smile at Krystyna as she carefully crossed several large boulders before finding one suitable to sit upon and leisurely gaze at the FALLS. Her fingers absentmindedly caressed a long string of beads, fashioned much like a Rosary, or Greek worry-beads. A peaceful expression touched her warm mahogany brown eyes as she raised her face to the patch of sunlight and blue sky that had moved above the FALLS. The remainder of the sky, by stark comparison, was dark and gloomy.

Turning to Logan, Krystyna found that he was staring intently at her, and not at the FALLS. His eyes glittered in the sunlight, reflecting the shimmering essence of the rolling waters. Krystyna had not, until this very moment, realized how stunningly handsome Logan's strong features were, softened by the full sensual lips, his statuesque muscular frame.

The roguish wrinkle curved at one corner of Logan's mouth. "There is something else I'd like to show you." He said, turning away, expecting Krystyna and Taima to follow him.

They rounded a curve along the rocky banks of the waters, walking side by side now, Taima's nose to the ground leading the way, the harmonious silence enhanced by the tranquil music of nature. Again, Krystyna felt a warm rush of peace touch her soul.

Logan reached out his hand, taking hers in his firm grasp. "We need to cross several of these larger boulders, so be careful with your footing, the rocks are slippery."

Cautiously, they approached a rounded slab of granite situated nearly in the middle of the waterway, the stone wet with spray, majestic bands of silver and gold glistening in the sunlight.

Scooping up a handful of water, Logan sprinkled it across the top side of the granite stone, the speckled markings contoured and naturally etched, springing to life. Krystyna leaned very close to see for herself the picture that had emerged

71

on the face of the stone. Time and the elements had converged together forming what appeared to be a horse, and upon the horse was a rider, a woman with long flowing hair, her body covered in what appeared to be an animal skin.

"Is this the young Native American woman who was lost so many years ago?" Krystyna asked.

"Some say that it is her, yes. But, as you can see, no human hand sculpted this scene. The meticulous attention to detail was crafted solely by nature. Uncanny, isn't it?" Logan asked.

"By all means." Krystyna closely scrutinized the life-like image. "Look here, at her outstretched arm."

A touch of arrogance caressed one corner of Logan's mouth. "Yes, I know. She's pointing to the town, WHISPERING FALLS. She was so close, yet so far away."

"Perhaps she's directing those lost to safety?"

"Who knows?" Logan said, finding an aura of pale blue in Krystyna's eyes, the occasional ray of sunshine painting a rainbow of colors through her long hair.

He reached for the ribbon that held Krystyna's thick chestnut curls in place, and pulled it free.

CHAPTER TEN

Orenda called to Logan and Krystyna from the water's edge. "We should go now. We need to prepare before the . . . appointment with Martin Braddock this evening."

Again, Logan held Krystyna's hand as they crossed the slippery rocks. She stole a glance at Logan. A dark and brooding expression covered his features, where a moment ago, something warm and magical had held them both.

Logan started to speak, "Mother, did you . . ."

"No, I heard no voices, I heard no words. But, I do feel more at peace; perhaps even a renewed sense of spirituality."

Half an hour later they arrived back at the Reed Ranch. Samuel was waiting for them at the bottom of the porch steps. Just as before, Orenda went to her youngest son and helped him up the stairs, a single step at a time, her soft voice comforting Samuel, his head buried in the curve of her neck.

He was a trembling mass of flesh and bones when they reached the top of the stairs. With the back of his quivering hand, Samuel wiped the sweat from his upper lip; silent eyes begging for forgiveness and understanding.

Orenda suggested Samuel take a few moments to compose himself and then join them for lunch. He could finish the last of the fence mending later that afternoon.

An hour later, Samuel was helped back down the stairs, and once his feet were firmly on the ground, he felt immediately more calm, the vigor of his youth gaining control and energizing him. He waved to his mother as he drove off in an old flatbed truck, the Reed Ranch insignia faded and peeling away from the doors, fencing materials and tools piled high.

Samuel was glad to go. He knew they were going to talk about SERENITY again, and he didn't want to do that. Work was good for the troubled soul, Samuel reminded himself. It kept your mind off other things; terrible things.

Once again seated before the fireplace, Orenda, Krystyna and Logan pulled their collective thoughts together.

"I'm afraid I can't second-guess what we might expect from Martin this evening." Krystyna began, turning to Logan. "Anymore than I can predict how your presence there will affect him."

"I'm aware of that. We cannot expect Braddock to divulge his secrets easily. Undoubtedly, we'll have to resort to other measures."

"I'm prepared to do just that." Krystyna said, her voice steady.

"Obviously," Logan said. "Braddock must be feeling a bit cornered. He must recognize something has gone wrong, some facet of his treatment plan has backfired. He may not be receptive to any questions posed to him, either from us, or anyone else for that matter."

An inspiring thought occurred to Krystyna as she offered a spirited smile. "Do either of you have a small tape recorder? One that would fit easily into my purse?"

"No." Orenda answered. "But, Garrett Chambers has one that he often uses."

Logan's chocolate brown eyes sparkled in the firelight. "What have you in mind, Krystyna?"

"I want to record what Martin says tonight. Believe me, he'll put us off guard, he'll confuse the issues. We can play the tape later, perhaps pick up on something concrete when we go over it again in depth, word by word."

"I'll call Garrett and invite him for dinner." Orenda offered, eager to spend an evening with Garrett under any circumstances; his mere presence soothed her soul. "He can bring the recorder with him."

"It's also a good guess," Krystyna continued, "Martin will not show us his entire operation at SERENITY. There are bound to be areas which will remain strictly off limits."

Logan leaned forward in his chair, elbows resting on his knees, his strong hands clenched together in a double fist. "This time, perhaps."

Meeting his intense stare, Krystyna realized the implication of Logan's words as she remained silent for a long and thoughtful moment.

"Krystyna, as much as I don't like the idea," a hint of Logan's roguish grin surfaced, "I think it exceedingly wise you accept the late dinner invitation Martin offered."

"No . . . it's not wise; not at all." Krystyna stated simply. "It's absolutely necessary."

After a lengthy discussion, nearly two hours later, alone in her cabin, Krystyna had bathed and dressed, choosing burgundy wool pants and a hand-knit sweater. She was slipping into her shoes when Logan knocked upon the cabin door.

Krystyna's breath caught in her throat as she took in Logan's tall lean frame, outfitted handsomely in a casual pair of charcoal colored slacks, black shirt and dove gray sportcoat snug against his broad shoulders. His eyes sparkled with excitement and raw intensity; Krystyna could not decide which of the two catalysts also inspired a heightened shimmer of mystery in those dark eyes.

"I'm a few minutes early, Krystyna. I hope you don't mind." Logan said as he stepped across the threshold.

"No, I'm ready to leave . . ."

"I wanted to have a moment alone with you." Her perfume reminded Logan of a seductive summer rain, alive and vibrant.

"Another question, Logan?" Krystyna asked, a hint of playfulness in her voice.

"No, not that." He found it terribly difficult to pull himself away from her incredible eyes long enough to think straight. This wasn't like him at all.

"I know this situation has been difficult for you," Logan said, "confronting another dark corner of Braddock's life, bearing your soul to complete strangers."

Logan paused again, suddenly nervous, the fingers of one hand combing through his raven hair. "You've gone through enough already. I'm just sorry that it had to be this way, Krystyna."

"I'm sorry too. But, I won't back down, not now when I'm so close to getting what I want."

"Aside from your divorce, what is it you want from life?" Logan asked, a subtle curve to his smile.

Krystyna had asked herself that very question again and again, the answer emerging during an emotional journey of self-discovery; a journey that undoubtedly would endure a lifetime. "I know with absolute precision what I *don't* want." She answered. "It would seem that all the rest is open for debate."

"Now that's a discussion I would personally find very interesting." Logan said, his roguish grin springing to life.

"Under the circumstances you know more about me than anyone else. I've suddenly realized that I know very little about you, Logan Reed."

"My roots are here, Krystyna, you know that. My family is here."

"Yes, but what about your dreams, your aspirations? What makes life worthwhile for you?" Krystyna stopped abruptly, pushing aside her strong desire to learn more about the mysterious and captivating man who stood before her.

"Perhaps I shouldn't be asking." Krystyna added quickly. "After all, we're little more than strangers."

"Strangers?" Logan repeated. "Not anymore."

Stepping over to the hearth, Logan folded his hands neatly together behind his back, staring into the fire. "But, as you are planning to leave on Monday, I can't see that it really matters one way or the other."

Krystyna wished he hadn't said that, his words having the same effect cold water thrown in the face would have been; a stinging edge of reality forced out into the open.

"I think it's time we go." Krystyna stated quietly, reaching for her jacket.

"As you wish."

Outside the cabin door Krystyna found Taima waiting patiently for her master, her tail wagging happily when she spotted Logan.

"I don't travel many places without my dog, Krystyna. And tonight is no exception."

"I certainly don't mind." Krystyna said, having now become considerably more comfortable around the dog herself.

"Here." Krystyna threw her car keys to Logan; he nearly missed catching them. "Let's take the Cherokee. You can drive and Taima can sit in the back."

Krystyna found words rather difficult now, a pensive mood overtaking her, smothering communications. There was too much on her mind. And tonight, of all nights, she was committed to spend time with Martin. A necessary evil.

They drove the quarter mile to the main house in heavy silence. When Logan turned the engine off, Krystyna reached over and placed her hand on his arm. "Would you mind if I didn't go in? Thank Garrett Chambers for the use of his recorder, and tell your mother that we'll talk later tonight or tomorrow. Just now, I need a few moments alone. Please."

Nodding, Logan went into the house and spoke briefly with his mother and Garrett. It took only the first sentence or two for Orenda to recognize the worry etched across her son's face.

"Logan, are you certain we're doing the right thing?" She asked.

"We're doing the only thing available to us. Our choices are quite limited, I'm afraid."

Garrett Chambers patted Logan's shoulder, handing him the microcassette recorder. "I'll stay with your mother and Samuel. I hope all goes well, Logan."

"Thanks, Garrett." Logan said, turning to his mother.

Orenda reached her arms tightly around her son. "Be very careful. I'll be praying for you and Krystyna."

Logan caught sight of the Cherokee from the large windows, and although it was dark outside, rain pelting down in torrents, flashes of lightning in the distance, the obscurity could not hide Krystyna's form as she sat rigid, seemingly cold as stone, staring out across the horizon.

Orenda looked to the window and back again to Logan. "How is Krystyna holding up?"

77

"She's strong, she's a survivor." Logan said.

"And?"

A long moment passed as mother and son exchanged meaningful glances. A sadness touched Logan's features. "In our eagerness to help Samuel and the others, we never stopped to think what following through on this would do to Krystyna. There's an emotional price tag connected to this meeting tonight with Braddock; one I hope doesn't end up costing her too much."

"Stay close to her, Logan. Don't let another innocent become another victim."

"Too late, Mother." Logan whispered as he closed the front door behind him.

Handing Krystyna the tape recorder as he slid behind the wheel of the Cherokee, Logan had a whirlwind of second thoughts about the entire evening. Nevertheless, despite his misgivings, he realized they must make good use of this golden opportunity to learn more about Braddock's method of operation. This could be their only chance.

Testing the recorder, Krystyna looked over to Logan, a renewed intensity in her eyes. "We'll find our answers."

"Yes, we will, Krystyna. And if not tonight, then . . . we still have time. It's important to remain positive."

"I promised your mother that I would do my best, and I will."

"I don't doubt you, Krystyna."

"Well, that's debatable. However, after tonight you will know with certainty who you can, and cannot trust."

A flash of lightning streaked across the night sky, illuminating the spirited twinkle in Krystyna's eyes. "After all," she added, "you're about to meet a living legend."

"Braddock is certainly not the only legend that lives in these parts." Logan said. "He's just one of many."

CHAPTER ELEVEN

"That white monstrosity to your left is apparently where it all happens." Krystyna said, pointing out the eccentric structure to Logan as they drove slowly before SERENITY.

"Continue down the road for nearly a mile; Martin's house is situated on the right. You can't miss it, it's the only house I've noticed out here on this lonely slope of the mountain."

"SERENITY is not what I had expected." Logan commented. "It doesn't seem to belong here at all."

"Neither does Martin." Krystyna remarked bitterly.

Taima had suddenly risen from her seated position in the back of the Cherokee, ears pricked up, pacing back and forth expectantly, only to pause, crouching, intense eyes scanning the darkened landscape.

"Why the need for such security, I wonder?" Logan asked, the guarded entrance gate at SERENITY fresh in his mind.

"That's a good question. I've never known Martin to take such precautions before. He always kept his notes safely concealed, yes, but nothing to this extreme. This is isolation itself; the mountains, for heaven's sake!"

"Perhaps Braddock is not merely concerned with keeping others locked out," Logan quickly suggested, "but has a greater need to keep something locked in."

Krystyna turned to face Logan, stunned at the frightening thought he had proposed. "What could that something possibly be?"

"I don't know. Himself, perhaps?" Logan suggested.

A prickly wave of cold air wafted across Krystyna. Or, she wondered, was her response an inner recognition of a grim and sober reality, far too ugly, far too profane to deal with on a conscious level?

When Logan pulled before the house, he immediately noted the odd similarities between the two structures. Without another word Logan and Krystyna got out of the Cherokee, Taima close on their heels, her nose catching the various scents and reading the air. Logan instructed Taima to wait at the front steps before he rang the doorbell. He looked over to Krystyna and smiled gently.

The massive front door opened. Dr. Martin Braddock and Stephanie, two mannequins with painted smiles, greeted them, stepping back mechanically into the foyer. Before Logan or Krystyna could move forward, Taima leaped in front of them at the doorway, a growl deep in her throat, her rigid posture a blatant threat.

Frightened of the dog, Stephanie quickly stepped behind Martin, peering over his one shoulder, her artificial aura of composure fragmented and exposed.

Kneeling down to Taima, Logan calmed her with his voice; the telltale heaving of her chest slowing with her master's assurance. Finally, Taima tossed her tail haughtily into the air, warily withdrawing back to the steps, her impassioned eyes never leaving the two strangers.

"I'm sorry." Logan said directly to Braddock. "Taima usually doesn't react quite so violently." Apparently she knew a bad seed when she saw one or two, Logan thought.

"Just see that *it* stays on the front porch." Martin suggested strongly, his words crisp. "I wouldn't want the dog to wander off and get into something it shouldn't."

"Of course not, Martin." Krystyna added, her tone decidedly stern. She casually slipped her hand in Logan's hand, pulling him with her rather aggressively into the marbled foyer, the hollow sounds of their footsteps echoing eerily.

Instantly, the house itself grated on Krystyna's nerves. It was all wrong.

"Martin, Stephanie, this is Logan Reed, a friend of mine." Krystyna began.

Extending his hand to greet Martin, Logan quickly added, "Dr. Logan Reed." A roguish wrinkle curved at his mouth.

Suddenly coming to life, Martin's fingers twirled the one end of his blonde mustache. "I see. I've looked forward to the day when there would be a little professional competition for me in this part of the country. Perhaps now you can provide that for me?"

"Actually, I'm a doctor of veterinary medicine. We're at completely opposite ends of the spectrum, I do believe." Logan stole a glance at Krystyna, the unexpected revelation clearly a surprise to her.

"That's a shame, Dr. Reed. Had you chosen another field of medicine, I'm certain you would have found it far more rewarding and enlightening." Braddock's emerald green eyes glowed with arrogance. "However, I'm glad to make your acquaintance, nevertheless."

Nodding, Logan found it very easy to dislike the man before him, all the way from his impeccable three-piece suit, right on down to what that flimsy suit failed to disguise; an overbearing and pompous attitude. And he especially did not care for the way Braddock incessantly stared at Krystyna, although as yet, Martin had not addressed her with as much as a single word.

"Nice to meet you." Stephanie stated indifferently to Logan, offering a cold contemptuous half-smile to Krystyna. "Martin will take your jackets. Let's go down to the living room. We can have something to drink, if you like."

Gracefully, Stephanie led the way down the marbled steps, her sleek blonde hair just touching the neckline of her amethyst silk pantsuit. She gestured to the expansive living room, her flagrant diamond engagement ring catching the light and tossing prismatic colors over the white leather furnishings. "Please have a seat. Can I offer you an espresso? Wine? Hard liquor?"

Sitting down beside Krystyna in one of three loveseats, Logan answered. "An espresso would be fine. Thank you, Stephanie."

"Make that two." Krystyna said.

A mechanical twist of Stephanie's mouth posed as a smile. Turning away sharply, half a dozen gold bracelets on a single arm chimed softly as Stephanie flashed her ice-blue eyes on Martin. "I'll be right back, Martin. Maybe you'd like to set the stage for your little tour?"

As she retreated to the kitchen, Stephanie found she was furious with Martin over this ludicrous arrangement, and she couldn't have cared less who recognized her sarcasm. She had the right to be angry. Martin wasn't pulling through on all his promises quite the way she had intended. And that would never do.

Although Krystyna had thus far avoided looking Martin straight in the eye, she could feel him staring at her. Now, he advanced toward her, an ominous shadow slithering across the room, unexpectedly seizing her hand. Merely by his towering position, Martin had given her no choice but to look up at him, no possible hope of evading him a moment longer.

"My dearest, Krystyna," Martin placed his hand ceremoniously over hers, dropping to one knee, his handsome face a portrait of compassion and understanding. "Just then, your expression was one I'd seen on your father's face a thousand times. I'd nearly forgotten how much you resemble him."

Pausing deliberately, Martin cleared his throat and continued. "I've not had the opportunity to tell you how very sorry I was to hear of your father passing away. You know how much he meant to me."

Krystyna was ill prepared when Martin brought up the subject of her Father. Unquestionably, Martin would know that it would always arouse shades of guilt for Krystyna, and naturally he would use this in an effort to further manipulate her, and throw her off balance.

Nothing had changed, Krystyna thought, pulling her hand away from Martin and meeting his eyes head-on.

No, she decided quickly. Everything had changed; herself, mostly. And this time she would not allow Martin to play his self-centered, ego-inflating games.

"Father's in a much better place now." Krystyna said in a controlled voice. "But, thank you for your concern."

Bringing himself to a standing position, Martin would not be brushed off so easily. "That you have always had, and beyond measure."

He paused again, as if with great purpose, commanding attention as he glanced over at Logan with an arrogant tilt of his head, returning finally to Krystyna. "Your wish has always been my command."

"Not every wish, Martin. You've forgotten the most important one. My divorce." A flash-fire of emotions swept over Krystyna, the flames fanned by her increasing anger.

Putting his hands in his pockets, Martin laughed easily, his deep voice echoing and bouncing off the dimly lit walls. "Never that one, my angel."

"You're toying with me Martin, and I don't like it one bit. Perhaps we'll pass on the tour after all."

"And deny me my chance to gloat? No, Krystyna. Just look at this as a golden opportunity for you to see what the future holds, the extraordinary ability to witness a true vision in the making."

Martin stopped abruptly, his mood sobering, a mask of feigned shock applied. "We're not retreating behind that infamous brick wall again, are we Krystyna? Where's that undying curiosity of yours? I always thought that one of your most endearing qualities."

Logan had remained silent long enough. He slowly and deliberately rose to his feet, a rigid muscle in his square jaw tightened and flexed. "You've insulted Krystyna one too many times, Braddock. I'm drawing the line right there. That will be the end of your nonsense."

The absentminded grinding of Logan's teeth further enhanced the dangerous undertone of his next words. "If it's a healthy return on your antagonism that you're after, then I'll give you back more than you can handle."

Putting his large hands on his hips, Logan continued. "You've succeeded only in disappointing me to the point of sheer boredom. All you've shown me so far this evening is that you're an egotistical, manipulative, insensitive jerk who poses as a scientist."

An emerald sparkle shone in Martin's penetrating eyes. "But then . . . that's my good side."

With a mock display of surprise, Martin laughed softly, an innocent little-boy smile surfacing. "Logan, I would have thought Krystyna would have told you that to know me is to both love and hate me."

"I'm a metamorphic miracle in the making." Martin said, winking at Krystyna. "An authentic Jekyll-and-Hyde kind of guy!"

CHAPTER TWELVE

A puzzled expression covered Stephanie's face as she carried a black enameled serving tray with espresso cups into the living room. "Martin," she said, "I should hope you're not giving away any trade secrets."

"Absolutely not." Martin answered quickly, perhaps even a bit too hastily, the fingers of one hand absentmindedly toying with his blonde mustache. "I've merely touched on the entertainment we've planned to provide Dr. Reed and Krystyna this evening."

Krystyna interrupted, the impatience building in her voice. "Just like your billboard advertisement reads; 'Expect a miracle at SERENITY'." Leaning toward Martin, her cold gray eyes were filled with contempt. "Well, I'm still waiting to see this . . . this self-proclaimed miracle of yours."

"Despite the doubt in your voice, Krystyna, I will nevertheless overlook that, and give you the straight facts, just as I've done with all my patients." Martin began, gesturing for Stephanie to take a seat with the others.

"Harold, dim the lights in the living room please." Martin said quickly. "We've installed a computerized security system, Harold, that also regulates a great number of other details. A sign of the times, you know."

Purely for emphasis, Martin chose to remain standing, drawing his suit coat together, intentionally painting the picture of a determined and serious professional before his captive audience. He'd done it enough times before, it came easy now, like a second skin crawling to the surface.

"Until very recently, patients with phobias were either misunderstood, misdiagnosed, or given up for lost by conventional physicians offering conventional treatments. Rehabilitation techniques employed, not only failed, but failed miserably. Those with phobias were doomed to an existence of excessive fear, progressing rapidly into major lifestyle problems. As a result, friendships suffered, marriages floundered, families were pulled apart; life itself dissolved into a fragmented maze held tenuously by a slender vulnerable thread."

Folding his hands together behind his back, comfortable now in his role, Martin continued. "Sigmund Freud believed that phobias and their resultant fears stemmed from repressed impulses or urges. The deeper the fear went, the more unrecognizable that fear became. Consequently, an endless host of physical maladies then manifest, disguising and concealing the true face of the phobia."

Martin stared soberly at Krystyna, his dark emerald eyes hard and uncompromising. "Can you imagine every day of your life filled with rampaging oceans of adrenaline, your heart racing wildly, hands turning ice cold, waves of perspiration damp and tell-tale, your physical body mobilized at every breath for fight or flight . . . never knowing which? Can you imagine the inability to sleep, night after weary night; your fears turning to nightmares far too unbearable to endure, at times unspeakable, unfathomable?"

Krystyna remained stubbornly silent as Martin carried on, his impassioned tone unbroken. "It gets worse. Those with phobias commonly develop digestive maladies often times accompanied by a dry mouth, dizzy spells, and bouts of severe nausea. There is also a high frequency of sexual disturbances in both male and female. Some experience weakness of their extremities, some crippling tremors. A few undergo blurred vision, or worse, tunnel vision. Fear inhibits a normally productive life. Phobics, regardless of their specific fears, have a strong predisposition to become social hermits. Due to the horrendous physical symptoms and the mental anguish of the fear, the patient soon refrains from driving a car, visiting friends and relatives, showing up for work, or shopping for groceries. They dig their heels in deeper, becoming more despondent, grief stricken, profoundly disappointed with life itself."

"You're painting a rather grim picture, Braddock." Logan stated flatly.

"It shouldn't come as any great surprise, Dr. Reed. Fear is merely an addiction. And there is certainly nothing glamorous about an addiction. Can you deny that?"

"No, I cannot." Logan said.

"This addiction, or fear, or phobia, or which ever label you choose, is driven by an insatiable compulsion; a compulsion borne of the original deep seated fear. Instead of recognizing their fear, examining it closely, tearing it to shreds and throwing it away, often times the patient cannot find the proper treatment, not without outside help, and certainly not without the tools to do so. Undeniably, the phobia stricken patients experience an internal tug of war; a war not easily fought alone."

"And that's where you come in, Braddock, the knight in shining armor?" Logan's observation was delivered through a sardonic grin.

"Indeed, it is." Martin smiled with great caution. He could ill afford an unwanted pause in the momentum he had so carefully created. Not to mention that the emotional roller-coaster ride he was savoring was elevating him to new and welcomed heights. And, he would not be denied the thrill of it all.

Hardly missing a beat, Martin pushed forward. "Society, as a whole, has dictated facets of human behavior for all of time. The society of today has consistently reinforced the issue of doing more, becoming more, pushing harder, getting farther ahead; overachieve in all you can. We've been bombarded by the baby-boomers who demand that we reach for the gusto, be all that we can be. Now, there's nothing wrong with that, to a point. And that point can reach saturation; beyond one's limitations, beyond our capabilities as human beings. However, let us never forget that we are not all movers and shakers, or the power elite. Years of research have led me to believe that this very super-achieving attitude is responsible for bringing out the deep-seated fears in those patients most easily influenced. In their eagerness, they've climbed on the merry-go-round and it's a downhill course from there on. To coin a phrase, they've simply come undone."

Although Martin was choosing his words carefully, altering his phraseology, it all sounded much too familiar to Krystyna. Listening to Martin's time-worn speech, she was suddenly reminded of the tape recorder concealed in her purse. She hadn't turned it on! Reaching into the purse, Krystyna pushed the ON button, at the same time pulling out her lace handkerchief, bringing it to her mouth as she forced a cough.

For what seemed a very long and awkward moment, Martin examined Krystyna curiously. In an attempt to further cover her actions, Krystyna spoke the first thing that came to mind. "Martin, isn't this where you give the little speech about the similarities between your patients and the mainspring of a watch being wound too tightly?"

It had more than crossed his mind, Martin thought; it was one of several pivotal points he had planned on bringing to light next. Indignant that Krystyna could have second-guessed him, even once, and perplexed with her newly acquired tenacity, Martin conjured up a detour down a road he knew Krystyna had never been.

"Well no, I hadn't intended on that." Martin said. "Perhaps later. For now, I wanted to . . ."

"Excuse me, Braddock, but I'm unclear on something here." Logan asked seriously. "You've referred to the super-achieving attitude of society as part-culprit and part-catalyst in the eruption of fears and phobias coming to light in people today. Is this correct?"

"Yes, but your definition leaves much to clarify. It's better expressed . . ."

"All right," Logan continued undaunted, his tone even. "Undoubtedly, members of this ultra-zealous crowd are highly educated individuals striving at breakneck speed to push their professional careers to the absolute limits. But, along with big corporate monies, come big headaches. In your opinion, are the stresses of this fast-paced life creating a breeding ground for excessive fears and phobias?"

"Naturally." Martin agreed, a strong hint of arrogance in his eyes.

"However, WHISPERING FALLS is as far removed from that city life as one can find these days." Logan emphasized strongly.

Standing up, Logan set his espresso cup on a glass and chrome table, stretching his long legs as he walked slowly over to Braddock. "The law of averages should tell you that you won't find those same stresses here. The people who live in WHISPERING FALLS have chosen to do so, desiring a slower, less demanding way of life. They keep busy doing more of what they really want to do."

The tone of Logan's voice was uncompromisingly rigid as he continued to make his point. "There shouldn't be a great need for your services in this quiet little town, Braddock. So, why are you here?"

"Apparently you've been misinformed, Dr. Reed. Contrary to your unscientific statistics, there exists an overwhelming need for my services here in WHISPERING FALLS. My extensive list of clients is proof enough."

"A list of innocent victims you have somehow coerced and manipulated into thinking they had severe debilitating phobias." A roguish grin danced around Logan's sternly set jaw. "If they didn't before, they certainly do now, Braddock."

CHAPTER THIRTEEN

The electrified tension in the room reached a fevered pitch as Logan and Martin stood facing each other, their expressions bold and combative.

Stephanie held her tongue as long as she could. She bolted from her seat, her usual grace forgotten in her anger, quickly stepping over to Martin. "Dr. Reed, I'll not have you speak of Martin's work in such a dark light!"

Logan turned sharply toward Stephanie. "Perhaps you have a reason to bend the truth to your liking. I do not."

Placing an arm around Stephanie's shoulder, Martin quickly decided that he didn't dare lose his composure now. Not now. He couldn't risk chasing Krystyna away too soon. No, that would never do. "Stephanie, I'm afraid you've put too much meaning into Dr. Reed's words."

Martin smiled at Stephanie; it felt awkward, surreal to him. Maybe it would pass. "Dr. Reed is a man of the sciences. I'd be terribly disappointed if he didn't offer me a heated debate. After all, it runs in our professional blood."

Although Martin sounded sincere enough, Stephanie found great difficulty believing him. She knew him better than he would guess. After all, wasn't he, in essence, her evil twin? She had always thought of him that way. However, under the circumstances, perhaps it would be best if she let Martin chart the course for this particular evening. It was his fiasco, not hers.

"Well," Stephanie said quietly, long graceful fingers twirling a lock of her blonde hair. "I'm certain that everyone here could easily understand if I thought Dr. Reed was being disrespectful."

Choosing to remain silent, Logan regarded Braddock with unabashed insolence. There would be no apology coming from him, Logan thought bitterly.

A telephone began ringing in the distance, the tone shrill as it echoed, scratching eerily across the marbled interior.

Stephanie flinched, quickly excusing herself to answer the call, thankful for a few precious moments alone.

In the space of this time, Martin looked over to Krystyna as she sat alone in the loveseat, distanced from the others. She looked small and frail to him suddenly; a host of long forgotten emotions flooding his senses, springing forth from a place Martin would have thought had dried up and withered away long ago. About three years ago to be exact.

Returning, Stephanie handed a cordless phone to Martin, her sapphire blue eyes troubled. Martin listened intently, the fingers of one hand twisting sharply at his mustache.

"No, you did the right thing. I'll be right there." He told the caller, a ragged edge to his words.

"That was the receptionist at SERENITY." Martin explained, addressing no one in particular. "I have to leave right away and I'm afraid this may take some time. Destiny has stepped in and canceled our tour."

In the same breath, Krystyna and Logan made eye contact. Their brief exchange only reaffirmed for Krystyna that this was an ominous reversal in their plans. From the onset of the evening there had been no room for error, this night representing what was perhaps their one and only chance to gain entrance to SERENITY, and find their answers. And now, the odds had suddenly been tipped heavily against them.

Refusing to let go of the golden opportunity at hand, pushing that sinking feeling away, Krystyna rose slowly from the loveseat, keeping her eyes deliberately riveted on Martin as she walked over to where the small group had gathered. "How disappointing, Martin. And we were just getting to the good stuff."

"There's so much more to tell you . . ." Martin started to say, unable to finish the sentence; his self-centered frustration displayed in naked sincerity.

"Perhaps you could show us instead." Krystyna suggested eagerly, a challenge in the making. "I have to say I find this new work of yours more . . . intriguing than anything you've touched on before. I was so looking forward to seeing it for myself."

Krystyna gave Martin a soft smile. "Now, I'm feeling rather cheated."

"I hadn't planned on our evening being cut short, Krystyna, or the tour, for that matter." Martin explained, the chain of circumstances now beyond his control.

However, Martin also recognized the likelihood of keeping the proverbial door open. A door he would again walk through.

Martin quickly proposed an offer. "Saturday evening, same time. And you shall, for all intents and purposes, experience SERENITY."

"Until then, Dr. Reed." Martin said abruptly to Logan, brushing past him.

Turning to Stephanie, scarcely looking at her, Martin mumbled a hastened, "I'll return when I can."

Before Martin was out of reach, Stephanie grabbed his one arm and held it steady, her sapphire blue eyes disagreeable. "Perhaps I should go with you if there's been an emergency."

Martin walked Stephanie over to a quiet corner of the room. "This is something I'm quite capable of handling, Stephanie. There's no need to worry." Forcing a smile, he added, "Perhaps our guests would like another espresso. I'm sure they'll be eager to return home soon."

"Don't try to pacify me, Martin. You should know better than that."

Indeed, he did. But, Martin was in a precarious position at best, and the last thing he needed was Stephanie creating more problems. "I'm not trying to placate you, Stephanie. I'm only asking for your cooperation."

A long moment lapsed before Stephanie responded. "Just don't push me too far, Martin."

"Of course not." Martin answered, a small voice in the back of his mind telling him to do just that . . . push her too far . . . but he ignored that small voice, as he had done numerous times before.

"I must leave." Martin whispered in Stephanie's ear.

Krystyna watched Martin take a dozen steps or so before he paused, turning his head slightly in her direction, peering over a single shoulder, an emerald eye glistening for a lengthy interlude.

It would seem there were moments when Krystyna could still read Martin, after all these years. And yet, that look of his told her everything, yet nothing. She hadn't a clue.

After the menacing stare from Martin, and needing a moment to herself, Krystyna asked Stephanie where the guest bathroom was located. As she made her way up the stairs, Krystyna overheard Logan ask Stephanie for another espresso, no doubt buying some much needed time.

Finding the bathroom easily, Krystyna flipped the light switch on and closed the bathroom door, stepping back into the hallway in one quick motion. Her eyes scanned the darkened area before her. Undoubtedly, all the doors leading off the passageway were bedrooms, but she had to be sure. She was looking for a particular room; a room that Martin would use as his personal study. Unfortunately, her search could only include the middle floor of the building in the stolen moments allowed her. The first and third floors would remain unexplored.

Quietly, Krystyna opened a door, the art deco colors of purple and teal predominant in what appeared to be a large unoccupied guest bedroom. Through the second door Krystyna found another bedroom; this room was unfinished, the barren walls and floors a gray wash. Rolls of wallpaper and cans of paint set atop an old splattered tarp in a single corner.

The study was the last room Krystyna walked into, silently closing the door behind her and turning on a small brass lamp, the soft light illuminating the shadows hovering in the darkened recesses. The expansive room was filled with bookcases, a half-dozen leather chairs, and an oversized antique walnut desk, the desk once belonging to Martin's father, Harold Braddock.

The usual assortment of staplers, pens, pencils, books, letters and forms were strewn about haphazardly. Manila folders, overplump with papers, were piled to one side of the desk. There was no computer on the desk and a thorough check elsewhere failed to reveal one tucked away in a neat corner.

Each drawer in Martin's desk was locked securely. Not a single file cabinet was to be found.

Sensing time was slipping away too fast, Krystyna hurriedly scanned the folders laid across the desktop, each labeled with a patient name, none of which were familiar, and certainly nothing regarding Samuel Reed. A stack of bills lay next to several phone messages written out on a memo pad; only one caught Krystyna's eye. It was a message from Michael Overby, the attorney who had drawn up their divorce papers, urging Martin to return his call at the attorney's home phone number. The date and time of the message was just that very day, Thursday. The phone prefix told her the attorney lived right here in WHISPERING FALLS.

Hadn't Martin explained that his attorney would be out of town and unavailable until Monday? Wasn't that the very reason for delaying the signing of the divorce decree? Had Martin lied, Krystyna wondered?

But, of course, she answered in her mind.

However, she must rejoin Logan and Stephanie before her absence drew any unnecessary attention. She used the last few moments she dared waste scanning the titles of the books laying randomly beside the manila folders on the desktop. Numerous well-worn bookmarkers were placed within the pages of the books. Quickly, Krystyna withdrew the tape recorder from her purse, bringing it to her lips, speaking into it softly, reading aloud the book titles:

ACCELERATED ELECTRONS,
QUANTUM MECHANICS VOLUME NINE,
COMPUTERIZED DATA-INTERPRETING SYSTEMS,
ELECTRONIC ANALYZERS,
REVERSE FEEDBACK IN THE TWENTY-FIRST
CENTURY,
THE RAREST OF RARE DIAMONDS,
THE POWER OF VIRTUAL REALITY,
THE ULTIMATE IN SOUND SYSTEMS,
EMPIRICAL METHODS OF TREATING MANIAS,

CONFRONTING PHOBIAS,
VISUAL PSYCHOLOGY

What a mixture, Krystyna thought wearily after turning off the small lamp and slipping back into the hallway. She again located the guest bathroom, also turning this light off and leaving the door open as she had found it earlier.

Descending the steps, she heard Logan's voice carrying softly from the living room, becoming louder and more clearly defined as she joined he and Stephanie.

Logan was not smiling but it was a reasonable facsimile. "Stephanie was just explaining to me the efforts she took designing and decorating both this house and SERENITY."

Without further prompting, Stephanie turned to Krystyna. "I'm quite pleased with the outcome. A treasure amid a bleak countryside of mediocrity, don't you think?"

Again, Krystyna's words camouflaged her true feelings about the structures. "Certainly, the style is decidedly unique."

The gold bracelets about Stephanie's arm chimed softly as she raised the espresso cup to her lips. "It will do for now." She said routinely, arching an elaborate brow.

Curious, Krystyna posed a question. "Undoubtedly, someone with your flair for design would naturally gravitate toward more challenging projects?"

"There are always new horizons beckoning to the creative side of some, yes."

"I would think your . . . creativity would be much sought after in the architecturally sophisticated cities of the world." Smiling, Krystyna watched Stephanie very closely as she continued. "Los Angeles, New York, Paris, London."

"That time will come, never fear." Stephanie said, her words edged in arrogance. It was time to change the subject. "Another espresso?" She asked, her tone cold and barren.

"No, thanks. Well, I suppose we should be leaving." Krystyna said, glancing at Logan, convinced nothing vital would be gleaned from further conversation with Stephanie. At least for now.

"Yes." Logan answered. "We'll return again Saturday evening, Stephanie."

"I'll see you to the door." Stephanie moved gracefully, her head held high, the heels of her sandals clicking sharply across the marbled floors. Logan and Krystyna followed her in silence.

A few feet away from the massive front door, Stephanie called out a command to the computerized system monitoring the security throughout the house. "Harold, unlock the front door."

The brass lock mechanism thumped heavily in the doorframe.

"Saturday." Stephanie said, even now straining with the social niceties expected of her.

Stepping outside, Logan and Krystyna were eagerly met by Taima, the thunder and lightning storm still in force, sheets of rain gushing down. The massive door closed behind them sharply as a muffled command to relock the door could be faintly heard.

Back in the Cherokee, both Logan and Krystyna were pensive, brooding in their own thoughts, each attempting to sort these very thoughts in the hope of an amazing discovery of the truth. However, this elusive entity proved not easy to grasp for either one of them as they began the drive down the mile long graveled road, the windshield wipers swishing back and forth at high speed.

Nearing SERENITY, Logan turned to Krystyna. "I'd like to stop at the manned entrance gate. Nose around just a bit. There's something about Braddock's excessive need for security that's still bothering me. I think we should check it out."

"Do you think that wise?"

"Does that matter at this point?"

"No, you're absolutely right. It's a good idea."

Logan turned into SERENITY, the elaborate entrance gate protected with an enormous network of iron and steel cables. A male figure was posted inside a small wooden cubicle, sitting comfortably before a desk, and to his left a wide bank of electronic equipment was within easy reach. All four walls were encased in glass, affording the gatekeeper a full three hundred and sixty degree view of the entire compound.

However, the guard did not turn and look at them until they pulled directly along side the cubicle.

In the back seat Taima did not bark nor did she growl. Instead, she put her face to the window and eyed the male guard very curiously.

"What's wrong, Taima?" Logan whispered softly as he stole a glance at her in the rearview mirror. He would never have suspected this complacency from her when approaching a total stranger in the dark of night. She was ordinarily far too protective and possessive to be modest or hesitant. True, an inquisitive sparkle shone in her eyes, but he expected a much stronger reaction. This unusual behavior only added to Logan's uneasiness.

Logan rolled his window down to speak to the guard. "Excuse me. Is this SERENITY?"

The guard turned to Logan, and as he did so a multitude of outdoor lighting was activated. Strong beams of illumination forced the darkness to scurry away in all directions; sparkling alabaster stars against a raven-black sky, Logan thought. Hope in the midst of agony; a guiding light. Logan was convinced Braddock would have planned it that way.

"This is SERENITY." The guard began, his voice deep and hollow sounding. "If you have an appointment, use your verbal code to enter through the gate. If not, you can schedule an appointment during our regular office hours by calling 332-6163."

"We've already met with Dr. Braddock earlier this evening at his home, but there was no mention of a code to enter through the gates."

"You must have your verbal code to enter SERENITY." The guard's voice was featureless as he stared vacantly through the glass enclosed cubicle. "If you wish to leave a message, you may do so now."

"No, that won't be necessary." Logan stated.

His own curiosity now set in motion, Logan slowly opened the driver's door and touched his feet to the blacktop, the rain drenching him quickly as he resumed speaking to the guard. "What are the office hours?"

"Eight to five, Monday through Friday. The office number is 332-6163."

Stepping close to the glass wall of the cubicle, peering in at the guard, Logan made a quick decision borne of intuition. Slowly, Logan walked the few steps around to the back of the cubicle. The guard never turned around.

"Okay. I have paper and pen now." Logan called out from the rear of the cubicle as he stood staring at the back of the guard's head. "What was that number?"

"332-6163."

"And the hours again, please." Logan requested, his jacket turning soggy with the rain.

"Eight to five, Monday through Friday."

Returning to the front of the cubicle, Logan stared a long moment at the guard, face to face. An ominous feeling in his gut just wouldn't go away.

Finally Logan asked the guard, "Unseasonably warm weather for an autumn night, wouldn't you say?"

Logan held his breath for a moment.

The guard's tone was lackluster. "Yes, very nice, unseasonably warm."

"Thank you." Logan called out as he joined Krystyna in the Jeep.

Suddenly, before they could drive away, a bloodcurdling scream reached them, cutting above the rain and the spiraling wind. It had come from inside SERENITY.

From the back seat, Taima's body tensed, the hair on her back rising, a low guttural warning emanating from her throat.

Another piercing, terror-fraught scream vibrated across the compound. It sang of sorrow, it sang of endless pain and anguish.

It was anything but sweet and filled with serenity.

CHAPTER FOURTEEN

The male guard sat rigidly, oblivious to the screams, a blank look to his pale face as Logan and Krystyna quickly pulled away from SERENITY.

Krystyna waited to speak until they reached the main road, the screams gradually dissipating, and SERENITY was completely out of sight. "I never thought I would again hear those awful cries."

"Krystyna, I won't suggest that we go back, there's nothing we can do at the moment. We can't even get into the wretched place."

"I suppose you're right. At least for now." Krystyna paused, her thoughts returning to the guard. "Logan, what do you make of the guard?"

"Rather mechanical, wasn't he?" The sardonic grin surfaced momentarily.

"Not only that, but was he blind as well? Couldn't he see there was a storm?"

"Apparently not, Krystyna, but I doubt he was blind. He would not be employed as a watchdog if that were the case."

"Then why didn't he realize you had walked around behind him?"

"I'm not sure, but the man clearly failed to notice."

"Logan, the guard behaved more like a cybernetic robot of some sort, programmed and all. Are you thinking along those lines?"

"That's a good guess." Logan answered. "But, I've my doubts about that possibility. I really don't know what to think."

"Did you notice he wasn't wearing a gun?"

"Yes, but he probably has one stashed in a drawer."

"Logan, do you think the guard was . . . human?"

He turned to Krystyna, his expression sober. "He looked as any man would. But human? Perhaps human-like, but not entirely. He didn't seem capable of thinking for himself."

"Maybe he doesn't . . . anymore." Krystyna said quietly.

Logan stepped more firmly on the gas pedal, eager to reach home and do what he could to soften the razor edge of sorrow slicing through Krystyna's voice. It seemed to cut through him as well.

At the Reed Ranch, Orenda and Garrett Chambers listened intently to the entire story retelling the events of the evening, and both were reeling from the drama of it all. Logan and Krystyna had been so close to their answers, and yet so far, Orenda thought in frustration. Much like the young Native American woman who was lost in the mountains, only to find death awaiting her at the Falls.

Then, Orenda's hopes were dashed further when she shared a few minutes with Logan in private. He had sarcastically referred to Dr. Braddock as a Jekyll and Hyde clone; a sinister and sleazy mix of masterful manipulation, insanely rabid with arrogance. Nevertheless, those character flaws were only a meager sampling of his bad side.

And yet, Logan confided with Orenda, Braddock had a soft spot in his callous armor, and that one weakness was Krystyna. Logan believed that Braddock still loved her, always had; deep from the heart, or what ever that maniac called a heart. Orenda soon came to realize that Logan's suspicions held in the same vein as her own.

During their private conversation, Orenda saw for herself that Logan also held strong feelings for Krystyna. There was little disputing that; it had brought out a vulnerability she had never before seen in her son. As well, a fierce hatred glowed in Logan's eyes when he breathed Dr. Braddock's name. There was a fury there, smoldering.

With this information, Orenda acknowledged Dr. Braddock represented a stronger threat than they could have supposed, merely because he was emotionally attached to Krystyna. And when emotions were involved, as Logan sternly pointed out to Orenda, the crime of passion, or love gone wrong, could become brutal and bad to the very bone. Unquestionably, they both

102

agreed, Dr. Braddock was the sort to suck the marrow right out and pick it clean.

Their group was nestled before the stone fireplace, Samuel asleep in a nearby bedroom, the mood somber, questions unanswered and dangling in the air; wispy tendrils of doubt disheartening.

It was the right time, Orenda thought, addressing Krystyna. "I think before we discuss anything further we should listen to your taped conversation with Dr. Braddock."

"I quite agree." Garrett said, absentmindedly rubbing his right thigh, his phantom pain throbbing as it often did, especially on cold wet nights.

Retrieving the tape recorder from her purse, Krystyna rewound the tape and placed it on an oak coffee table for all to hear. She pressed PLAY. She remembered the moment well, could again feel her apprehension, her disrespect for Martin rushing through her. Martin's deep voice, a mesmerizing, melodious, silvery tone, one she could identify forever, startled her nevertheless. A cold sweat again covered her skin.

Garrett looked over to Orenda for her reaction and her perception of the mad scientist. She sat stiffly in her chair, her mahogany brown eyes staring at the recorder.

Or, perhaps that was disbelief Garrett saw in her eyes. What ever it was, Garrett didn't like it; it didn't suit Orenda. Not in one whose eyes always painted warmth and compassion, a wisdom borne to only a precious few. Orenda was deeply concerned, and that made Garrett squirm in his chair.

His leg, despite its absence, ached all the more.

From his place at the hearth, Logan stepped over to Krystyna, sitting beside her, wrapping an arm around her cold shoulders. She turned slightly toward him. The pained look in her gray eyes exposed her frail emotions; the prisoner about to reenter the prison and face the evil warden.

Braddock's impassioned words saturated and swallowed the room. "Can you imagine every day of your life filled with rampaging oceans of adrenaline, your heart racing wildly, hands turning to ice, waves of perspiration damp and tell-tale, your physical body mobilized at every breath for fight or flight . . . never knowing which? Can you imagine the inability to sleep, night after weary night, your fears turning to nightmares far too unbearable to endure, at time unspeakable, unfathomable?"

They listened with their hearts, or perhaps even with their souls.

There it was again . . . the voice.

He knew it was "THE" nightmare right away, the same one, a hideous repetition that made his skin crawl no less each and every time.

Strangely enough though, he knew to hide in the dark crevasses of his mind, or try just the same, and he called that instinct.

Unfortunately, that only worked in . . . daylight.

At night, the subconscious part of his mind took control, taking him, again and again, defenseless, to the brink of his deepest, darkest fear.

And then there was the voice, silky and smooth.

He desperately didn't want to go!

But he had been told that he must. It was the only way to be cured.

He still didn't want to go to the rooftop and look down. He had been told to face his fear. Feel his fear come alive, exhumed from its vile and musty place, reaching its cold clammy fingers around his heart, clenching tightly, more tightly still, until he was forced to surrender to his fear.

Yes, he was told, welcome his fear as a blood brother.

But, his fear took his very breath from him; stole it away like a thief in the night.

He entered the room, doing just as he was instructed, sitting down in the emerald leather chair; the single piece of furniture to be found in the windowless and otherwise empty room.

The door closed, hard.

Then came the verbal command to secure the deadbolt.

Click, the lock was engaged.

There was no other way out.

He closed his eyes tightly, knowing what would happen next. After all, hadn't this been tailor-made just for him?

Yet, his eyes would not stay closed for long. The music was the first to touch his senses; soft violins created soothing melodies both calming and serene. Pictures on the walls came to life; comforting colors splashed across a field of vibrant flowers, sprinkled with sunlight, clouds dancing like ballerinas in the background of a porcelain blue sky. A graceful forest of evergreen trees swayed gently in a slight breeze.

It was utterly peaceful; a clarity borne from only nature. It reminded the young man of the FALLS. Or, a comforting arm wrapped snugly about his shoulders.

Then, as always, the colors of the scene burst into three-dimensional form in every direction; to his left, to his right, before him and behind him. He was surrounded with a living, breathing realism.

There was no way out now.

This was as real as real gets.

The room with a single chair as its only furnishing, ceased to exist.

In its place, a new world had been sculpted, energized into existence as any other creature enjoying life.

And now, this new world belonged to him.

He wanted no part of it.

The walls held a heartbeat; a slow, steady throbbing that the young man felt deep in his bones, the blood in his veins pumping neatly with the rhythm. The glorious sunlit sky beckoned to him, the voice telling him to step into the light and relish the warmth of the sun upon his upturned face. The voice told him to dance among the flowers with the butterflies. Drink in the essence of purity. Cherish the bird's sweet songs.

Rising from the leather chair, he did as he was told.

Still, his legs shook, waves of sickly tremors draining his strength, but he pushed himself deeper into the field of flowers before him. A bee buzzed at his ear for a noisy moment. The young man bent over to pluck a white daisy from the brilliant carpet of colors, the sap from the broken stem sticking to his fingers.

He had done this before, precisely this way, even to the daisy.

Next, he knew the sky would darken.

He trembled again, hot acid rolling in his queasy stomach.

The scene would become, not a field of wildflowers, but an asphalt jungle. And the voice of the big city beckoned to him; come face your fear, come feel your fear.

The scene changed instantly around him. He no longer felt the warm rays of sunshine upon his face. Gone were the flowers, the birds, the sweet music. Gone were the blessed trees. The city wrapped her arms around him and held tight.

There was no corner of his mind in which to hide now, the young man thought.

He walked on and on, solid pavement scrunching under his shoes, and along the streets, it seemed to him, at least a million buses, trucks and cars, spat their toxins into the air, screeching their tires, honking. The deafening clamor of the city vibrated all around him.

The people of the city brushed past him without looking at him, a blank stare to their pallid faces. Certainly no one answered his pleas for help. He was ignored.

An ebony veil smothered the lingering shreds of daylight, the field of flowers now worlds away. For a fleeting moment the young man longed for the solitude of the tall building. But only for a moment until he realized with a sharp twinge of panic that the tall building did not offer him a sanctuary. No, never that.

That was where his fear lived, an evil thing that threatened to devour him.

He slowed his pace, feeling the elusive hand of destiny drawing him to the tall building, the skyscraper, his will and freedom of thought . . . lost, as he was.

This is where it happens, he screamed, a mewlish cry uttered through clenched teeth. But, there was no one to hear him. He knew that as well. There was never anyone else in the building. He was always alone, so alone.

Standing still now, feet braced firmly apart, the massive mouth of the skyscraper opened to allow him entrance. He bent backward, craning his neck to look up at the tall building, the rooftop disappearing into the night sky. Yet, no beacons of light shone through the haze at those heights. Up there . . . it was always dark.

When he failed to enter the building immediately, a silent hand tugged at his shirtsleeve, a serpentine voice urging him forward.

As he moved across the threshold, his tennis shoes squeaked sharply along the polished floors of the foyer. If only he would have been allowed to take the stairs to the rooftop, he thought, maybe that would have made the ordeal easier. But, it was against the rules of the game. He must ride the elevator up dozens and dozens of floors, being propelled at a nauseating speed until he was certain his heart would stop.

He just knew that he couldn't go through with it.

He wasn't the only one with this phobia. So, why pick on him? Couldn't he be afraid, just like millions of others? Wasn't it okay?

No, he had asked to be cured. He had agreed to this.

My God, what had he done?

What had the doctor done?

What about all the others?

The elevator doors beckoned to him; they wanted to fly him up to the rooftop, his stomach plunging to the bottom, the blood vessels in his head suddenly feverish and pulsating painfully. Once there in the small cubicle of the elevator, he wouldn't be capable of hanging onto the railing, his hands slippery, powerless against his fear.

He knew all of this. He'd been here before, many times.

The elevator doors were not quite twenty feet away now.

107

He walked stiffly over to the elevator doors, doing as he was told, his tennis shoes screeching along the floors in a failed effort to dig in his heels, the protest he felt visible in his rigid posture.

All too soon he stood directly before the elevator doors. Beads of sweat formed on his upper lip. The hair at the back of his neck was damp.

The doors opened, the elevator car empty.

Or was it, this time?

His heart pounded fiercely in his chest.

His eyes felt they would burst.

The doors remained patiently open, a black sea of evil swirling in the distance, whispering his name.

Samuel.

Samuel.

Samuel.

CHAPTER FIFTEEN

Suddenly, the group heard penetrating screams coming from Samuel's bedroom. Logan was the first to respond, his adrenaline quickly igniting him into action. He ran to the bedroom, flinging the door open, turned on the overhead light, only to find Samuel crouched in an alcove between a dresser and a chair; Samuel's fetal position a devastating portrayal of his emotional pain.

When Orenda, Krystyna and Garrett reached the bedroom, Logan was cradling Samuel in his arms, rocking him gently. Orenda knelt beside her two sons and rocked with them, grieving for the harm done to Samuel. This was a silent exchange of hearts where no words were spoken in this delicate and frail moment of hopelessness.

Witnessing their pain brought cruel and bitter tears to Krystyna's eyes. Garrett noticed the effect this was having on her, so he drew a fatherly arm around her shoulders, and gently guided her back into the living room. This would allow Orenda and her son, Samuel in particular, a few moments alone. Garrett knew that Orenda would guide them well with wisdom.

Garrett also realized this was Logan's first experience in witnessing the aftermath of Samuel's nightmares. And Braddock had the audacity to call this serenity? The mere thought disgusted Garrett. It was incomprehensible to him.

For Krystyna, the anguish of the scene in the bedroom tore at her resolve, forcing memories of the past to life; similar scenes exorcised from the dead, but not forgotten, and now fresh as the fear on Samuel's grimacing face.

However, this time the pain went deeper, much deeper. Krystyna had allowed herself to become involved with this family. She cared what happened to Samuel, a dear sweet young man who was just beginning to enjoy adulthood. She cared what happened to Orenda, an endearing friend, a loving mother, a woman of natural grace.

And there was Logan. Her heart more than went out to him, it was filled with him. But, she could not allow herself to think beyond that, for now. Krystyna was not going to see this family torn apart any longer. Not only had she made a promise to Orenda, she had come to WHISPERING FALLS on a promise made to herself, and to this promise she added yet another. Krystyna would stop Martin from hurting vulnerable human beings for his own selfish purposes.

Yet, the prices to pay for stopping Martin would cost dearly, likely to include Krystyna's personal fears of him.

There it was; she had finally admitted it to herself. Krystyna was afraid of Martin. Plain and simple, really.

But the worst of it was that Martin had always known, had used it against her all these years. Was still using it against her, manipulating her, toying with her, experimenting on her as if she herself were a patient. Martin, the zealous exploiter of human weaknesses.

Enough was enough, Krystyna thought. "Garrett, I need your help."

"Anything in my power."

"There must be someone in town who would be willing to talk to me about Martin; someone whose knowledge was acquired on the inside of SERENITY. An employee perhaps?"

Garrett's thoughts ran through a mental list of town residents who had remained, refusing to flee from their homes. The list was pitiful and few. And among that list, most of the residents were terribly . . . afflicted, caught up in the evil web Braddock had woven so carefully, unable or unwilling to describe the treatments. He wasn't even sure who still worked for Braddock, if anyone.

"I'm sorry," Garrett answered, "but I can't think of a soul."

This was terribly frustrating for Krystyna. "Surely, there must be someone."

Garrett shrugged his shoulders. "You've seen a few for yourself. William Fairchild, the workaholic from the hardware store, is oblivious to his surroundings for the most part. His mind is running in a circle while he scrambles around like a trapped mouse in a maze. The same goes for Virginia Pedersen, the compulsive cleaner of the clothing store. The only difference is there's a can of disinfectant in her hand. To varying degrees, all are lost in their own little worlds, thinking everything is fine. They think they are fine."

"They've been convinced of that, Garrett."

"Some convincing, huh?"

Krystyna felt a sudden chill. "And Samuel heard Martin's voice on the recorder, and hearing his voice stimulated a nightmare, acting as a catalyst?"

"It would seem." Garrett answered. "And now that he's awake, I wonder how much he remembers?"

"I remember more than I want to." Samuel said, entering the room, drawing close to the stone fireplace, rubbing his cold hands together before the flames.

Logan and Orenda had followed him into the room, Orenda an arm's distance from Samuel, and Logan claiming the seat next to Krystyna. Each and every one waited for Samuel to continue speaking.

"I'll tell you what I know." Samuel began, "I just hope you can figure it out."

Admiring Samuel's strength and courage, Krystyna asked in a gentle tone. "Are you certain you want to tell us?"

"Yes. I want it over with." Samuel answered, his fingers beginning to fidget with the belt of his robe.

Krystyna turned to Logan. His jaw was set firmly, his anger held in bitter restraint, his large hands opening and closing anxiously into clenched fists. When he failed to turn to her, Krystyna reached her hand over to his and squeezed softly. He squeezed back although he continued staring at Samuel. She wanted so much to erase his pain, all of their pain.

Clearing his throat, Samuel began. "Next year I'd planned on attending college. I wanted to go as a man, not as a child, and not with a silly fear of heights! No, it's not silly. I know that now. But I thought it would make the difference, thought it would make me a whole person. I made the decision to visit Dr. Braddock and see for myself if he could help me with my fear of

111

heights. A friend of mine was getting good results, or so he believed. We were told others were getting good results. They'd taken the cure. So, I went to SERENITY and during the orientation I was convinced this treatment was for me. I could go away to college and leave my fear of heights behind. Braddock would wave his magic wand and I'd be cured."

As Samuel smiled, his blue eyes remained cold and somber. "I knew that mother would never agree to my receiving treatments at SERENITY, and I'm sorry to say I went behind her back . . . lied to her . . ."

Orenda began to speak but Samuel politely motioned her to remain silent. "It's necessary for me to explain."

Samuel paused, collecting his thoughts. "Dr. Braddock made it sound like he had all the answers, and what answers he didn't have, our subconscious did, according to his theories. It was a visual thing, he explained, and what our minds accepted as visually real, was just that, real. So, Dr. Braddock made the pictures somehow . . . I'm not sure what he uses, but the outcome was . . . so real, so frightening. I was already there in the pictures. I saw myself in them; faded blue jeans, tennis shoes, my favorite old green sweater. I walked into the scene and merged with my reflection. The pictures in my nightmares are a carbon copy of the pictures created for me at SERENITY. It's like seeing the same movie over and over again."

Samuel went on to describe the treatment room with the single chair, the door that was locked behind him, and in greater detail the pictures, and how he got lost in those very pictures. For all he knew he became one with the pictures, taken to the very edge of that skyscraper, standing precariously on the very edge, looking down, frozen with fear, a bloodsucking dizziness draining him of his courage.

He had been told that he would one day leap from that tall building, willingly, happily, joyfully, finally ridding himself of the fear and the frustrations and symptoms that accompanied his phobia. The pictures created for him would serve as a training ground, boot camp, a dry run, until one day when he would stand at the top of the skyscraper and look down without fear, knowing that fear no longer held him in its death grip.

"And now," Samuel said quietly, "I have nightmares of the tall building, the same picture scenes over and over again, my fear gnawing at my gut, breathing down my neck. It's worse than ever, full blown, larger than life. I wouldn't wish this on anyone."

Claiming a chair, Samuel looked to his mother. "I know you're trying to find out how Braddock is doing his treatments, and I can't help you there. I haven't a clue what he uses to produce the pictures; pictures so real you can feel the ground beneath your feet, you can touch a tree and feel the roughened bark, you can smell the summer air, and believe me you can, without any question, taste your own fear! It lives in those pictures. It lives in that room."

Samuel added quietly, "Welcome it as a blood brother."

"What did you say?" Logan demanded.

"Braddock said the picture worlds he created were a mirror image of ourselves, blood of our blood, created from a part of us he referred to as the Theater of the Mind."

Krystyna had heard this phrase from Martin before. "Martin Braddock is right to a point about that, Samuel." Krystyna said. "The answers are within ourselves, and to look within ourselves is fine, but not in his way, not with his brand of help."

"I'll see that you get the proper therapy." Logan offered. "I'll find a qualified doctor to treat you. He or she will be nothing like this wandering, self-proclaimed miracle man with magic up his sleeves! I'll scour the countryside for the right person."

"But what about the others?" Samuel asked. "What about my friend, Allyn? What about his mother, his father? They took the treatments, only to run away in the night, leaving their belongings, weeks ago. What about our neighbors who have been affected? Logan, what about them?" There were tears forming in Samuel's soft blue eyes.

"I don't know, Samuel, but I assure you when this is over, Braddock will never again perform this treatment on anyone. We'll see that he is never allowed to do so."

Samuel smiled faintly, his spirit lifting as his anger forced courage into his heart. "I'd like to lock Dr. Braddock away in one of his own picture worlds! Freeze him in a single frame! Make him stay there forever, a prisoner!"

"Who knows?" Logan said. "Maybe you'll get your wish when everything is said and done."

Krystyna's smile was serious. "Martin a prisoner, forever? Death row for the devil? Yes, I rather like that."

CHAPTER SIXTEEN

As he talked further, Samuel became less anxious, the trauma of his nightmare less visible in his eyes, that haunted look dissipating. Krystyna could see that he felt a sense of great relief, a heavy lonesome burden eased a bit from his shoulders. She watched Orenda who sat quietly, also observing Samuel very carefully, Orenda's determined expression rallying strength to all those around her.

Orenda told Krystyna she was convinced in her own mind that Samuel would weather this storm, despite the enormity of potential, just as well as any other. She had faith in her children, and in the men they had become.

As a group they continued talking for quite some time, the mood considerably lighter, the conversation turning to other events in their lives; a mutual need to balance the evil with an element of wholesomeness.

They brushed on happier times in the Reed household and Krystyna learned of Evan Reed, the statuesque Scandinavian man who came to WHISPERING FALLS on a fishing expedition, and never chose to leave the pristine emerald countryside again. Evan Reed, blonde and blue eyed, had fallen deeply in love with Orenda, marrying her after a mere twelve days, years later fathering Logan and then Samuel. Krystyna could see for herself that Logan resembled his mother, and after viewing the family photograph albums, she determined that he had also inherited his father's tall stature and rugged good looks. Samuel had assumed Evan Reed's fair skin, blonde hair, blue eyes, and mild mannerisms.

Theirs had been a happy childhood, Logan and Samuel. A loving mother and father who provided a solid and structured home life, acres of land to call home, an entire countryside of wonders for two young boys to explore. Orenda explained to Krystyna that Logan's interest in animals had become apparent as a very young child, his first casualty brought home in an old shoebox, a robin with a broken wing. Samuel had shown strong carpentry skills at an early age, Orenda had gone on to say, repairing his wooden toy chest at age four.

Garrett seemed quite comfortable speaking of Evan Reed, apparently knowing him a few years before Evan had succumbed to cancer. It was further apparent to Krystyna that Garrett held Evan Reed's memory dear in his own heart, having a profound and abiding respect for not only the man, but for Orenda, and her two sons. Garrett's emotional attachment to Orenda was a tangible thing, Krystyna thought, easily recognized in their interactions with one another. To a degree, Orenda mothered Garrett, and he let her, but in a sweet and caring way. Krystyna could easily envision the two of them living happily together for the remainder of their lives.

Krystyna could not, however, envision if WHISPERING FALLS would still be there for them, or anyone else for that matter. Martin's experiment was threatening to devour all in its path, sucking everything down, pulling like quicksand.

Also, it was not easy for Krystyna to dismiss the smoldering rage she saw gleaming in Logan's embittered eyes. Krystyna was increasingly fearful of what Logan might do to right the situation with Braddock.

At the same time, the more Krystyna learned of Logan and his life, the stronger her insatiable desire for him became, a burning curiosity that could not be subdued. This earthy, sensual man, stormy one moment, silent the next, and yet had captured her emotions as no other. Looking through the photographs of him as a young boy, she recognized his sardonic grin, even at age three, the incredible sparkle in his chocolate brown eyes at age nine, the tenderness he showed his dying kitten at age eleven.

Now as a man, Logan had carried with him, a profound sense of spirituality, strict moral codes, and an enduring emotional bond with his mother and brother. Logan clearly respected his bloodlines, at the same time respecting his fellow man, and what his fellow man held near and dear to their own heart.

Again, Krystyna remarked to herself of Logan's unending compassion. It was a warm thing, and when he looked at her, that very compassion shone in his eyes.

Krystyna returned Logan's smile. He'd been staring at her again; a soulful look, long and meaningful.

For the first time since her own treasured childhood, Krystyna felt at home. Perhaps it was the cozy fire at the hearth, or the compassionate human beings in her presence, or Taima on the floor snuggled about her ankles, fast asleep, contented. Taking a deep breath, Krystyna wished that the moment could last forever. But, she knew it wouldn't.

Tomorrow was Friday. She had planned on leaving WHISPERING FALLS Monday immediately after signing the divorce papers.

That left only a few days, too few.

But, Krystyna would make each day count as if they were her very last.

Tossing and turning, Krystyna did not sleep well. Visions of Samuel falling from the roof of a tall building crept into her dreams that night, and finally she decided to get up, shower and dress. The hour was early, not quite seven, and she left her cabin and headed for town in the Jeep Cherokee, feeling the need to do something, anything.

Deciding she should speak further with Garrett, Krystyna realized Garrett's bookstore would not open for another hour, so she used the time to slowly drive along the lonely streets of the town. Not a solitary soul walked about, nor did she pass another car. Nothing, it would seem, lived.

Stopping at the police station, Krystyna found a handwritten note, nearly illegible, undoubtedly scrawled in a hurried moment, taped to the entrance doors. The note said:

CLOSED UNTIL FURTHER NOTICE.
IF YOU HAVE AN EMERGENCY AND NEED ASSISTANCE,
PLEASE CONTACT THE COUNTY SHERIFF AT 332-1400.

It appeared the police chief had been one of the first to leave town, Krystyna determined, judging by the stack of rolled newspapers, yellowed and tattered, at the doors. A thick film of dust covered the windows, one large pane showing evidence that someone had written with their finger through the dust:

THE CAPTAIN'S JOB IS TO GO DOWN WITH THE SHIP,
NOT BE THE FIRST TO ABANDON IT!

Krystyna pulled the Jeep before the one and only restaurant, hoping that a cup of black coffee wasn't too much to ask for in this all but deserted ghost town. A brass bell jingled sharply as she closed the restaurant door behind her, entering the establishment, calling out as she claimed a seat.

"Hello?"

There was no answer.

Again, Krystyna called out. Again, no answer.

The rich aroma of fresh coffee filled the air, and behind the yellow Formica counter she spotted a coffeemaker with a pot on the burner. She stepped quickly behind the counter, and was about to pour herself a cup when she heard the bell chime at the door. Krystyna turned to look at the man who entered the restaurant. Middle aged, he was dressed in tan slacks, a garishly patterned plaid jacket, and a camel hair overcoat was missing three leather covered buttons. He also carried a battered briefcase.

The man tossed his mouse-brown hair away from his eyes, peered at his watch, tapping an impatient finger to the crystal. "I'd have a cup of that, please." He said to Krystyna, not really looking at her as he claimed a booth nearest a large window.

Why not? Krystyna commented to herself. She filled a cup with coffee, and as she walked over to the man she noted he had opened his briefcase and was rummaging through an untidy pile of papers. There were official documents, affidavits, and various legal papers from what Krystyna could see.

Documentation that an attorney would surely have in his possession, she quickly surmised.

The man did not look at Krystyna as she set the cup of coffee on the table before him. When he failed to respond, other than a perfunctory thank you, Krystyna remained in position, waiting for him to look up at her.

Another few seconds later, he did. "Yes?" He said, reaching into his pocket, withdrawing a dollar bill and placing it on the table absentmindedly, his eyes quickly drawn back to his pile of papers.

"Michael Overby?" Krystyna asked, a slender ray of hope filling her heart.

"Yes." The man answered, raising his head, expressionless, clearly not knowing or caring who Krystyna was.

She extended her hand. "I'm Krystyna Kramer-Braddock. I think we have business to attend to, you and I."

Nearly choking on his cup of coffee, Michael Overby paled before Krystyna's eyes. His handshake was weak as he mumbled, "Krystyna Braddock, oh yes, Martin's . . ."

"Wife." Krystyna said evenly, sitting down across from the attorney. "I'm his wife. That is . . . until Monday."

"Yes, Monday. I can only assume Dr. Braddock explained I was called out of town unexpectedly."

"That's what I've been led to believe." Krystyna's eyes were gray clouds of suspicion. "And now, just as unexpectedly, you're here."

"Just returned, actually." Shades of guilt were written across the attorney's mildly attractive features.

"However," Michael Overby said quickly, rushing now, taking a hurried gulp of coffee. "I've had to squeeze in other appointments that I've missed these past few days, and I'm booked solid until Monday as a result."

"Yes, I'm quite certain this thriving metropolis holds your legal services in high demand these days. But, that's quite all right, Mr. Overby. Monday will suit me just fine. We'll sign the divorce papers as planned." Krystyna said, her smile effectively throwing the attorney off guard.

"Nevertheless," Krystyna added, her smile shrewd and secretive. "There is one small favor I would ask of you now. I know it's within my legal rights to obtain a complete listing of Martin's assets, a list that would include even the walnut desk he inherited from his father."

Krystyna watched the man's bloodshot eyes widen nervously as she continued. "I'd like to exercise that option available to me." Krystyna said firmly, her smile vanishing as she finished the sentence. "Now, right now."

"Now?" The attorney repeated, hastily deciding that the woman who sat before him would never agree to sign on Monday, willingly signing away her fair share of a blockbuster fortune in everything from high-dollar real estate holdings, to Braddock's impressive collection of rare diamonds. When Krystyna Braddock fully understood what her husband was really worth, she'd never sign, he thought. Merely human nature, he assumed, thinking his judgment of people extraordinary accurate. But, this time it had to be different. He knew that this particular divorce must be finalized, at any cost; there had been explicit instructions to this end. All in all, several people were depending on this divorce, himself one of them.

"Now is not a good time, Mrs. Braddock. I might suggest that you look over Martin's list of assets on Monday prior to your signing the final decree."

"Not good enough, Mr. Overby." Krystyna answered flatly. "Today . . . now . . . this very moment."

Krystyna paused again, her harsh tone unconditional. "Or, I must consider leaving WHISPERING FALLS immediately, postponing the signing of the divorce papers for perhaps another . . . year . . . or two."

Michael Overby quickly made a decision, against his better judgment. "Now would be perfectly fine. After all, it shouldn't take too terribly long to find the papers you're asking to see. I have them at my office and I was just on my way there."

"Good. I'll follow you in my car." Sliding out from the booth, Krystyna smiled once again as she stood waiting for the attorney, his fingers shaking nervously as he stuffed his documents back into the battered briefcase.

After returning to his small and untidy office, Michael Overby handed Krystyna the list of Martin's assets; it was detailed over sixteen single-spaced pages. She looked the list over carefully as she remained standing, refusing the chair the attorney had offered. Indeed, she was truly amazed at the contents of the list.

"Very interesting, Mr. Overby."

Oh no, he thought, cringing inwardly at Krystyna's impish expression; now she'll never agree to the terms of the divorce, and worse than that, maybe not to the divorce at all! Holding his breath, Michael Overby's hand eagerly reached out to take back the papers.

"No." Krystyna commented casually, folding the papers and placing them into her purse.

Like a stone statue, Michael Overby's arm remained extended, his hand open, empty.

"I'll be taking these with me. I'll have a chance to read over Martin's assets and have time in which to . . ." Krystyna smiled innocently. "Reflect."

"Just keep in mind, Mrs. Braddock, your husband is more than willing to give you . . ."

"Give me?" Krystyna crossed her arms before her, a stern twist to her words. "Martin never gives anyone anything. He always wants something sacred in return."

"I wouldn't know about that."

"Not yet, you don't."

"I think Mr. Braddock is offering you a very fair and equitable sum. I might suggest you not push him for more." Michael Overby said.

"That's for me to decide."

"Of course, Mrs. Braddock."

"I may . . . or . . . may not see you on Monday." Krystyna said soberly, her words strong and even, her hand now resting on the doorknob.

The attorney desperately needed to know more. "Second thoughts, Mrs. Braddock?"

"For whom?" Krystyna answered, offering the attorney a mischievous grin. "I won't keep you any longer. Thank you for the list, Mr. Overby. It's been very . . . enlightening."

CHAPTER SEVENTEEN

Krystyna decided it best to leave Michael Overby with the distinct impression she was having second thoughts about the divorce. In truth, she never had. Just as sincerely, Martin's money meant absolutely nothing to her. And this was something Martin could never quite understand, incapable of appreciating her willingness to pay any price for her freedom. Martin had become enormously incensed over the matter in the past, clearly frustrated at his inability to gain further control of her; Krystyna, out of reach, unobtainable.

It was also inevitable that Michael Overby convey Krystyna's apparent hesitancy directly to Martin Braddock, who would then likely share this with Stephanie. Not entirely certain what their responses might entail, she realized that at the very least, both Martin and Stephanie would be forced to strongly reconsider what action Krystyna was contemplating.

Let them wonder, she thought. Let them squirm.

On another score, the list Krystyna had obtained from Michael Overby was undeniably a true shock. It would seem Martin had acquired wealth beyond her wildest expectations, and another cursory look at the list drilled another chard of realism through her. As long as Martin had this kind of money to support his fanaticism, he would continue using vulnerable human beings for his experiments.

Martin's wealth enabled him to do what he chose to do. It gave him a power Krystyna would not credit him without.

Martin's wealth had always been his backbone.

Back on Alder Street, Krystyna drove to BOOKENDS, ETC., hoping to speak with Garrett Chambers. He seemed quite pleased to see her, a subtle hint of loneliness in his startling blue eyes.

"Glad for the company, Krystyna. There's a tomb-like silence around here these days and I'm afraid I've all but lost my clientele. Let's see now," Garrett said, his wooden leg scraping across the floor. "In the last three days I've counted at least a dozen families who've left town."

"It's frightening how fast evil can escalate and devour, but I refuse to believe that all is lost." Krystyna paused, changing the subject. "I had a chance encounter with someone rather interesting this morning; Michael Overby. He's Martin's attorney, the one handling the divorce. What do you know of him?"

"Very little, I'm afraid. Keeps to himself, blends in with the woodwork. Since most business in WHISPERING FALLS has all but withered and dried up, I would sooner think he's sitting around, twiddling his thumbs, waiting, just waiting."

"Waiting for what, Garrett?"

"For . . . the end? I don't know. Maybe his cut?"

"That's a thought. He certainly wasn't the man I was expecting. Michael Overby appeared a bit too meek and mild for an attorney, but now that I've mentioned that, he's just the sort Martin could most easily manipulate. True to his form, Martin preys on the weak."

"Braddock's puppet?" Garrett suggested.

"More than likely one of many." She agreed. "However, we could reason that most camp followers have already taken their leave, throwing in the towel long ago."

"I wonder how many remain?" Garrett asked.

A brief but penetrating picture of SERENITY flashed through Krystyna's mind. She could envision that, at the busiest of times, there would have been an employee securing the guardhouse, perhaps someone standing inside monitoring the front entrance, an assistant or two, and a part-time janitor. Other than a cook and possibly a maid at Martin's personal home, she doubted the existence of an armed guard solely because Martin had installed the sophisticated security system.

"A handful of watchdogs, at best." Krystyna finally answered thoughtfully. "But still, too many."

She continued, her words a mere whisper. "One too many."

Regretfully, Krystyna recognized that Martin was a lethal army in and of himself; a stand-alone savage.

Garrett brought Krystyna's thoughts back into focus as he asked, "So then, what did the attorney have to say?"

"Michael Overby seemed rather anxious I sign the divorce decree on Monday and not make any waves."

Krystyna opened her purse and withdrew the papers listing Martin's assets, handing them to Garrett. "I'll be signing away my legal share. I've insisted it be this way."

Taking his reading glasses from his shirt pocket, Garrett read the list carefully. Minutes later he gave Krystyna a sober smile. "I'm impressed."

"Without all this, SERENITY would never be."

"Krystyna, it's too bad you couldn't take it all away from Braddock, every last cent."

"Yes, and do some good with it, but I doubt even that would stop Martin. Come what may, he would obstinately pursue his evil work to the extent that if he had to sell pencils on the street corner to do so, he would, and with a shameless smile."

Krystyna turned to peer through the windows overlooking Alder Street. "We can't ever forget that desperate people do desperate things, and Martin, despite his aura of composure, can't deny something has backfired, and it's his doing. And now, he's recklessly trying to fix it before it destroys him. Martin . . ."

Movement on the street caught her eye. A dark brown late model Oldsmobile sped down the road, heading east, and behind the wheel was Michael Overby. Krystyna continued to stare after the brown car as it cleared the bend in the road, spiraling drifts of dust in its wake, the dust evolving into phantom-like apparitions.

"It would seem Michael Overby is certainly in a hurry to meet with someone." Krystyna said, turning to Garrett, a mischievous sparkle in her eyes. "Garrett, can I borrow your car? Just now, I don't want to be seen in mine."

"Well yes, it's out back, the keys are in the ignition, but . . ."

"Good." Krystyna said, running to the rear of the shop. "I've got to hurry."

Garrett ran his fingers through his thick gray hair. "Good Lord, girl, be careful!"

Krystyna was out the back door before she could hear the last of Garrett's words. After starting the car she accelerated hard, due northeast, with an early assumption that Michael Overby was going straight to Martin. Krystyna wanted to know if, as a collective group, they had felt it important enough for a hastened meeting. If so, then perhaps Krystyna had more leverage than she once thought.

As she encountered the brown Oldsmobile a reasonable distance ahead of her, Krystyna slowed her pace, noting they had already passed the turn for SERENITY. Where then was Michael Overby going?

Not terribly familiar with the roads, Krystyna found her sense of direction was thrown off balance as the brown Oldsmobile veered south, or what she thought was south, taking a little used gravel road. Within minutes dense towering evergreens suffocated the landscape on either side, arching heavy branches across the narrow roadway, forcing the daylight to grow dim. Krystyna saw the brown car brake and make another turn. She followed, keeping as much distance between them as she could allow.

Soon, she began to recognize the architecture of the land. She was certain the FALLS were somewhere near, and as she rolled the window down, Krystyna could easily hear the rushing waters, brisk in their descent, the pungent musty aroma of the river with its muddy yet fertile banks.

Eventually, Michael Overby pulled the Oldsmobile into a small roadside parking area that had been provided for tourists wishing a closer view from the top of the FALLS. Krystyna continued driving, stopping several hundred yards further down the road, and turned into the circular driveway of an abandoned home. She parked Garrett's green Ford, well out of view from the road. She ran through the woods, backtracking, keeping a parallel line with the road, the surging waters echoing in her ears, the evergreen trees thick, slowing her pace.

Sudden movement in a small clearing ahead caught Krystyna's attention. She stayed precisely in place, dropping down to her knees, further concealing her position. From this vantage point she could easily watch Michael Overby as he paced back and forth, eventually leaning against a wrought iron railing which had been secured on an outcropping of solid rock.

The view from this secluded spot was magnificent, but Michael Overby seemed not to notice, his interest focused on a solitary figure fast approaching him.

The figure, clothed in a dark blue raincoat, the hood brought up and over the head, raised a bold arm toward the attorney. Michael Overby flinched, taking a hesitant step back as he mumbled something.

The raised arm then fell to the figure's side.

An apparent argument ensued between the two, harsh comments muffled by the tempestuous wall of water. Eager to learn what she could, unable at this distance to decipher actual words, Krystyna crept closer.

Now repositioned, she was hardly better off. She could merely depict that the figure in the raincoat was exceedingly angry, the arm raising again, tempted to strike out, much like a snake's tongue slashing through the air with its venomous message.

Yet, Michael Overby's body language told a bit more. Undeniably, Michael Overby was angry, given his multiple attempts at throwing his own hands up into the air in utter frustration, consistently shaking his head in disagreement. As the heated debate began to flicker in intensity, the slump of Michael Overby's shoulders signified his reluctant acceptance of a situation conceivably out of his control. All the while, the figure stood tall, composed, words delivered softly, secretively, even in the midst of isolation.

As the figure turned to leave, Michael Overby reached out to touch the figure on the shoulder. The retreating person stopped, whirled around, the hood of the raincoat slipping away as he or she faced the attorney.

The figure smiled at the attorney; a contrived smile, Stephanie Robert's smile.

CHAPTER EIGHTEEN

Earlier, nestled among the evergreen trees, Krystyna was fairly certain the figure was Martin. Now, it seemed very significant that it was Stephanie, and alone, who had responded to the emergency meeting with the attorney. Perhaps Martin had been otherwise occupied in his laboratory, his attention required elsewhere, another patient crisis. Still, it seemed odd to Krystyna; Martin much preferring to take care of business himself, one of the legacies he assumed long ago as a self-made scientist. This had left him with a death grip on each and every gruesome detail, an insatiable need to be in control and handle any given situation personally, very personally. If at all possible, Martin would never trust another in his place, allowing someone else to wring a sadistic pleasure from his own dirty deeds.

Then again, it was within the realm of possibility that Martin was unaware of this meeting, purposefully kept in the dark. That, in itself, opened up all avenues of thought for Krystyna.

It had become brazenly apparent that Michael Overby assumed Krystyna was showing telltale signs of strongly reconsidering her financial position. The simple fact an urgent meeting had been orchestrated, confirmed this for Krystyna. That's good, she mused, let them hang in doubt, questioning her next move, confusion clouding their perspective.

And, wasn't it interesting, Krystyna reflected, that a select few were suddenly exhibiting a voracious interest in the monetary settlement of her divorce? She was not among that group, however. Amazingly, neither was Martin. Change the color of his soul? No, never. It was merely out of character for one who always regarded his great wealth only as a means to an end. Beyond that, Martin couldn't have cared less.

After greater thought, Krystyna was forced to conclude that Stephanie stood to gain a lifetime of financial security once she married Martin. Undoubtedly, someone with a cold and calculating heart would want the estate and effects to remain as they were now, whole and undivided. Krystyna wondered if Stephanie was truly that greedy. Certainly, Stephanie must have realized if Martin were to lose half of his financial holdings tomorrow in a poker game, there would still be plenty for everyone.

Why then, Krystyna questioned, did a settlement continue to be an issue? She reasoned there was something else, aside from Martin's money, that he dared not lose, something that, to Martin, was far more endearing and precious. But what?

Pulling her thoughts back to the moment, the figure now unveiled, Krystyna watched as Stephanie cast a dubious frown at the attorney. More words were exchanged, smothered by the much larger sounds of the FALLS.

Frustrated, still unable to hear their conversation, Krystyna stood up, shielding her body against a nearby cedar tree, edging closer to its neighbor, stepping lightly, carefully, noiselessly, from tree to tree.

Gaining better than thirty feet, Krystyna could now decipher an occasional word or two, a half-phrase, a split sentence, the tone still vague, warbled at this distance. Risking discovery, leaving the seclusion of the trees, Krystyna moved silently over to a grouping of large granite boulders, hunkering down close against the cold gritty stone, the graveled edge of the outlook and its pathway directly before her, Stephanie and Michael Overby not twenty feet away.

The word "divorce" reached Krystyna above the rumbling sounds of the water, Stephanie's tone now shrill, her voice carrying ever so slightly, followed by "you gave it away" and a minute later "SERENITY".

Quick to intervene, the attorney made a heated reference to "Martin's will," his thin lips held tense, the remainder of his sentence obliterated.

Regardless, what ever he had said, hit an exposed nerve, and hit hard. Stephanie's embittered expression froze on her face as she listened further to the attorney, stubbornly silent for several volatile minutes.

Finally, a brittle scowl curved at Stephanie's mouth. "I'll not be placated with fruitless promises. You know what to do. Do it!"

Something else was added, Stephanie's voice evaporating into the air as her head turned away, her dominant body language conveying the paramount of importance she placed on her cause.

In response, Michael Overby paled considerably, stepping back, the heel of one shoe grinding sharply in the graveled path, tripping slightly, and narrowly missed reaching the wrought iron railing for support. He then lowered his head as one trembling hand clutched the frigid iron. His last words, although muffled and unrecognizable, were delivered obediently without a hint of his earlier resistance.

Stephanie Roberts turned away sharply, silently declaring the discussion terminated, unaware that for a brief ugly moment the attorney caught a glimpse of her twisted smug smile.

Now, an instant later, Michael Overby was already wishing he had turned away first, wishing he had been spared Stephanie's corpse-like look of scorn; a wicked and toxic picture that would undoubtedly haunt his dreams. A part of him knew it would be lurking in the cobwebbed corners of his darkest fears. It was just a matter of time. He cringed at the thought; elusive ice-cold fingers touching him in vulnerable places.

The defeated slump of Michael Overby's shoulders only confirmed his surrender as he retreated down the graveled path leading away from the overlook.

Stephanie now stood alone, peering heedlessly at the cascading wall of water, too absorbed to notice the fine spray misting her raincoat. Her thoughts were heavy, pondering priorities which she realized would take considerable time to think through. Ultimately, Stephanie also saw the need to clear the way of all obstacles. The good news, however, she thought, was that obstacles took considerably less time to deal with. When an exacting plan was put into action, Stephanie could erase an obstacle in no time at all. Martin had taught her how, and with a precision few possessed.

Impatient, Krystyna waited for Michael Overby to drive away before she withdrew from the boulders and approached the overlook, effectively closing in on Stephanie. Eager for a confrontation, one that could provide something concrete, Krystyna called out to Stephanie, halting just short of the wrought iron railing. "Hello, again."

Cool blue eyes surveyed Krystyna with unquiet distaste. Inside, Stephanie recoiled in shock; the person most on her mind suddenly materialized before her very eyes. "Isn't this a neat and tidy coincidence? And just when I was thinking of you, Krystyna."

"Funny how one's name can keep popping up, and at the oddest of times, the strangest of places." Krystyna said, half-smiling.

"Yes, funny." There was nothing humorous in Stephanie's flat and tedious tone.

"I don't suppose you know the history of the FALLS?" Krystyna asked, wondering where to begin, glancing out across the sweeping waterscape.

"Some fool's tale; no doubt the result of a drunken binge."

"If that's what you believe, Stephanie, then why are you wasting your time here?"

The gravel crunched loudly beneath her feet, Stephanie quickly turning, her voice raised, clearly irritated. "Are you following me, Krystyna?"

"No, of course not." Krystyna smiled through her lie. "I happen to enjoy the FALLS. This is my second visit."

Pausing, Krystyna stared curiously at Stephanie. "Why do you hold so much animosity toward me? You shouldn't feel the need. Essentially, we both want the same thing . . . my divorce from Martin."

Stephanie's eyes were cold and suspicious. "It's not settled in my own mind whether, at the last possible minute, you won't insist on a healthy share of Martin's assets, taking advantage of his kinder, generous side."

"And if I did? What would that really matter?" The smile on Krystyna's face was genuine now. "Nevertheless, you'd have seen the last of me."

"Yes!" A slow hiss escaped Stephanie's contorted lips. "No more delays, no more wretched setbacks."

Instantly, Krystyna recognized that Stephanie harbored a seething impatience, a visible restlessness to get on with much more important things. Get, instead, to the glory.

It fit Stephanie, to Krystyna's way of thinking; decidedly, in a big hurry for fame and fortune.

"What does Martin expect to shock the world with, this time?" Krystyna found herself asking.

Stephanie's upper lip curled arrogantly. "I would think it obvious, to you especially."

"Martin's earth shattering discoveries have never been particularly obvious, not to anyone." Krystyna's smile quickly evaporated, her defiant tone now challenging. "My bet is that it's something hidden."

"Well," Stephanie's shrewd eyes were sarcastic. "If it was hidden in plain sight, you'd see it then, wouldn't you?"

Instinctively, Stephanie's deceitful words pricked at Krystyna's heart, telling her there was more here, right now, listen carefully, remember well. "I'm sure of only one thing Stephanie; I'll see far better once I learn how to decipher those ludicrous tidbits of misinformation you seem so terribly proud of offering me."

Catching Stephanie's crestfallen expression, Krystyna continued before a rebuttal could be raised. "Usually it's a matter of how deep the secret in question is actually buried. You've just told me it's not hidden, not really."

"Who would be fool enough to leave their secret out in the open, big as life, and twice as ugly? Certainly not Martin. You're merely jumping to wild, baseless conclusions. I've told you nothing, Krystyna. I've led you nowhere." Stephanie dearly hoped that was the case. How she hated being placed in this situation!

"That would be just like Martin." Krystyna said, nodding her head absentmindedly. "Hide the goods in plain sight, out in front of everyone, no one thinking to look at the obvious."

Krystyna, now gravely serious, stared a long moment at Stephanie. She compiled all of her uneasy assumptions into a single guess, hoping for some important feedback, a reaction, or better yet, a confirmation. "I guess it's all in how you look at it. We could ask some of Martin's patients where they think the secret is hidden, if indeed it is at all. Above all others, they should know, deep down, Martin having manipulated their minds into accepting a custom-made picture as the absolute truth. Force-feed the eye, the body and mind will quite naturally respond."

Krystyna paused, Samuel's own words and theories strongly in her mind. "I know this much. It's not virtual reality but . . . visual reality."

Stephanie's penciled brows knitted together sharply, a nervous twitch to one brow, as Krystyna's words echoed in her mind; visual reality, visual reality, visual reality. Somewhere, a tiny demon screamed! Did the woman realize just how close to the naked truth she was? Alarmed, Stephanie knew she must immediately change the subject, take control, evade if necessary, alter the course of this conversation.

"I know why you're here." Stephanie whispered, her tone frostbitten.

Returning her icy stare, Krystyna spoke almost carelessly, lightheartedly. "Then do, please, inform me, by all means."

"Undoubtedly, once you heard, you just couldn't resist!"

"Heard what? Resist what?"

"The real reason you're here."

"And what reason is that?"

"Don't play the fool, Krystyna. It's not very becoming."

"You've lost me, Stephanie. I haven't a clue. This is getting us nowhere."

Stephanie tapped her foot impatiently. "Martin's acquisitions made headlines the world over, for God's sake. How could you not know?"

"I've made it a point to lose track of Martin."

"Krystyna, you can't expect me to believe you?"

"You'll believe what you want, regardless of what I say. Right now, I'm calling an end to this pitiful excuse for a conversation." With a wave of her hand, Krystyna motioned as though she were about to leave immediately, forcing Stephanie to divulge what was on her mind now, or forget it.

"It's the diamonds, isn't it?" Stephanie demanded.

Initially, Krystyna failed to respond, overwhelmed, confused.

Stephanie gritted her teeth as she repeated her question, her voice a low guttural growl, alarmingly animal-like and threatening.

A moment later, Stephanie flashed a brief but tormented smile. "I've yet to see any one, man or woman, who could resist diamonds such as Martin's diamonds! They're overpowering, intoxicating, sensual. It's no wonder you were tempted."

Krystyna was quite literally stunned. What diamonds, she wondered, were so all-important? *THE* diamonds? The diamonds from Martin's list of assets? Who cares? I don't really care, Krystyna thought.

Yet, what remained very clear was Stephanie's apparent high regard for them. Why? And, Krystyna contemplated, what was so special about Martin's particular diamonds?

Krystyna spoke in an even, straightforward manner. "Stephanie, I don't know what you're talking about. However, I'm certain I could get a direct answer from Martin about these . . . diamonds."

"Don't bother Martin!" Stephanie snapped. "Since I'm in a generous mood today, I'll have him give you a pair of them; one diamond for good luck, and another for good riddance!"

CHAPTER NINETEEN

"And, don't think for a moment." Stephanie continued, "that I'm tossing you a worthless trinket! Any one of these extraordinary diamonds would yield a small fortune."

"I want nothing from you."

"That remains to be seen."

Both Krystyna and Stephanie stared at one another, the only sound the falling waters pounding on the jagged rocks.

Eventually, Stephanie drew the mist-covered raincoat more closely around her shoulders, suddenly feeling very drained of energy, offering a final comment. "Perhaps we'll present the diamonds to you tomorrow evening after your tour of SERENITY. That would be an appropriate time, actually; something to highlight the evening's end. Until tomorrow."

Burning questions, unspoken and thereby unanswered, turned cold and lifeless on Krystyna's lips as she watched Stephanie disappear from sight. Drinking in several deep breaths, Krystyna attempted to calm herself. She was angry, frustrated, and immensely concerned, feeling the oppression of a black cloud hovering over her, closing in, suffocating.

The conversation Krystyna shared with Stephanie played over and over again in her mind, particularly her hidden-in-plain-sight concept, to which Stephanie had tried to side-step, succeeding only in reaffirming the concept's believability. Along the same vein, the label Krystyna used to describe the methods employed at SERENITY, visual reality, proved to be yet another theory Stephanie sought to evade.

Krystyna was convinced she had guessed at something conceivably near the truth. And in those moments she had watched Stephanie grow increasingly, suspiciously nervous.

Krystyna had strayed too close for comfort.

Unfortunately, none of the little bits Krystyna had gleaned amounted to much of importance; a few pathetic pieces Stephanie had thrown her way.

Krystyna added it all up, forming a single sentence in which she struggled to find a touch of sanity or a morsel of meaning. The secret of SERENITY was hidden, at the same time visible to everyone, and Martin's diamonds may or may not have any bearing.

Exasperated, Krystyna fought back tears. Actually, she didn't know whether to laugh, instead. It was all ludicrous. It made little sense.

It made even less sense when she remembered Michael Overby's reference to Martin's "last will and testament." Krystyna found this perhaps the most intriguing, if not perplexing, of all. What "will" were they referring to? She knew of none.

And, what of the diamonds? Where did they fit in? Were they meant to? Krystyna drew a complete blank.

Standing there at the top of the Falls, Krystyna peered out at the majestic sight, the continuous spray of water creating rainbows of light, sprinkling colors randomly, as emotions rose and fell in her own heart. She thought of her life with Martin, the loneliness of recent years, and the precipice at which she now stood. There would be no future worth having unless Krystyna could figuratively bury the dead, putting to a final rest all that remained of her marriage with Martin.

At this juncture, it seemed equally important that she do what she could to stop Martin cold, preventing him from hurting any more innocent people. Innocents like Samuel. And Krystyna could sense events were spiraling at an accelerated reckless pace toward a critical conclusion.

The biggest problem was that today was Friday. Time was slipping away.

There was a part of Krystyna that longed to return home as planned on Monday; home being that safe haven she had built for herself which included a cozy two bedroom apartment situated above the modest bakery she owned and operated. She had discovered great personal enjoyment as a pastry chef, welcoming the warmth of the ovens, the scents of yeast and fresh bread baking. There was also the orange tabby cat she inherited along with the building, a small furry friend who greeted her at the end of each day. Miles from Seattle, the suburban atmosphere was tranquil, an easy-going life, and Krystyna had made a few good friends, both male and female.

But there had been no one special.

Krystyna allowed herself to think about this at length. Many sleepless nights she had wrestled with this question, speculating whether or not she would find in one man the love she so desperately craved.

After Martin . . . it wasn't easy to trust.

It was, at times, impossible to believe in the good of man . . . after Martin.

Before long, Krystyna's thoughts turned to Logan. Somehow she could not envision a future without him, the lure of his sardonic smile having captured an eternal place in her heart and soul; a place she had not known was there . . . uncharted territory.

Krystyna returned to the bookstore, calling out to Garrett Chambers as she entered through the rear quarters. She quickly found him embroiled in an unsettling discussion with an auburn haired woman. A few feet away from them, the leaded glass and oak door stood wide open, forgotten, while great gusts of frigid air tumbled in. Immediately, Krystyna could feel the tension in the room.

Garrett's hands reached out to the aggravated woman, gripping her firmly by the upper arms. "You must remain calm! Your mother needs your strength now."

The woman's eyes grew large, panic covering her grief stricken face. "Yes, yes, I know. If only she had told me! We talked often, long distance of course, from Arizona, but I had no real idea, no clue." The woman raised her arms in frustration, pushing Garrett from her. "She never let on. If it weren't for our surprise visit today, I may never have known my mother was suffering a mental breakdown!"

"You must not blame yourself and you must not jump to any conclusions. I don't mean to alarm you, but I'm not certain you should define this as a typical breakdown."

"What would you call it then? You saw her just now as they forced her into the ambulance, screaming obscenities about germs and cleanliness, the rantings and ravings about pictures on the walls. For God's sake, Garrett, she nearly ripped the ambulance attendant's face off when he tried to touch her, let alone restrain her!"

The bitter anger in the woman's eyes flared, but as her line of sight moved over toward Krystyna, the woman's expression turned to one of genuine embarrassment.

"Excuse me." Krystyna quickly said. "I assumed Mr. Chambers was alone."

"We've had a family emergency and Garrett has been kind enough to arrange for an ambulance." The auburn haired woman said, her lower lip beginning to quiver as she cast her tear-filled eyes to the floor.

Garrett did not hesitate to intervene. "Krystyna Kramer, this is Judy Bosh, Virginia Pedersen's daughter." He motioned with his eyes out beyond the large front windows. "Virginia Pedersen from across the street."

Yes, Krystyna remembered the clothing storeowner, Virginia Pedersen, the compulsive cleaning-machine. Another of Martin's victims, pushed too far.

"I met your mother just a few days ago." Krystyna stated simply.

"How was she? Lucid?" The woman asked breathlessly, her hands coming together in a tightly fisted ball.

"Virginia seemed unusually preoccupied with her cleaning duties around the store."

Judy stared hard at Garrett and Krystyna. "I'd been led to believe that was a big part of her therapy."

"Perhaps so," Garrett commented, "but I can assure you, not to this extreme."

"Mother told me very little about her treatments, and I never pushed her for details. We're not as close now that I have children of my own, living a good distance away, but I know that Mother had all the faith in the world in this place called . . . SERENITY. I didn't think there was reason to question her judgment."

Judy Bosh instinctively brought one cold hand to her mouth; somewhere deep inside a scream begged for release. "My God, what have they done to my mother? I want to know who's responsible?"

"These are questions we've asked ourselves numerous times, Judy." Garrett's response was gravely serious. "Unfortunately, we're short on answers."

"Judy," Krystyna said, "we've concluded those in charge of SERENITY have been treating patients in an inappropriate manner, a manner not approved or regulated through standard channels. We're in the midst of gathering evidence to provide the proper authorities."

"Are you telling me the treatments given my mother were beyond illegal, but . . . unethical?"

"Yes, I'm afraid so; experimental, unproven." Krystyna nearly choked on her words, knowing they would provide Judy Bosh with the truth, yet it would be an ugly and callous truth.

The blood drained from Judy Bosh's face. A tall slender man walked through the open door in this moment, and without hesitation Judy ran to his awaiting arms. David Bosh, the woman's husband, introduced himself to Krystyna, his brief handshake tremulous. He comforted Judy, gently explaining their need to leave immediately; her mother was being transported to a hospital nearly sixty miles away, and he felt it best they follow, ensuring a chance to speak with the physician on call.

David Bosh's red-rimmed eyes communicated silently with Garrett. "Judy," he said, turning to his wife, "why don't you check on the kids. I'll meet you at the car."

"All right." Judy said quietly, slipping out the opened front door.

David Bosh stepped to the door, closing it behind his wife, turning back to Garrett and Krystyna. "When we pulled into

WHISPERING FALLS this morning, only to find Judy's mother incoherent, unmanageable, I was at a loss what to do. Thank God you were here, Garrett. This place has turned into a ghost town! I didn't think we'd find anyone to help."

"Didn't you try William Fairchild next door?"

"Sure, I went to the hardware store first. There wasn't any answer."

Something ominous flashed in the blue of Garrett's eyes. "How can that be? Young Fairchild's always there; he's an unnerving workaholic."

David Bosh shrugged his shoulders. "The place was dark, the door locked." Checking the time on his watch, he extended his hand to Garrett. "We must leave. Garrett, thank you again. Undoubtedly, Judy and I will insist her mother live with us in Arizona, once she is well, so I very much doubt our paths will cross. That being the case, good luck to you, my friend."

David Bosh nodded his head to Krystyna; there was pain in his eyes.

Another great gust of damp bitter cold swept into the bookstore as the oak door opened and closed.

Krystyna turned to Garrett, a burdensome thought tugging sharply at her. "Let's step next door," she suggested, "and check on William Fairchild."

"You read my mind, girl."

Turning to leave, Garrett placed a hand on Krystyna's shoulder. "I've a bad feeling about this."

"Me too, Garrett."

CHAPTER TWENTY

As they approached FAIRCHILD'S HARDWARE, Krystyna focused on the tattered sign in the window: WE NEVER CLOSE. It quickly brought to mind the day she arrived in WHISPERING FALLS, and the innocent face of William Fairchild; dark brown hair, cut neat and precise, and energetic blue eyes. If the unassuming, average looking young man had not spoken, Krystyna would never have otherwise guessed at his anguish.

However, William Fairchild's tension riddled words had given away his strange compulsion that first meeting, the moment he declared the hardware store would never close, would remain open for business regardless of the holiday, regardless of the time of day or night.

Fairchild exuded a sense of eerie desperation.

Although it was already mid-morning, filtered daylight weaving through a thick mantle of rain clouds, Krystyna and Garrett could discern obscure shapes, aisles of merchandise upon which cardboard boxes had been stacked to the ceiling, leaning precariously, tilting at odd angles.

Garrett tried the front door. It was locked. He knew of a spare key that Fairchild kept hidden in a crevice of a handmade cedar mailbox. A moment later the door was opened, Krystyna and Garrett stepped across the threshold, old wooden planks underfoot groaning with their arrival. After instructing Krystyna to stay positioned where she was, Garrett fumbled his way through the gloom, looking for the switch that would provide light for the numerous overhead florescent fixtures.

Once the hardware store was illuminated, Krystyna joined Garrett, taking a long moment to study the maze of merchandise before them. It was clear that William Fairchild had in his store every imaginable product a hardware retailer could possibly stock on hand, and what space was there, had been utilized to its maximum capacity. It would seem Fairchild's supreme purpose of preparedness had driven him to this excess.

Amazingly, a semblance of order prevailed amid the chaos; everything seemingly in its proper place. Rather like William Fairchild himself, Krystyna thought, at least on the outside.

Nevertheless, it did not appear William Fairchild had been at the store in recent hours, Krystyna confirming that the furnace was turned off, not down, the temperature gauge having dropped into the low forties. A hurried check through a stack of sales receipts nearest the cash register revealed William Fairchild's last sale was three days previous.

The remnants of a half eaten sandwich lay discarded in a trash can, a resultant repugnant stink filling the air; a large blue-black fly crawled lazily over the garbage.

"Garrett, I don't like the looks of this." Krystyna said, continuing to scan the mountains of durable goods. "Where do you think Fairchild might be?"

"Well, it's obvious he's kept the store just as always, ready for a customer. It's also obvious Fairchild's not been here for several days. That's very unlike him. This store is the man's life, his home away from . . ."

Garrett turned sharply and looked to another door situated at the rear of the establishment. The door had been left slightly ajar.

"Home?" Krystyna asked, finishing his sentence, her eyes drawn to the door as Garrett had been.

"Yes." Garrett answered. "Fairchild moved his meager belongings into a back room here at the hardware store soon after his behavior became . . . changed."

"Garrett, you mentioned William Fairchild was once a lazy, freeloading, unproductive worker."

"Yes, that was before SERENITY, before he got help." Garrett answered, a hint of sarcasm to his voice. "Some help, huh? Turned Fairchild inside out. Spun him into some kind of hyperactive drone who needed nothing more than the elixir of work to feed upon."

"Maybe Fairchild came to realize his condition had actually accelerated, and that he, like so many others, must leave WHISPERING FALLS before . . ."

A sudden cold chill caressed the back of Garrett's neck; butterfly kisses of a delicate yet volatile evil. "God, I hate to think where this might end, Krystyna."

His right leg dragging stiffly, Garrett walked over to the partially opened door where he hoped to find young Fairchild. His back to Krystyna, there was an expression of hopelessness he dared not allow her to see. He could at least spare her that. He could not, however, shield her from what horror may or may not lay beyond the door.

That bad feeling Garrett had experienced earlier had grown into a vile beastly impression, one which left him with a sour taste in his mouth, slightly metallic, and a sick knowledge that the feeling was no longer just merely bad, it was worse than bad. It was now thoroughly intimidating, bordering on lethal, with a startling dose of insanity.

Stepping inside the slightly opened door, the adjacent storage room revealed additional mountains of merchandise. There was a tiny recess that housed a shower stall, toilet and sink, and a workbench area was littered with an assortment of tools.

Yet another door remained in another corner.

Garrett entered what he felt represented William Fairchild's personal quarters. A single cot, the bedding neatly arranged, was situated beneath the only window. Inches away, Fairchild had placed an ice chest atop several shelves filled with canned goods and staples. Next to this a double-burner hotplate served his simple cooking needs. A blue enameled bowl, coffee mug, single knife, fork and spoon, had been left to air dry on a clean terrycloth towel.

At the foot of the cot was an old steamer trunk, the leather surface scratched and scuffed, upon which lay a half dozen, precisely folded, blue jeans. The now familiar FAIRCHILD'S HARDWARE logo could been seen on a white cotton smock draped ceremoniously across the back of a dilapidated chair, the button at the waist secured. Another smock, this one quite soiled and smudged with dirt, had been tossed into a paper bag. Two pair of running shoes peeked out from under the cot, and a worn-out brown leather slipper, the mate nowhere in sight, lay abandoned, upside down, in the middle of the cracked linoleum floor.

There was little here William Fairchild could have amused or entertained himself with, Krystyna decided. There was no television or radio, no books, not even a magazine. No letters from loved ones were strewn about, no telephone, no newspapers.

There was, however, a vast collection of alarm clocks to be seen, each one set at differing times, precisely an hour apart. Overhead, a bared lightbulb cast an unappealing gray wash over the already stunningly somber room.

For a long breathless moment Garrett was unaware Krystyna had crept up behind him and was peering over his shoulder, taking in the meager contents of the lifeless cave Fairchild had called home.

Their attention was drawn to an immense blackboard that occupied an entire wall, literally from the floor and extending to the ceiling.

Suddenly, words escaped both Garrett and Krystyna.

If there were to be a heartbeat found in Fairchild's habitat, it was within the blackboard. Here, chalk in hand, the young man had written notes to himself. They included lists of items yet to be ordered, even longer lists of chores yet to be done, and each listing was broken down into increments of time required for each chore or work detail. A few check-marks accompanied the varying items, and an entire column labeled SLEEP, had been crossed out. No time for sleep had been scribbled in large eye-catching letters.

Krystyna noted the handwriting at the top of the blackboard appeared quite legible, carefully penned, but as their eyes gazed down, toward the last of the entries, an urgent scream for help jumped out from the childish scrawl.

At approximately the halfway mark, all direct references to the hardware store, supplies, or chores, stopped abruptly. Instead, William Fairchild scratched out his innermost thoughts, his dreams, his nightmares, and it would seem that Fairchild's worst nightmare had come true.

He had written: be prepared. Always open for customers. Never closed. Be prepared. I am. Always. Never . . . never not here. Always . . . working. Always waiting. What am I waiting for? It's not a good thing, I know that.

The penmanship changed; letters erratically formed, the writer's hand shaking. I'm waiting for . . . the pictures. I'm waiting for the pictures . . . to stop! The images on the walls . . . become images in my mind. Stop the pictures.

A hand drawn scene portrayed a human figure with a multitude of arms and legs, each limb performing a specific task in unison with its neighbor. The head of the figure had been merely outlined, the interior shaded subtly, signifying nothing remained there. An arrow pointed to the hollow area of the head, and broken sentences followed the lines of these arrows. The sentences read: nothing here now, no thoughts of my own. Where have I gone? Is there anything left to save? Stop the pictures . . . please.

William Fairchild had written further, his penmanship forgone, the words barely readable: lost and alone. One of the few left now. Gone too far. My reality . . . is no longer reality. The pictures have swallowed me up, eaten me alive.

Gone too far.

Stop the pictures.

The room with the chair.

Stay out of the room.

Never sit in the chair.

The lights in the pictures . . . too real.

The pictures . . . gone too far.

Then, near the bottom of the vast blackboard, a single sentence had been written, over and over, until the last word faded into oblivion, the illegible scrawl little more than a toddler's doodling. The sentence read: SERENITY sucked the life out of me. SERENITY . . . sucked . . . the life . . . out of me. SERENITY . . .

CHAPTER TWENTY ONE

Krystyna broke the heavy silence. "Regardless of Fairchild's frame of mind, he's decided, and rightly so, to leave WHISPERING FALLS."

She took a last look at the somber living quarters. "I doubt he's coming back."

"I fully agree." Garrett said. "But, I'd feel a bit better if we drove out to his father's home, it's a mere three or four miles down the road; see if either one of them is there."

"Good idea."

Garrett put a CLOSED sign in his bookstore window, redundant though his action was, and minutes later they arrived at the home of William Fairchild senior. No other vehicles were parked before the dark brown shingled house, the front porch sagging to one side, an antique rocker, the caned back split open and in sad need of repair, the only visible sign of a possible occupant.

After knocking on the door numerous times, Garrett turned the knob; the door opened with ease.

"Hello. Fairchild, are you here?" Garrett called out.

Despite the darkness inside the house, enough light filtered through the windows to quickly assess the situation. Someone had left in a hurry, and this was evidenced further as Garrett and Krystyna walked from room to room; dresser drawers were pulled out, items retrieved, the drawers left open. A half-eaten breakfast of scrambled eggs had congealed and dried on dishes remaining on the small kitchen table. A copper-based teakettle sat on the stove, the water long gone, the bottom scorched and blistered, the burner turned to low. Several cupboard doors were thrown wide; someone had carelessly rummaged through their contents, leaving a chaotic rubble in their wake.

"They've both have the good sense to get out." Garrett said, more to himself than to Krystyna.

"Yes, it would seem."

"Now what, Krystyna?"

"The right thing would be to contact the police, file a missing person's report."

"Of course we should do just that, but the local guys have left town, remember?" Garrett said. "We could call the county sheriff, mention Braddock and SERENITY, and casually file a missing person's report on nearly the entire town. Yeah, I can see their eyes glazing over now."

Garrett smiled softly at Krystyna. "Girl, you can bet Martin Braddock has smooth-talked his way all over the neighboring counties; he's already a big name in these parts. Undoubtedly, he's been very convincing."

"Oh yes, I'm-the-good-guy-act." Krystyna's arm reached to an opened kitchen cupboard and slammed it closed. "Just doesn't leave us many options."

"For now, Krystyna, let's get out of here."

Back in the Jeep, Krystyna dropped Garrett off at the bookstore with a promise they would meet later that day at the Reed Ranch. She realized, as a group, they desperately needed to bring all their thoughts together and formulate a plan. There was also a nagging suspicion about the remainder of the tape recorded conversation with Martin; they had not finished listening to the tape and she sensed it was important to do so.

Checking her watch, Krystyna found it was nearly lunchtime and she had much to share with Orenda and Logan. The mere thought of Logan brought a flashflood of emotions into her heart; she experienced an urgent need to hear his soft yet sturdy voice. The touch of his hand on hers . . . meant everything, everything that truly mattered in this world.

Something quite out of the ordinary had happened to Krystyna where Logan was concerned, and she accepted this. In these present days of realities being turned inside out, Krystyna felt she had gained a slight advantage, something solid with which to build upon. A tiny spark of joy rushed through her.

Krystyna no longer felt alone.

Returning to the Reed Ranch, and after a warm and wet welcome-home from Taima, Krystyna followed Orenda into the cozy kitchen. Logan was pacing back and forth across the well-worn oak floors. He spotted Krystyna, flashed a sardonic smile. "We've been . . . worried."

She felt a faint blush cover her face. "I should have let someone know where I was going. I didn't mean to worry you unnecessarily."

"Well, you did."

Krystyna feigned an expression of surprise. "What? Can't I sleuth about on my own?"

"Definitely not." Logan offered a boyish grin, seating himself at the table, taking a long sip from his coffee mug. "It's much too dangerous."

Orenda, keeping herself occupied as she prepared lunch, interjected a comment. "Logan's right, Krystyna."

Hearing the slightest edge of alarm in Orenda's voice, Krystyna sat down at the oak table beside Logan. "Nothing's happened since I left this morning? Is Samuel okay?"

"Nothing happened. Samuel is . . . the same." Logan confirmed. "Regardless, we need to take every preventive measure available to us. You must allow me this."

Although Logan's words were patiently delivered, Krystyna caught a strong underlying cautionary note. She looked from Orenda and back to Logan. "You can't be thinking that I'm personally at risk?"

Logan answered much too quickly to be convincing. "No, but I'm not willing to take any chances. Absolutely none."

The stakes had changed and Logan had the good sense to recognize it. He was not willing to sacrifice Krystyna for Samuel's sake, or make any sacrifice of his loved ones, whatsoever. In the space of a few days, Logan's priorities had been drastically altered, but more importantly, he had allowed himself to care. It was as simple as that, and he welcomed this new caring with open arms. And, it had everything to do with Krystyna Kramer, the beautiful stranger who appeared on their doorstep, out of the blue, the stranger with the chestnut curls, and whose dove-gray eyes could never lie.

Krystyna recalled for Logan and Orenda the events of her busy morning, which included her stormy encounter with Stephanie, and spying on her and Michael Overby as they met secretively at the Falls. With a strong impression of dread, she told of the search for William Fairchild and their discovery of the eerie blackboard. Leaving nothing out, leaving no detail thrown to the imagination, Krystyna explained, at great length, her assumptions, and what few educated guesses she had formed. They further discussed the diamonds, and their potential part in the drama, and also their theories on visual reality, and its close associate, virtual reality.

Garrett arrived shortly after lunch, the afternoon sky growing surprisingly turbulent, and hours passed of deep probing.

Well into their discussion, Samuel returned from his fence mending, only to sit with them and fuss and fidget. That was all he could handle, trying to sit still while he listened to them speak of Braddock and SERENITY. He excused himself from the group, explaining he really needed to resume his work on the fence.

By late afternoon, a brutal wind rose against a frenzied charcoal-colored sky. Krystyna drove the Jeep to her cabin, tossed her jacket across a chair after a hurried glance at the dreamcatcher, and laid down for a nap on the feather bed.

Dinner was a rather elegant affair, Orenda having prepared a sumptuous meal, including a chocolate pie for dessert. As was their established custom, coffee and beverages were taken before the hearth in the great room, Orenda in her comfortable, perfectly broken-in overstuffed chair, Garrett next to her, his right leg propped up on a leather ottoman, Logan and Krystyna seated together on the sofa.

Their discussion began nearly where they had left off earlier in the day. It was the general consensus that Braddock would

152

give his secret away, only if certain conditions were met; perhaps a corner Braddock could not back away from, or a dedicated stand representing a worthy threat to his method of operation. Perhaps, better yet, direct exposure of his improper deeds.

It always came back to the bottom line. Something had to give, and give in a big way, before SERENITY and Braddock could be brought down.

Throughout the conversation, dozens of thoughts were exchanged, invariably circling back around, returning again and again to the crux of the matter; Krystyna was the only real link to Braddock and the truth. Only through her could they succeed.

They listened to the remainder of the taped conversation with Martin and Stephanie, and the room around them instantly turned deathly quiet, the recorded voices penetrating the air, their violations subtle and not so subtle, the emotions resurrected and embodied with life once again.

When they came toward the end of the recording, Krystyna quickly jotted down the titles of the books she had read aloud into the machine when she crept into Martin's den. Quantum Mechanics, Accelerated Electrons, The Power of Virtual Reality, The Ultimate of Sound Systems, The Rarest of Rare Diamonds, Visual Psychology, and Confronting Phobias, to mention most.

"Strange collection of books, each one by itself." Logan said. "I can understand to some degree Braddock having a need for the material, but all these titles together . . ." Logan allowed the end of his sentence to hang suspended, open for debate.

Garrett frowned, his bushy gray brows knitting together. "Sounds more like Braddock built a movie theater than a clinic."

"My God, Garrett, you might be perfectly right." Krystyna said, pausing, her thoughts spinning. "SERENITY, a very sophisticated theater with spectacular lighting effects, life-like realism, phenomenal acoustics. Each patient sequestered and isolated. That's with great purpose, mind you. Subversion tactics. Ungentle persuasion. Brainwashing."

"Brainwashing?" Orenda asked, a film of panic covering her mahogany brown eyes.

"Martin must have incorporated subliminal messages in the pictures he produced and tailor-made for his patients, infusing specific information into the patient's mind." Krystyna answered.

"Subliminal messages?" Logan was staring at Krystyna.

"It must be. There is no other answer."

"But," Logan hesitated, trying desperately to understand. "How does Braddock produce pictures showing patients doing various acts they have never done before, pictures showing themselves in places they've never been?"

"Logan, I haven't a clue how Martin engineers these pictures, but I do know he's found a way in which these pictures greatly affect the person watching them. It's purely visual. Remember what I said before? Feed the eye and the body and mind will respond. That's one of Martin's favorite theories."

Pausing, Krystyna looked from Orenda to Garrett, and then to Logan. "That's why Stephanie grew especially nervous when I broached the hidden-in-plain-sight concept. The pictures are in plain sight. Our answers lay in what's hidden in the pictures."

"Or," Logan suggested, "more specifically, how those very pictures are made."

"Precisely, be that computer generated, animated graphics, infrared film, whatever. If we knew what it was, we might also know how Martin's plan came to backfire." Releasing a long sigh, Krystyna's voice was etched in sadness. "Unfortunately, we're back to square one. We still know little more than we did at the beginning."

An ominous air of hopelessness washed over the room.

Eventually, the group disbanded, Garrett returning to his home, Samuel feigning sleep in his room, Orenda tidying up in the kitchen.

Logan, suddenly very quiet and withdrawn, drove Krystyna to her cabin in the Jeep Cherokee. At her door, Krystyna paused, wishing Logan would reveal more of what lay beneath the veiled darkness in his eyes. There were a multitude of questions she yearned to ask him, personal things; answers she felt were necessary, timely. There were unspoken words begging to be shared.

Most of all, Krystyna needed to know how Logan felt toward her.

Instead, Logan absentmindedly bid her goodnight, Taima's nose nuzzling at her fingers, and she entered the small cabin wondering if sleep would evade her as well. It was going to be a long, bitter cold night.

Krystyna finally dropped off to sleep after an hour of fretful tossing, her thoughts churning wildly, and her dreams came at her in bits and unconnected pieces. It was in the early morning hours that Krystyna first heard the soft tapping at her door. Groggy, half asleep, her initial thought was that Logan had come to her, now ready to say what was on his mind, and she scrambled to get to the door. She turned the deadbolt, opening the door wide for Logan to enter.

A tall figure stood at the threshold, the facial features obscured in the twisting ebony shadows.

Krystyna's heart lurched in her chest.

A silky-smooth voice curled around the figure's words. "Krystyna, my angel!"

It was too late now, the door stood open, the figure entering the cabin in a take-charge manner.

Through the opened door the glint of a black Mercedes caught her eye.

In an instant she realized her vulnerable position.

The blood drained from Krystyna's oval face.

The late night caller was Martin.

CHAPTER TWENTY TWO

Before Krystyna's shock could abate, or alternatively push her into action, Martin had a strong hand cinched around one slim wrist, an impassioned madness rising in his eyes. "Please Krystyna, hear me out!"

Krystyna squared her small shoulders, frantically searching for a way out of this impossible situation. She avoided making eye contact; it would do no good for Martin to see her fear. Later, she would gain some element of control.

For now, Martin had caught her when she least expected it. After the fact, it was easy to see it coming. Krystyna really should have known better. Didn't those years of living with Martin teach her anything about the man?

Another thought which kept running through Krystyna's mind was silly, inconsequential even, when compared to the full scope of the moment; her eyes were incessantly drawn to the opened door.

She then remembered this was the second time in a single day she watched an opened door remain long forgotten, unimportant, while a human tragedy unfolded. What ever happened, Krystyna knew the cabin door must remain open.

If all else fails, keep the door as it is.

Gusts of frigid, bone-beating cold air coursed through the room, providing a constant reminder for Krystyna.

Keep the door open.

Maybe Logan will hear her screams.

"I've come to speak with you, Krystyna . . . just you and I."

"No Martin, and that's emphatically no!"

Slowly, very slowly Krystyna brought her eyes closer to his. "We spoke yesterday and we'll speak again Saturday for the tour, concluding our business together at Overby's office on Monday."

Now, she locked determined eyes with Martin. "That's all the communication with you I could possibly stomach."

Immediately, Martin let go of her wrist.

Nevertheless, he had decided he would stay a while.

Martin walked over to the fireplace, reaching out toward the smoldering embers to share what little warmth they retained.

Keep the cabin door open, Krystyna thought. Perhaps Martin will just say his piece and that will be that.

Krystyna folded her arms together, a hard chill settling over her, shaking her. "Martin, I'd like you to leave now." She bit down hard to keep her teeth from chattering.

"Krystyna, my angel . . ."

"Don't call me that."

"Anything you wish, Mrs. Braddock."

"Leave, now."

"I'm sorry, but this happens to be a good time for me." Martin said, twisting one end of his blonde mustache. "It'll just have to work for you."

"I'll have you thrown out then."

"By whom? Your friend, Dr. Logan Reed?"

Krystyna looked over to the opened door, the wishful thought locked in her heart. The brisk, frigid air, whipping into the room, burned a path across her skin, the lightweight nightgown and robe offering little warmth.

Roving bands of moonlight slanted in through the large front room windows, yet Martin was not quite satisfied with the lighting, reaching over to a small stained-glass lamp. Yes, Martin thought, more light, and all the better to see you with.

Something unnerving had flashed in Martin's eyes, just then, as he leaned over the lamp, and in those emerald eyes Krystyna thought she had seen . . . a glimmer of stark intimidation.

Now it dawned on Krystyna that Martin had traced her whereabouts through Logan Reed, and the Reed Ranch, easily putting two and two together. It mattered little at this point, yet Krystyna couldn't fathom why.

Martin interpreted Krystyna's long silence to be a false front of courage. A hurried glance around the tiny cabin confirmed the front door stood open, but more importantly, Krystyna was quite alone, and that meddlesome Reed character was nowhere to be seen.

"Okay," Martin said. "Let's leave Dr. Reed's name out of this, shall we? This is between us."

"Martin, there's nothing unfinished between us, nothing worth saving, nothing . . ."

"I'll never believe that, Krystyna, not for a moment."

"How can you think otherwise?"

"Seeing you again has brought out feelings I once chose to bury, and as a result, I've undertaken some very frank confrontations with these personal truths, Krystyna."

"Stop right there. I don't want to hear any of this, nor do I care about your personal truths."

"You should. They have everything to do with you."

"No!" Suddenly, Krystyna thought Martin's emerald eyes closely resembled those of a blood-sucking, flesh-eating, vulture-like predator. She cringed, directing her sight elsewhere, anywhere.

"Why do you suppose I fought our divorce every step of the way?" Martin asked.

She stood mute, hurling defiance at Martin with her stubborn stony silence.

"Answer me, Krystyna." Martin's tone was demanding.

The cabin door remained open. Sharp needles of bitter cold wind pricked at Krystyna's shivering frame.

"I'll tell you why." Martin said, a quieting of his grimacing facial features occurred miraculously, instantly. "Krystyna, I've never come to grips with losing you."

Anger flared through Krystyna. "That's an insult! I was never yours to begin with!"

"Not so."

"You have a new life planned with Stephanie. Let it be, Martin, for God's sake."

"Stephanie has been . . . among other things, convenient, loyal, ingenious. But, she'll never be my angel."

Martin quickly stepped toward Krystyna, leaving two or three feet between them, emotion tugging at his voice. "You are the only ray of innocence that touches me . . . anymore, the only good thing going in my miserable life. There is a purity about you . . . something I've always treasured. I hoped some of it would rub off on me, suppress my evil side."

"You kept me around hoping I would change you, Martin. That's all it ever was. Well, it didn't work. We're two people better off living in opposite ends of the galaxy."

"No Krystyna, I've come to a different conclusion."

"I will not discuss this further with you! Please leave."

Undaunted, Martin's voice was empowered with a renewed enthusiasm. "Seeing you again showed me what I refused to see all along. I love you, Krystyna."

Stunned, unsure if she was hearing Martin correctly, Krystyna was very confused. Martin had never spoken those three words before, not in the nearly ten years she had known him.

However, confusion quickly settled into black and white portions of validated truths. Martin did not love her, he merely needed her. She somehow balanced the scales of injustice, to Martin's depraved and wicked way of looking at things. In his deepest desires and dreams, oddly enough, Martin really wanted to help his fellow man. He'd only become bent in the process. It was subtle, he had later explained to her, nothing he could put a finger on.

Krystyna recognized that Martin's brand of love equated to the ownership of chattel, a prized porcelain possession, one that would absorb, without complaint, any verbal abuse, and one smart enough to look the other way should Dr. Jekyll decide to experiment. Painfully, emotionally, he extracted what he needed from Krystyna's soul, or at least had tried, and still could not leave her be in peace.

She wanted to scream.

Krystyna looked again to the opened door.

Krystyna also recognized that Martin's particularly fragile male ego had been bruised.

Worse yet, Martin could never accept that Krystyna no longer wanted to be his wife.

Never again to feel his touch.

Never again to hear his sweet cries of pleasure.

Never again to witness Martin's raging obsession seize him most unexpectedly; another face, carved with rage, turning to her in the dark corners of a cold-blooded night.

An endless wave of chills took control of Krystyna. "I want no part of what you sacrilegiously call . . . love!"

Without a moment's hesitation, Martin grabbed Krystyna by the shoulders, his grip firm, unyielding. "I can't lose you. Not again."

Krystyna pushed hard against Martin's chest with her hands. "It's over, Martin, it's long over."

"Everything, I've done for you. All for you."

"Stop right there! I don't want to hear another word. Leave, now."

Something ominous lurked in Martin's emerald eyes. "Reed is using you. Can't you see that?"

"I told you to leave, Martin." She wriggled about, failing to wrestle out of Martin's ironclad hold.

"Reed is using you to get to me."

Krystyna's next words slipped easily and honestly. She wouldn't have taken them back, even if she could; she only hoped they stated the ultimate of truths. "And get to you, we will!"

"I see." Martin said soberly, a dark brooding expression quickly forming. "Why would you do that, Krystyna?"

"Because your experimentation is wrong, morally and ethically wrong. I'll do whatever necessary to bring your operation down. Someone has to do it. It may as well be me."

"Krystyna, your attitude surprises me, and after what I've done for you, and of course for your . . . father."

"What you did for my father has nothing to do with this. You chose to help him. I never twisted your arm. I owe you no favors. So, stop your pathetic mind games and listen up."

Krystyna glanced over Martin's shoulder toward the opened door; ten lonely feet separated her from the entrance. "Martin, I'll destroy you, once and for all. And I'll do it for me, for the Reeds, for the atrocities you've committed."

"You'll change your mind, Krystyna, when you see for yourself what I've discovered."

"You mean, see what you've destroyed. No, nothing will change my mind."

"It matters not, my angel. You'll never figure it out on your own."

"Don't be so sure, Martin. You've made mistakes before, and you've made a whopper here in WHISPERING FALLS."

"You make it sound like it's all a matter of time, Krystyna."

"It is."

"But time is on my side."

Movement at the opened door caught Krystyna's attention. Instantly, she offered Martin a smug smile. "Not any more."

His eyes followed hers to the opened cabin door.

There, in the entryway, stood Logan. At his side was Taima, her large wolf-body held rigid, her growl a menacing scream, long white fangs exposed, glistening in the moonlight. There was an urgent hunger in her amber eyes.

CHAPTER TWENTY THREE

Krystyna wrenched her shoulders from Martin's grasp. "Now, will you leave?"

Another threatening growl echoed across the frigid room.

"You've left me no choice." Martin said quietly, cautiously pulling further away from Krystyna. "But only for the moment, I assure you."

Logan stepped just beyond the threshold, and to one side of the opened door. If need be, Taima had a straight shot at Martin's pale white throat. A snap of Logan's fingers would send the dog into a white-hot frenzy.

Martin stared at Krystyna, his impending retreat clearly not what he had in mind. He vacillated back and forth with his options for a long tense moment.

"Do it, Martin. Make a move toward me." Krystyna said finally, challenging Martin. "Taima will stop you before you can draw a single breath."

Enraged, Krystyna took a step closer to Martin, completely unaware she had done so. "Do it, Martin. It'll be over in a few minutes. Do us all a favor."

Taima inched her rigid frame through the doorway, penetrating eyes locked on Martin, saliva dripping a mad dance down the length of razor-sharp fangs.

"You'd like that, wouldn't you, Krystyna?" Martin asked, the incredulous thought slowly becoming a hard reality. He had never known Krystyna to be so . . . cold-blooded. Strangely enough, however, this would not dampen Martin's resolve. Rough edges could always be smoothed out, if given the time. He could still, as yet, mold Krystyna as he wished. He had the power of the pictures to wield as he saw fit; an awesome power. Slightly unpredictable, but awesome nevertheless.

Incredibly, Martin burst out in maniacal laughter, throwing his head back gleefully. "Does this mean you won't be attending the tour?"

Krystyna stared at Martin evenly, her composure unshaken. "Logan and I wouldn't miss it for the world."

"Tonight. Eight o'clock." Martin said, tilting his head nonchalantly at Logan. "Now, call off your dog, Reed."

"In a moment, Braddock. First . . . a warning from my dog. Never dare trespass on her property again. Second . . . a warning from me. Stay away from Krystyna. That's fairly simple. I think you can comprehend. If not . . ." Logan raised his fingers to Taima, gesturing then toward Braddock.

Taima's menacing growl heightened it's intensity, her body language conveying an unparalleled desire to be the first to spill Braddock's blood.

"I don't normally take to warnings, Reed," Martin said, "but in this instance, I'll back away. Just keep in mind, that won't always be the case."

Martin turned around to Krystyna with a maddening smile. "Tonight, my angel."

Stepping to the doorway, arrogance to his gait, Martin paused to glare at Logan. Instantly, he knew he shouldn't have tried to have the last word.

Logan grabbed Martin's jacket front, twisting the sturdy wool fabric into a tight ball at his neck, slamming Martin's body into the timber-framed doorjamb. The sheer force of the blow caused Martin to momentarily lose his breath, a wave of pain slicing deep into his back. His peripheral vision darkened. He fought down the urge to bring his hands before his face to block another possible assault. He knew he could not win this way, and definitely not with that flea-bitten creature, *the dog*; the dog who had now caught the edge of his jacket in its voracious teeth, gnarling and chewing the cloth into tattered shreds.

"Maybe I didn't make myself perfectly clear, Braddock." Logan gave another hard twist to the knotted fabric around Martin's neck. "Don't interfere in any way with Krystyna. And never, never touch her again."

Faces inches apart, Logan gritted his teeth together. "I personally won't tolerate it."

Releasing his grip slowly, Logan finally brought his hands to rest on his hips. As if by silent command, Taima withdrew to her master's side, her amber eyes never leaving Martin.

Shaken, Martin gathered what dignity had been left him, and retreated to where his Mercedes was parked. It was there Martin arrived at a decision and made a secret promise to himself, one monster to another.

The emotion packed moments suddenly caught up with Krystyna. That, and the intense frigid air gusting through the opened door, began a series of shaking chills she could not stop. Weakened, she gave into them. Logan quickly grabbed a warm afghan from the sofa and wrapped this around Krystyna's trembling body, checking also to make certain she wore slippers.

"Come with me, Krystyna."

He led her outside to a little used footpath, a thick, crunchy carpet of fragrant pine needles beneath their steps, moonlight and Taima guiding their way. They soon encountered a pair of secluded cabins, the shutters closed, the doors heavily boarded over. Another hundred yards further along the path, Logan's cabin came into view, the rooftop of the log structure outlined against the luminous starlit sky.

Entering the cabin, Logan guided her to a loveseat, stealing a glance into Krystyna's tearful eyes. Immediately, a sharp emotional pain pierced through him, and it hurt him in a place he'd never been hurt before.

He quickly turned away.

Instinctively, Taima claimed her post near the foyer, amber eyes alert, ears pricked up, listening, anticipating the possible return of the unwelcomed stranger.

Logan insisted Krystyna take the brandy he offered her. She accepted it wordlessly. Although the cabin already felt comfortably warm, Logan added several logs to the fire, tending to the embers carefully. Any residue of a chill was soon smothered from the room. They sipped at their drinks in silence, each sorting through their own thoughts, Logan standing at the

165

rock hearth, Krystyna on the loveseat. The flames of the fire danced with the flickering shadows; an illusion of topaz ribbon-like shapes weaving gracefully across the spacious interior.

Logan, greatly affected by Martin's impromptu visit, had been left with a strong relenting impression; he could still feel his eager hands twisting at Martin's neck. Even though Logan detested situations that required violence, he had to admit he experienced a small thrill of satisfaction when he jerked a second time on the man's neck.

But, not nearly the satisfaction Logan would feel when Braddock was completely out of Krystyna's life.

Thinking back, Logan estimated a mere ten minutes had lapsed since Taima had awakened him, her wet tongue on his fingers as he lay sleeping, nudging his arm, a soft whine in her throat. He knew her cry was urgent. A minute later, hastily clad in jeans and a sweater, he was drawn to Krystyna's cabin, Taima leading the way, following the trail of harsh words and the scent of danger in the air. A black Mercedes was parked boldly before Krystyna's cabin, the plates reading SERENITY, and Logan easily concluded the intruder was Braddock.

However, emotionally, Logan was not at all prepared to walk into the cabin and find Martin's rough hands mauling Krystyna. Although he credited a higher power of wisdom providing him the strength to hold back the worst of his anger, and, yes, jealousy, it had been one of the more difficult moments in his life.

Like Taima, Logan wanted the taste of Martin's blood.

Everything came into focus in that single moment for Logan; the repercussions of one's actions, the concept of right and wrong, his beloved family, his hopes and aspirations, and now, too, his deep feelings for Krystyna.

He looked over to Krystyna, seeing that a faint tinge of color had now returned to her face. The chills had ceased. "Are you feeling better?"

"Yes." Her voice was a soft whisper.

"Did Braddock hurt you?"

"No, but . . ."

166

"If there's more, I need to know."

"No," she quickly assured him, "he didn't hurt me physically. Martin was simply being himself; a master manipulator and an emotional terrorist. It's no wonder I'm left feeling rather . . . abused. But, I thought I may have seen something far more intimidating in his sadistic eyes, and it frightened me."

Krystyna felt herself wanting to cringe at the dark memory, but she took a deep breath, concentrating, willing the ominous thought right out of existence. "Bottom line, Martin can never be trusted." She said. "I know, I lived his two-faced truth."

"What reason did Braddock give you for his . . . trespassing?" Logan asked.

"I can't explain the actions of a madman any more than I could guess at his motives."

"Krystyna, that's not an answer to my question." Logan found, to his surprise, that he had been holding his breath. He locked eyes with Krystyna. "He's still in love with you, isn't he?"

"Or so he claims."

"And, he's profoundly sorry to have lost you?"

Krystyna nodded to Logan. "I told him I was never his to begin with."

A whisper of a smile tugged at the corner of Logan's mouth. He breathed much easier now. "Is there anything else I need to know, at least right away?"

"No."

"Good." Logan said, focusing on Krystyna as she set her empty brandy glass on a table, rubbing her cold hands briskly together. He moved to the loveseat, taking her hands in his, warming them for her, allowing himself something he had wanted to do since . . . since the day Krystyna arrived.

Leisurely, not wanting to rush in the least, Logan looked deeply at Krystyna, memorizing for all of time the gentle slope of her shoulders, the long sweeping eyelashes, the hint of a dimple at her small chin. He caressed her gleaming chestnut hair, reveling in the silky texture, bringing the curls to his face, drowning in the essence.

He then concentrated on Krystyna's emotion filled eyes. He stayed there, one soul to another soul, silently communicating and embracing the undeniable bond that linked the two of them together.

It was then that he literally gave himself up to Krystyna, come what may, realizing that if she should leave, the biggest part of his heart would go with her, and stay with her forever. He'd never be the same again.

Logan leaned toward Krystyna. "Please, don't say anything more."

He reached out and brought her face closer to his. "Let's leave the world at large out of this. Don't talk about how you're leaving on Monday, let's not mention Braddock or SERENITY. Put that all aside . . . for a while."

Krystyna started to speak, Logan quickly intervening, his lips drawn to hers in a kiss that would alter the course of everything, and in the quiet passage of a minute or two, words became useless, bloodless entities.

Logan found Krystyna's lips to be soft, warm, and deliciously inviting. Giving into the passion, he tasted and explored, leading a trail of kisses down the slender curve of her neck, to her moist lips again, engraving into his memory every detail of Krystyna he could possibly savor.

Somehow they found themselves moving to the plush carpeted floor, a dozen pillows tossed about, a comfortable but hastily made bed before the fireside. Through the gown and robe, Logan felt Krystyna's heart pounding, racing, as she moved against his chest.

"This is about you and I, Krystyna." Logan said, breathlessly, unwilling to tear his lips away from her silken skin for any measurable moment of time. He'd never known desire, such as this.

Krystyna's robe was set aside, a single pink ribbon now holding the neckline of her gown. Logan looked at Krystyna laying beside him, her shimmering hair lustrous in the firelight, her delicate smile his personal slice of heaven.

"This is about accepting what's right before our very eyes." Logan said, his voice thick.

He bent over her, kissing where her heart should be, asking of his God that a blessing be put upon this union, and he asked with a humility and a sincerity born of a spiritual warrior.

Krystyna, trembling, but not with cold, pulled at the ribbon of her gown, the fabric falling open to her waist. Their eyes met and lingered for a long moment.

"I love you, Krystyna."

It wasn't the brandy that made the room start to spin for Krystyna, it was the knowledge that the man she loved, loved her in return. She allowed this truth to be absorbed, luxuriating in the warmth of her happiness.

Logan was right, Krystyna thought, no mention of Martin now, there was nothing sinister to taint their golden moment. She pushed the ugliness and frustration and fears aside, welcoming instead something truly beautiful and sacred to take its proper place.

Logan felt Krystyna's fingers tug at his sweater, pulling the garment up and over his head. His jeans were next. There was an urgency in her kiss now, a determined hunger, Krystyna molding her body to his. He heard her moan softly, guiding his lips to her breasts as she arched her back, drawing him closer still, a satiny sheen covering their nakedness in the dancing firelight.

Running her fingers along Logan's well-muscled body, Krystyna felt his body tense, her caresses tantalizing, provocative, increasingly demanding.

Each touch, each kiss, each movement vibrated with expectancy.

Their eyes met once again.

The moment was here.

CHAPTER TWENTY FOUR

The voice, silky and smooth, was calling Samuel's name.

It was the nightmare again, he soon came to realize, and this time it began with the elevator doors of the skyscraper opening up, a dark hungry mouth that would transport him straight into the womb of his greatest fear.

As always, he desperately didn't want to go.

Knowing what lay ahead, Samuel's instincts screamed to him of the dangers. Just the knowing left him weakened, trembling, lightheaded.

But, he must surrender to his fear of heights. And the rooftop of the skyscraper was where his final surrender would take place.

A silent hand pushed him into the elevator; the darkness swallowed him as the steel doors closed with what sounded like a growl. This was followed by a sudden lurching motion. Samuel's stomach soured, churned, cramping. He felt like he could vomit.

Instead, he concentrated on grasping the handrail, his sweating palms preventing a decent grip, one frail attempt after the next, as the elevator car rocketed upward at a dizzying speed. The rough jarring motions of the elevator caused him to lose his balance and he bounced into one wall, and off another.

Each terrifying moment seemed like an hour to Samuel as the elevator creaked and groaned against the forced jettison, swaying side to side, rocking about like a small lifeboat fighting enormous ocean waves.

Stop! He screamed.

Little good, his screams. He knew they were useless, here in the picture world.

The closer to the rooftop he came, the more violent the elevator ride, so much so that he held his clattering teeth together, his mouth impossibly dry, the shaking felt deep in his bones.

Suddenly the brakes were applied and the elevator car came to a screeching halt. Samuel had nearly reached the rooftop of the skyscraper.

He stared at the steel doors for a long tense moment, the elevator car seemingly suspended in the air, hovering at a terrifying height. However, the elevator doors remained closed.

Finding the courage to stand, Samuel pressed the open button on the elevator's control panel. Nothing happened. He pressed another button; main floor. Nothing happened.

It never did.

Samuel had tried pushing the buttons each and every nightmare, but the result was always the same; no up, no down, no stop, no open. Out of his control.

He desperately didn't want to go.

Then, as if laughing at him, the elevator doors opened wide. Although shadowed in a veiled darkness, the relative safety of the building's interior was a blessed sight. Samuel prepared to jump through the opening, but he didn't trust the doors not to close too quickly, pinning him between their jaws.

The elevator, to Samuel, was a living thing.

He stood there, on the edge of panic, caught between reason and recklessness. His decision was made for him when the elevator doors began to close, and he lunged forward, grateful for something relatively solid beneath his feet.

At least, Samuel thought, he wasn't trapped in the elevator hundreds of feet high above the ground, at the mercy of . . . God only knew what. He wasn't sure. He really didn't want to know.

Samuel breathed easier now, but he knew this was merely a brief quiet moment until . . . until the next step. Now, he must climb a staircase the final leg of the journey.

He desperately didn't want to go.

The staircase was just as he had last seen it; decrepit, unstable, the only access to the rooftop, with huge gapping holes in the steps. And he knew better than to steal a look down through those holes . . . too far down, endlessly down.

Lightheaded again, Samuel rested against a cool marbled wall, and waited. It was no use thinking he could outsmart the pictures, foolish to imagine a way out of the skyscraper. The only way out was down . . . from the rooftop. Six hundred feet down . . . maybe seven. A very ugly thought.

Samuel fought the unending waves of terror that seized him, a part of him resigned to the fact he must walk out to the very edge of the rooftop and face his fear. He must look over the edge, his toes overhanging, his heart in his throat . . . he desperately didn't want to go!

The silent hand pushed Samuel to the darkened staircase, one trembling step at a time, his bloodshot eyes drawn upward, concentrating with all his might not to look down. A swirling rush of wind, created by the down-draft inside the staircase, whipped and pulled at Samuel, the icy fingers of cold air stinging his face.

It was a small eternity before he reached the landing at the top of the staircase, the door to the rooftop before him, the wind whistling in his ears.

No going back now, Samuel thought.

As if ever there was a choice!

His quivering hand met with the cold knob of the door, at the same time pushing with his shoulder and body weight, knowing that the door to the rooftop does not budge easily. The momentum of Samuel's action propels him through the threshold and into another world.

The rooftop, a flat ebony desert, beckons to him. Samuel puts a hand before his eyes and cannot see his fingers for the suffocating darkness. There is a small pinpoint of light to be seen coming from an unknown source, far away, lurking at the unseen edge.

It is that very edge that Samuel must confront intimately, and with a prayer in his heart, Samuel moves slowly toward the outer perimeter of the skyscraper's rooftop, the light pulling him along, calling out to him, reeling him in with a silent seduction.

He desperately wants to go home.

He'd like to be anywhere but here.

But, the nightmare wasn't done with him . . . yet.

Samuel forced himself to keep walking toward the lighted edge of the rooftop. Soon, he remembered, he would catch a glimpse of a neighboring skyscraper and he would know just how high up he really was. Once his eyes registered the sight, he would be doomed, his fear of heights overwhelming him, controlling his faculties.

It happened, just as before, his gaze catching the night sky. Samuel was instantly stripped of his dignity as tears streamed down his face, the salt of his tears mingling with the repugnant taste of his fear, and he moved, reluctantly, to the edge of the rooftop.

Fifty feet from his destination he could easily hear the clamoring noises drifting upward from the street; horns honking, brakes squealing, voices speaking, babies crying. There was little darkness now, the lights of the city enveloping the sky in a gloomy haze.

Too soon, Samuel would look over the edge and see these sights for himself. At this distance the people would look more like ants, the cars, buses and taxis miniature toys, and the ground would rush up and . . . swallow him if he wasn't careful.

Dear God in heaven, Samuel began to pray, but just then his toe stubbed against the ledge of the great abyss. He had finally reached the place where he must welcome his fear as a blood brother.

A short wall two feet high had been built around the perimeter of the rooftop and Samuel stepped up onto this wall, realizing that it was barely wide enough to stand upon.

He held his breath, wiping his tear stained face with the back of a trembling hand. At these heights the wind whipped viciously at his body.

All he had to do now was look down.

Samuel didn't want to.

If he did, the world would spin, faster and faster, his sense of balance lost, and he would topple over the edge.

Samuel moved his feet several inches, the toes of his shoes seeking substance, but finding none. Only thin air.

If he should lean but a few degrees forward, he would fall, his body plunging helplessly, his breath stolen with fright, grappling for a handhold of any kind, but finding none.

Would he die, Samuel wondered, before he collided with the ground in a ruptured heap of blood and shattered bones? He didn't want to know the answer as he stood on the precarious ledge.

Although he tried to keep his line of sight on the horizon, he could feel his fear build inside him, gnawing away at his dwindling resolve, growing into a large beast that would surely devour him.

In a moment, Samuel knew that it would come down to the beast . . . or him. The internal tug of war began in earnest.

Now, only inches separated Samuel from a certain death.

A strong gust of wind could easily push him over the edge.

But, was that silent hand truly the wind?

Samuel wasn't sure . . . anymore.

CHAPTER TWENTY FIVE

Krystyna's last recollection was of crawling into Logan's featherbed. Now, it was nearly eight o'clock and she could hear birds singing their cheerful morning songs. Logan, sleeping soundly, lay nestled against her. She lay there content, warm, with a smile on her face. Krystyna was deliciously happy.

She slowly moved away from Logan, pushing the bedcovers carefully aside, not wanting to wake him.

In the living room their makeshift bed of blankets and pillows remained before the stone hearth. Krystyna found herself smiling again as she added more firewood to the smoldering embers.

Taima offered Krystyna an affectionate greeting as she stood by the door waiting to be let out.

After drawing the front room draperies to the side, a dismal windswept day was easily revealed beyond the windows. Nevertheless, Krystyna saw only the promise of sunshine.

Once in the kitchen, she made a large pot of strong coffee. The pantry held a decent assortment of staples and she quickly set about to bake some croissants. In no time she had cleaned up after herself, the croissants baking in the oven, and she wandered around the cabin, finding and appreciating bits and pieces of Logan just about everywhere she turned.

A pair of scuffed leather moccasins were placed next to his favorite chair. An impressive collection of glass-blown paperweights was situated atop a small pine desk. His now familiar, hunter-green suede jacket was suspended from a neat row of brass hooks near the entrance.

Several family portraits hung on the walls; Orenda and Evan Reed on their wedding day, Samuel at around age three, learning to ride a small pony, and Logan, attired in football jersey and helmet, the picture probably taken late in high school and again displaying his sardonic grin.

In the bookcase she found a scrapbook filled with short notes and long letters from his client's families, thanking Logan for the exceptional care he had taken of their beloved pets; dogs, cats, horses and many exotic animals as well. Another scrapbook held a vast assortment of photographs depicting overjoyed families reunited once again with their pets, many animals still bandaged, limbs splinted.

A stack of papers next to the albums told more of Logan's veterinary practice he shared with two associates. The animal hospital was apparently located in Spokane, fifty or sixty miles from WHISPERING FALLS, yet despite his long hours of work, Krystyna knew that Logan came home to visit his mother and brother quite frequently; his cabin regularly cleaned and liberally stocked with all the necessities.

A partially finished scale model of a clipper ship had been placed on the dining room table; bits of wood, fabric, twine, and vials of paint were nearby in an old shoebox. There was great attention to detail here and Krystyna marveled at the patience required to undertake such a delicate project.

Krystyna smiled again, her hand lightly touching the model, imagining Logan's hands at work.

She, too, was memorizing every detail of Logan that she could; keepsakes to hold forever in her heart.

The aroma of freshly baked goods wafting down the hallway and into Logan's bedroom, was more than enough to wake him from a sound sleep. Logan soon appeared in the doorway of the kitchen, a terrycloth robe wrapped around him. "What smells so good?"

Krystyna smiled. There was an impish sparkle in her eyes. "Croissants. I thought I'd surprise you."

He drew nearer her, placing his hands at her waist. "And, that you did." Logan bent to kiss her lightly.

"Are you hungry?" She asked.

"Do you dare ask me that question?" There was a flirtatious sparkle in Logan's dark eyes.

"I'll ask you again after you've eaten your croissants." She answered.

Their eyes met for a long moment, Logan reluctantly drawing away, but they continued to talk while they set plates and knives and forks on the eating bar. Krystyna poured coffee into two heavy mugs, adding a single spoon of sugar to hers, cream in his. A pitcher of freshly squeezed orange juice was the finishing touch and they began to eat their meal.

Later, dishes washed and dried, they moved to the loveseat in the living room, sipping on the last of the coffee.

"There's something very important I need to say." Krystyna finally said.

"What's that?"

"You wouldn't let me tell you . . . last night."

"Last night I was afraid . . ."

"Logan, you were afraid I did not love you in return?"

"Yes."

Krystyna set her coffee cup aside. "Logan, I do love you, with all my heart and soul."

"Krystyna," Logan whispered in an emotion filled voice, bringing his eager arms around her, holding her close to him. "My greatest fear is to lose you, just when I've found you."

Tears slipped down Krystyna's face. She felt a mixed blessing of heady joy and exquisite pain. "First, we have to get through tonight and tomorrow. Then . . ."

"Don't say it, Krystyna." Logan whispered in her ear, a sense of desperation overwhelming him at the thought of what tomorrow might bring. Or, worse yet, take away.

They held each other tightly, hope-filled prayers in their thoughts. After a time, Krystyna smiled as she rose to her feet, reaching out for Logan's hand. Her hand suddenly felt extraordinarily small and vulnerable in his.

"Krystyna," Logan whispered. "My heart will go where you go."

By the time Logan and Krystyna arrived at the main house, Garrett had already joined Orenda, and the two of them were seated at the oak table in the kitchen. It was early afternoon.

"Orenda," Garrett said, "you must also consider the possibility that Braddock might get away with all of it . . . never to be brought to justice, or the justice you'd like to see done."

Orenda now noticed Logan and Krystyna, gesturing for them to join their discussion at the table. "I was just explaining to Garrett my frustrations about Samuel being drawn into all this, and I'm feeling very angry right now."

Krystyna responded, placing a compassionate arm about Orenda's shoulders. "I understand, Orenda. Perhaps we should place another call to Dr. Jonathan McCabe."

"Do." Orenda said. "We must try something . . . anything."

In a matter of minutes, Krystyna was speaking with Dr. McCabe on the phone. She did a good deal of listening before other aspects of the situation were discussed. Finally, she concluded with a somber statement. "I want you here. I want you to see for yourself Martin's other side; the dark side of the human animal you always knew was there."

The conversation ended soon thereafter, Krystyna turning to Logan and the others. "Well, Jonathan McCabe and one other board member will be here in WHISPERING FALLS tomorrow. They're catching the first flight out in the morning."

Logan cast a doubting look at Krystyna. "That easy? A second phone call and they're on their way?"

"Not quite, Logan. They want irrefutable proof. That is precisely what they are expecting."

"I'm not sure I like the sound of that." Logan said.

Krystyna avoided looking at Logan. "I had to promise I could deliver Martin's notes."

"That may be impossible! You know that!"

"Yes, but . . ." Krystyna began, suddenly turning toward the sound of stumbling footsteps near the entrance to the kitchen.

There stood Samuel, clad in pajama bottoms only, the entire left side of his face severely bruised and swollen, the eye puffed up and closed. Mottled streaks of black and blue extended down the left side of his neck and the length of his left arm. There were cuts and abrasions on both of his feet. Blood trickled out the corner of his mouth.

Orenda muffled a cry as she rushed to her son. "Samuel, what happened to you?"

Intense pain filled Samuel's tormented eyes. "The nightmare again, mother."

"The rooftop?" Orenda questioned, her words a whisper.

"Yeah . . . the rooftop!" For Samuel, the nightmare had been as real as real could possibly get. He still trembled. "The nightmare . . . " Samuel's hand touched his swollen face and he winced in pain. "I did it, mother!"

"What did you do, son?"

More droplets of blood eased from Samuel's lips. "This time I was brave. I welcomed my fear as a blood brother." Samuel swallowed hard. "It was simple, really. This time . . . I jumped."

CHAPTER TWENTY SIX

Orenda helped Samuel to a chair while Logan hurried to retrieve a first-aid kit and his black leather medical bag. In minutes Samuel's cuts and abrasions were cleaned and bandaged, his injuries carefully assessed by Logan and determined not to be serious enough to warrant hospitalization.

It soon became obvious the left side of Samuel's body had impacted with the ground in his nightmare, and as a result, his left arm and leg were both badly bruised and sprained. Samuel had been fortunate, Logan went on to explain, the contusions of soft tissue in these limbs would heal completely in a matter of weeks. The sprains could conceivably take several months. Also, the blood trickling from Samuel's mouth was actually a small cut from where he had inadvertently bitten his tongue during the fall.

Wracked with pain, Samuel eagerly accepted the two blue capsules Logan offered him. Soon, a bit of color returned to Samuel's pale grimacing face even though his hands still trembled when he drank from a glass of milk.

Shortly, the medication easing the pain just a bit, Samuel began to explain of his ordeal. The room became deathly quiet as all of them learned the ugly truth.

"How could this have happened?" Samuel kept repeating.

However, no one could explain how Samuel's injuries occurred while he innocently slept in his bed, deeply involved in a toxic nightmare.

"At least I survived the fall," Samuel concluded, "and as much as I don't want to admit it, I did face my fear."

"But not this way, Samuel." Orenda said, worry etched across her brow.

"No, not Braddock's way. It's too . . . drastic." Samuel's words were becoming thick, slurred. "SERENITY . . . what a joke!"

"You're exhausted." Logan said. "That's to be expected . . .considering your journey."

Logan helped Samuel to his feet. "Come along. You need to lie down, elevate your arm and leg."

Samuel eyed Logan suspiciously as he was gently led from the room. "I don't want to dream again."

"Don't worry, I doubt you will. The medication I gave you is quite strong. If you sleep, it will be peacefully." Logan explained. "Let's help you to the sofa in the living room. That way, should you need us, we'll be very close. I'll be in shortly to put another ice pack on your arm."

Samuel's blue eyes fixed on Logan. The two brothers were alone now. "Get Braddock for me, Logan. Would you do that?"

"That's just about to happen." Logan answered, quickly explaining about Jonathan McCabe and the Board of Ethic Sciences. Logan only wished he felt more confident about the outcome.

"Thank God." Samuel said with a sigh of relief.

Logan covered Samuel with a warm blanket, adjusting several pillows to support and elevate his injured limbs.

"I wish there was something I could do . . ." Samuel whispered.

"Don't worry, Samuel." Logan said. "With any luck at all, by this time tomorrow, it will be over."

"Krystyna's leaving soon then, isn't she?" Samuel asked.

"It would seem." Something cold rolled over at the bottom of Logan's stomach. "But, enough of that. Rest, Samuel. Get your strength back."

Samuel grabbed Logan's arm. There was something he had to tell Logan . . . before he lost the thought and before he fell back to sleep. It had to do with the single chair in the empty room, didn't it? Suddenly, he couldn't remember, his thoughts fuzzy, disjointed.

"Logan, please don't go to SERENITY tonight. I'm afraid for you. Afraid for Krystyna." Samuel yawned, his eyes closing. "Don't . . ." What was he trying desperately to remember? Samuel's eyes fluttered open for an instant, only to close again.

Logan looked closely at Samuel. He had fallen asleep in mid-sentence.

When Logan returned to the kitchen, Orenda was pacing the floor, a hard expression on her face. "This has gone completely too far, Logan! I cannot sit and do nothing while Samuel . . ."

"I know better than to insist you stay put tonight." Logan said, glancing over to Krystyna and Garrett.

"Good," Garrett commented. "Let's put a plan together. I'm willing to do whatever is necessary."

"Okay. Now that everyone has a part, let's start with some ideas." Logan suggested.

"First of all," Krystyna answered, deadly serious, "we need to strike when Martin least expects us to strike."

"What are you saying, Krystyna?" Logan asked.

"You and I are going on the tour, certainly, but that's only the beginning." Krystyna said, going on to describe her rationalizations, and over the course of the next four hours, an intricate plan was formulated, polished and repolished.

As a group they took into consideration the variables and the obstacles which could occur, and it appeared nothing would daunt their optimism. If they should waiver, all they had to do was remember the terror Samuel was forced to endure when he jumped from the rooftop of the skyscraper.

No one needed more incentive than that haunting picture. None of them would ever forget or forgive.

Regardless, Krystyna realized it would be close to dawn by the time they returned home to the Reed Ranch.

So be it, Krystyna thought. It will be done.

Logan and Krystyna returned to their respective cabins with over an hour to spare before they were due to leave again. Logan would call for her when it was time.

Meanwhile, Krystyna paced through the cabin, roaming aimlessly from room to room, wrestling with the bruised and bloodied picture of Samuel all too vivid in her mind.

Indeed, Samuel's own question repeated itself; how could this injury have happened in a mere dream?

Sadly, Krystyna had no answers. The pictures provided for Samuel had become a warped reality, Martin's brand of reality.

Feed the eye, the mind and body will respond, Krystyna remembered.

Subliminal messages?

Pictures within pictures?

She must find out before tomorrow . . . somehow.

Krystyna peered through a window. She felt chilled to the bone. Outside, a bitter cold wind whipped at the trees. The vague silhouette of a full moon was mostly hidden behind the raging turbulent sky, a sky that had darkened hours ago, heavy with rain. It seemed an ominous sign.

She felt better after a warm shower, taking care with her make-up and leaving her hair down, brushing it well. As planned, she wore a borrowed dress from Orenda, an exquisite hand-beaded ankle-length dress, a dress closely resembling the one Orenda would wear. She opted for comfortable black flats, realizing they may meet fairly rugged terrain on this dark night. She chose not to wear any jewelry.

Soon, there was a knock at the door and Krystyna felt her heart suddenly leap in her chest. However, this time she was certain it was Logan.

He entered wordlessly, his eyes dark, somber. He was alone. Taima had a role, elsewhere, for now.

Krystyna felt herself being drawn into Logan's arms, at the same time stepping forward naturally, without thought. They did not kiss. They merely held on to one another, gathering strength.

The first to pull away, Krystyna was slow to smile. "Well, Dr. Reed, have we forgotten anything?"

"Garrett's recorder?"

She reached for her purse. "Right here."

"Pen and paper?"

"Also right here."

"The silent dog whistle?"

"It's in my bra."

Logan flashed his sardonic grin. "Why there?"

186

"In case I lose my purse."

They were both smiling now. It seemed to ease the tension.

"Did you find the spare key to the Jeep?" Logan asked.

"Yes. We'll drop it off with your mother as we leave."

"There's a flashlight in the Jeep, isn't there?"

"Yes."

"Good."

"Logan, what about your tools?"

"Everything I should need is in a duffel bag stuffed behind the driver's seat of Samuel's truck."

"What did you decide about the gun?"

"Garrett will have it with them."

Krystyna shivered at the thought of the gun, a nine-millimeter automatic. "They may have a worse need for it than us."

"This is true."

"How long do you anticipate Samuel will be left entirely alone? That's still bothering me."

"Not long, Krystyna, an hour, perhaps a bit longer. He'll do fine. He's slept most of the last twenty-four hours, so he'll have no trouble staying awake. Besides, Samuel has a way with shotguns."

"You've left him your cellular phone?"

"Yes. Just in case."

"And you fueled both the Jeep and Samuel's truck?"

"Yes." Logan answered, suddenly remembering something else. "Here's a spare key to Samuel's truck as well."

"I won't have a need for this."

"Krystyna, in the event you and I are separated, I need to know that you could escape in the truck. It's only a precaution."

Her dove-gray eyes widened. "I'm not leaving SERENITY without you!"

"You'll do what has to be done." Logan said, a stern edge to his voice she'd never heard before.

With great reluctance Krystyna took the key from Logan's hand, slipping this also into her bra.

Logan grinned. "Maybe you should use a larger purse."

187

Krystyna returned the smile.

"It's time to leave, Krystyna."

The moment had finally arrived and Krystyna felt the apprehensions of going into battle nearly empty handed; leaping, on blind faith alone, straight into a black swirling vortex called the territory of the enemy.

Suddenly, she felt very much like Samuel, a trusting soul, standing on the edge of the rooftop, vulnerable, peering down into the unknown.

She whispered a humble prayer.

CHAPTER TWENTY SEVEN

Logan raised his arm to the doorbell, glancing over to Krystyna. There was a fierce determination in his dark eyes. "Act one."

She nodded in agreement. She was ready.

Wasting no time answering the door, Martin Braddock stepped back into the foyer, allowing them entrance. He gave them a brief, benign smile. "Good evening Dr. Reed, Krystyna."

"Harold, lock the front door." Martin repeated the verbal command to engage the security system.

After taking their jackets, Martin decided to offer an apology. It was the best he could muster under the strained circumstances. He also wondered why he felt the need to apologize for something over which he had no true regrets. "Sorry about last night, Krystyna. I suppose I should have called first. How inconsiderate of me."

Krystyna knew this was about all Martin would mention of the episode. It was typical for him to ignore, right out of existence, his own faults and selfish deeds. She looked over to Logan who wore an expression of disbelief. He, too, was astounded at the pompous unnerving attitude of Martin.

Logan made eye contact with Martin. "Braddock, I won't waste my time repeating my earlier warnings to you, but I will tell you I'm looking forward to enforcing them, nevertheless."

The sneer on Martin's face was a failed attempt at a smile; he knew it himself, didn't even bother to cover it up. He really did not like this irksome Reed character! "I see the furry force behind your threats decided not to join us this evening?"

Instinctively, Krystyna laid a hand on Logan's arm, wordlessly reminding him not to fall into Martin's traps. They dared not lose their tempers. They needed to stay calm and clear-headed.

Forcing his animosity aside, Logan's voice was steady. "That's correct. Taima decided you weren't worth chewing up and spitting out. That's one of the things I love most about my dog; she's an excellent judge of character."

Martin twirled his fingers around one end of his blonde mustache. "Well, Stephanie is waiting for us downstairs. Drinks before dinner, perhaps a little conversation, then we can conduct our tour in earnest at SERENITY."

Moving to the marbled staircase, Krystyna was struggling over which obscenity to scream at Martin first. Instead, she counted the steps as they joined Stephanie in the white leather and chrome living room.

Poised on a loveseat, Stephanie raised the wineglass in her hand. A blood red droplet spilled from her glass; it went unnoticed. "So, our guests have arrived. Dr. Reed, nice to see you again."

"And you." Logan said without conviction.

Stephanie turned to Krystyna. "Lovely dress."

"Thank you." Krystyna answered, sitting down beside Logan on one of the loveseats. Surprisingly, she thought Stephanie's compliment sounded genuine.

Martin seemed to enjoy his role as bartender, suggesting several different wines, liqueurs, and assorted alcoholic drinks with long fancy names. Both Logan and Krystyna opted for a glass of Cabernet Sauvignon.

Feeling Stephanie's eyes on her, Krystyna returned the stare. "Is there something wrong?"

"No, I was just thinking how unlike Martin and you are. I truly have a difficult time imagining the two of you living together."

Krystyna smiled easily. "Yes, I know. I have a difficult time with that also, Stephanie." She glanced over to Martin. "Just consider it along the lines of a bad dream. It wasn't real to begin with."

"Let's not get off to a bad start, ladies." Martin said, attempting to inject some cheerfulness in his words.

"Oh, we wouldn't do that," Stephanie blurted out. "We're like old friends, by now. We've met in places you'd not ever guess!"

A puzzled expression touched Martin's emerald eyes. He looked from Stephanie to Krystyna.

"It's true, Martin, but that's strictly between Stephanie and myself." Krystyna said. "Leave it at that."

This announcement made Martin instantly uncomfortable, and Krystyna saw the uneasiness creep into his face, the liqueur glass brought to his lips and held there, without taking a sip, forgotten.

Good, Krystyna thought, let's give him something else to ponder.

"However," Krystyna concentrated on Stephanie, "I've become very curious about the . . . collection you mentioned the other day. Perhaps you'd be willing to show them to us?"

Stephanie's smile brightened her entire face. She was glad to see that there was an ounce of class in the other woman Martin had once married. More than that, she could not deny the opportunity to gloat before Krystyna. "I would be very pleased."

Setting their wineglasses on a nearby table, Krystyna and Logan rose from the loveseat, their motions unhurried, casual. Neither one wore a readable expression.

The sudden dawning of what was about to transpire, hit Martin and hit him hard. It now appeared that Stephanie told Krystyna about the diamonds; the single subject he was not in favor of divulging to anyone! His mind raced for a solution. He must draw their attention away, somehow, immediately.

Martin was too late.

Already, Stephanie was leading their guests toward the photograph gallery, their backs to him, and twenty feet to the far side of the gallery was the vault encasing his prized collection of diamonds.

Martin, thinking quickly, credited neither Logan or Krystyna with the smarts to put it all together. In any event, he would deal later with Stephanie.

Stephanie's heels pounded sharply across the wide expanse of tile floor. Eventually, they rounded a corner, entering a long, rectangular shaped gallery, complete with built-in spotlighting, revealing a vast display of the Braddock family photographs.

There were photographs of generations going as far back as the seventeenth century. Both sets of Martin's grandparents were there, numerous portrait oils of his father and mother, Harold and Marie Braddock, and a long deceased brother, Thomas, the photo taken in happier times.

The group passed along the photographs slowly, with no particular interest, until further along the gallery and nearly to the end, a grouping of photos caught Krystyna's attention. She swallowed hard. There on the wall had been hung pictures of her mother and father. Stunned, she stepped closer finding several photos of herself; one as a chubby toddler, another as a third grader, later as debate team captain, and dozens taken during her married life with Martin.

Krystyna was compulsively drawn to a single photo of her beloved parents. Tears came instantly. Seeing their faces, so alive and carefree, brought the loss of them back into focus. She hadn't expected this.

Watching Krystyna closely, Logan lightly touched her shoulder, guiding her further along the gallery, whispering in her ear. "Be strong."

When Logan turned back to Braddock and Stephanie, he caught a calculated and scheming expression pass between them. He didn't like it.

Giving into the fact that his precious diamonds were about to be viewed, Martin thought it wise he go along with it; to do otherwise may call undue attention. So, he decided he would conduct the viewing in his own controlled fashion. He certainly could not leave this up to Stephanie. She was already on her third glass of wine.

"Here we are." Martin said, stepping to the side, turning to face Stephanie and his guests. He donned a proud stance, squaring his shoulders. He pointed to the single large photograph of SERENITY, the picture set apart from all the rest, occupying a sacred place. "Behind this picture is the vault."

Martin continued, drawing his hands together in a solemn pose. "Let me ask you, Dr. Reed, Krystyna, what is nature's most sought after treasure?"

Pausing, Martin wasn't expecting an answer. He smiled. "Diamonds, of course; lumps of carbon, the hardest substance to be found on earth. The cause of greed, murders, and wars. The diamond is the greatest worker in science and industry. And it's said they are a girl's best friend. I only know they have bewitched and bedazzled all those who've laid eyes on them, from primitive man to the sophisticates of today."

Martin reached to pull the photograph frame aside, temporarily blocking Logan and Krystyna while he worked the combination lock. The vault clicked softly, the locking mechanism released, and he opened the heavy door, pushing it far to the side. Martin extracted a large black velvet box, holding it reverently as he turned to face the others.

"I was exceptionally fortunate," Martin began, "to be at the right place at the right time, and as a result I now own a small yet significant part of history."

Inching forward, Stephanie wanted a closer look. She had always found them to be . . . hypnotic.

"Please Stephanie," Martin snapped, "allow our guests first chance to see for themselves."

"Now," Martin continued, his tone softening, "let me ask if you know of the infamous Peace diamond?"

Krystyna looked to Logan, shrugging her shoulders.

"Apparently not." Logan stated simply.

"This is my favorite of all the diamonds." Martin smiled. "The Peace diamond, originally over four hundred carats, has been dedicated to the peace and uplifting of the human spirit. Naturally, since it was unearthed, all those in ownership have associated this diamond with good fortune, and untold success in all endeavors. You can well imagine the great race of mankind to procure this specific diamond. As with all the priceless diamonds of the world, it was cut down to a more manageable size, a mere hundred and thirty carats, the excess pieces sold to the highest bidders."

"Martin," Krystyna said, "can we assume the smaller cut portions of the Peace diamond would have changed hands numerous times?"

"Indeed they have, and as I've said, I was fortunate to obtain several fully faceted diamonds from the original."

Stephanie interrupted, wine glass in her hand. "But, that's not the only piece of an original that Martin has acquired!" She poked Martin in the ribs playfully. "You've saved the best for last, haven't you? Tell them about my favorite."

Martin cleared his throat, fighting an impulse to reach out and slap Stephanie senseless. It wouldn't, he thought, take much. "As I was saying," he continued, "another diamond in my collection was a small paring from another original, one I'm certain you will both recognize; the Hope diamond."

Krystyna's mind was attempting to compute all she could remember about diamonds, and she knew that the Hope diamond was the largest blue diamond in existence. Aside from that, she was desperately seeking a correlation between these diamonds and SERENITY. She was feeling hopelessly lost, and by Logan's disgruntled expression, he was not faring much better.

"As with the Peace diamond," Martin explained, "the Hope diamond was pared down from its original size, these smaller pieces changing hands over the centuries. However, there is no good fortune associated with this particular diamond. Quite the contrary! The history of the Hope diamond relates evil influences, bloodshed, and was directly held responsible for many mysterious intrigues. Yet, I am privileged to own my portion of the Hope diamond."

"Well?" Stephanie urged Martin. "Peel back the velvet and let them see!"

Although Martin detested Stephanie for rushing him, he complied obediently, opening the top drawer of the black velvet box. Inside the numbered and labeled compartments, were loose diamonds of all sizes, colors and shapes, utterly brilliant, sparkling with clarity.

"These are from the Hope diamond," Martin said, handing an entire drawer of compartments to Krystyna, extracting a second drawer and likewise allowing Logan to view them closely. "And these are from the Peace diamond."

The diamonds were truly a magnificent sight, Krystyna marveled. She looked over to Logan. He was visibly impressed with the diamonds, the charismatic colors a spectacular display, yet he chose not to comment.

A third black velvet drawer was removed from the box, only to reveal another dozen compartments filled with other, less prized diamonds.

Stephanie could feel the smug smile on her face.

Then a fourth and finally a fifth drawer opened revealing a literal fortune in diamonds. Stephanie reached out to touch one. It felt silky, cool, crisp.

Stephanie looked intently at Krystyna, taking a sip from her wineglass. "The offer still stands; one diamond for good luck, another for good riddance."

Amazed at Stephanie's congenial mood, Krystyna gently smiled, whispering. "I'll still pass."

"As you wish." Stephanie said quietly, sipping at her wine, mesmerized at the glorious sight of all those diamonds. She asked Martin if she could again see her favorite, the Hope diamond.

Finally, the drawers were put back together into the black velvet box, and returned to the vault. Martin then suggested they move to the dining room for dinner.

"Before we do that, Martin, I wanted to ask you something." Krystyna said. "I'm curious to know if any of the legends, good or bad, have accompanied your pieces of the Hope or the Peace diamonds?"

"I've had unusually good luck. What more can I say?"

Martin leaned closer toward Krystyna, emerald eyes gleaming. "With Hope, Peace and SERENITY on my side, how could I possibly lose?"

CHAPTER TWENTY EIGHT

Typical, Krystyna thought, Martin was in his infamous mood whereby he could not, despite all the bleak and bold facts, and would not, admit failure. "Martin, you sound insanely optimistic!" Krystyna said. "I think you need to take a good hard look around you."

"I have! That's what keeps me going."

Stephanie looked over to Logan, rolling her eyes. "How boring; they're going to be at it again. Let's leave them to their squabbling, Dr. Reed." She hooked an arm through his. "Come along to the dining room. I need a fresh drink anyway."

Casting a hurried glance at Krystyna, Logan waited for a signal from her. She lightly touched the sapphire blue beads at the neckline of her dress. Soon, Stephanie and Logan disappeared, their footsteps echoing across the vast spaces.

Shaking her head back and forth in frustration, Krystyna continued. "Martin, in case you haven't noticed, most, if not all, your patients from WHISPERING FALLS are gone."

"They'll return, Krystyna. You'll see."

"I'm afraid I don't."

Martin twirled his fingers around one end of his blonde mustache. "It's a very big and prosperous country, Krystyna."

"By that, am I to assume you intend on treating patients elsewhere?"

"You could, yes."

"But why? It's not working, Martin."

"That, my angel, is a matter of opinion. In the beginning I had enormous success."

"Perhaps. What about now?"

"I won't disagree that something went wrong."

"Then how can you justify continuing with the same treatments, knowing full well they could easily backfire?"

"I've nearly figured it out, Krystyna."

"That's not good enough, and you know it!"

"What I know will astound you." A wicked twist pulled at Martin's mouth. "Krystyna, what would you say if I told you I'm doing little different than the government itself?"

Krystyna took a step back. Her eyes resembled cold marble. "I've heard this before."

"No, you haven't. Believe me when I tell you this is something relatively new and different. Yet, the government has secretly worked on perfecting this . . . method for their own devices, namely warfare through means of psychological conditioning. Few are aware of the existence of this method."

"Even now, I find it hard to believe the government would use human beings as guinea pigs."

"Krystyna, how naive you are, my angel." He smiled gently. "They always have and they always will. However, this method is so unique, so powerful, I wanted to see it put to good use. Help instead of hinder. I soon realized it would be years before anyone else took it as far as I have."

"Too far, Martin. Always too far."

"My intentions are for the good of man."

"That's debatable."

Right before her eyes, Martin changed his colors.

"Krystyna," Martin whispered eagerly, "is there a chance we might speak alone?"

"We are, at the moment, quite alone." Krystyna said, peering over his shoulder down the long photograph gallery.

"No. I meant . . . later."

"There's no reason . . ."

"Yes, my angel, there is."

"Stop that angel crap right now, or I won't give your request a single moments thought!" Her voice was suddenly shrill. To her amazement, the fingers of her right hand contracted and curled like claws.

"All right." Martin whispered quickly. "I'll not push."

Krystyna fought for control of her anger.

"You never answered me."

Good, she thought, Martin was doing just as she had hoped. "Let me think about it."

"I'll settle for that."

She gave him a long cold stare. "You'll have to."

Krystyna turned away from Martin, drawn to the distant echo of voices drifting from the dining room.

An hour later, the meal finished, the group moved back to the living room. Everyone had coffee except for Stephanie. She felt like having another glass of wine, sobering somewhat after dinner. She much preferred the evening in a dream-like state. It would be over soon, Stephanie promised herself, seeking a sense of detachment, realizing she really didn't want to be there. She was impossibly bored, especially with Martin.

"Well," Martin said, "if everyone is agreeable, I think we should begin the tour of SERENITY."

Logan rose from the loveseat, stretching his long legs. "We'll follow you in Krystyna's Jeep."

"Let's retrieve your jackets." Martin said, gesturing to the marbled staircase.

"Run along," Stephanie whispered to Martin. "I'll catch up soon enough."

Martin eyed Stephanie suspiciously. "I want you there."

"I will be," Stephanie answered, seeing their guests were halfway up the marbled steps leading to the front foyer. "I just want to freshen up."

"Don't be long."

I'll take as long as I want, Stephanie muttered under her breath, reaching to refill her wineglass.

Martin's hand closed down painfully over hers. "You've had enough to drink, Stephanie!"

"Just a last sip, Martin. You need not worry."

"I'm already worried."

"About what?"

"About you. You and your mouth!"

"Oh?" Stephanie said, pulling away from Martin, taking her wineglass with her. "You're upset because I told Krystyna about the diamonds."

"What did you expect? That I would be overjoyed?" Martin laughed, the eerie sound dancing ghost-like around the cavernous room.

"Krystyna would have found out, regardless. She has a complete list of your assets."

Martin was no longer laughing, yet a sinister smile had survived. "You know how I feel about that imbecile attorney. Don't mention him again this evening."

"Of course not, Martin."

"We'll discuss all of this later."

You bet, Stephanie thought. That, and more. She had a belly full of complaints to lodge, preferably right down Martin's throat! Maybe, just maybe, tonight was the night.

Turning on his heel, Martin glanced back at Stephanie. "You have a lot at stake here, yourself. Remember that."

Minutes later, Stephanie was alone in the house. Her mind whirled. She needed another drink.

Following the sleek black Mercedes, Logan and Krystyna watched Martin as he spoke with the uniformed guard manning the entrance of SERENITY. Their exchange was brief, the Jeep then pulling forward, the guard stating they had been cleared for admission. As before, there was an odd vacant look to the guard's lackluster face, his affect wooden and tedious.

As they neared SERENITY it became amazingly clear the mammoth proportion of the incongruous structure. The building loomed high and wide, resembling a blood-dark phantom with arms held open. A maze of windows stared out into the stormy night, and lost against the shadows became an interlacing web of sinister and sparkling eyes. At its foundation, the rain-splattered asphalt of the vast parking area appeared much like an endless, midnight sea.

Logan reached to take Krystyna's hand. "You look frightened."

"I am." She felt Logan's assurance as he squeezed her hand.

Krystyna stole another glance at SERENITY.

They ran through the drenching rain to find the front entrance standing open; two sets of glass doors, one serving as an airlock. Martin was inside hanging his soggy overcoat on an elaborate wrought iron stand, and when he spotted them, he motioned for them to enter.

Once inside, the ivory ceiling soared thirty feet overhead. A burgundy tiled foyer met with an elegant reception area of sapphire blue leather chairs and sofas, arranged in small intimate groups. On a large windowless wall a glass display case housed a replica of the florescent pink billboard advertisement Krystyna had seen in several locations scattered about WHISPERING FALLS. She read the sign again:

EXPECT A MIRACLE AT "SERENITY"
CELEBRATE LIFE IN PERFECT BALANCE!
LEARN TO LOVE YOURSELF AGAIN!
DISCOVER INNER PEACE!
CONTACT DR. MARTIN BRADDOCK
GUARDIAN OF HOPE, MESSENGER OF
ENLIGHTENMENT
1212 HILLSIDE DRIVE, WHISPERING FALLS,
WASHINGTON

Krystyna finally turned to Martin, chuckling. "Guardian of Hope?"

Martin's smile was twisted. "Rather appropriate, wouldn't you say?"

No, I wouldn't, Krystyna thought! Yet, this confirmed for her a correlation between Martin's diamonds and his work at SERENITY. What that correlation in fact was, remained elusive.

Branching off the foyer and reception area, several plush carpeted hallways disappeared into the darkness, snaking away in all directions. Martin motioned for Logan and Krystyna to follow him along one hallway that further revealed three distinct doorways, equally spaced apart.

The first door had a brass engraved plaque: INTRODUCTION.

Martin opened this door, speaking over his shoulder to Logan and Krystyna as they entered. Martin's attention elsewhere, Krystyna reached into her purse and turned the tape recorder to ON.

"I thought I'd start here, just as though you were patients about to experience SERENITY for the very first time." Martin gestured to the opened space before them; a semi-circular arrangement of seating, easily accommodating a hundred occupants, positioned and focused on a sunken black marbled podium.

Leading them down to the front row, Martin then took his place at the altar he so loved. With deliberation, he took a long moment to adjust the electronic panel within easy reach of his fingertips.

Clearing his throat, Martin began, the image of perfect control. "Fear. We, as humans, fear. We each search to destroy that monster hiding in our personal closets, or lurking under our beds. None of us are unaffected or untouched by the gripping cold hand of fear."

He continued in greater detail, describing again for Logan and Krystyna the maladies associated with fear driven individuals, the resultant pitfalls, and the unwelcomed lifestyle changes. He touched on the many phobias he had treated; fear of lightning, fear of spiders and bugs, fear of the dark, fear of just about everything imaginable.

Krystyna watched closely as Martin became enraptured with his own words, caught up in his insatiable drive to care and to cure.

"Each patient is interviewed at length by myself personally, establishing and setting recovery goals and methods to achieve those goals. All aspects of their fears or phobias are addressed. All questions are answered. The patient is then instructed to avoid alcohol, caffeine, nicotine, any chemical stimulant. If indicated, we enlist the patient to monitor a well balanced diet and help ensure a natural vitamin regimen. These steps are carefully tailored to each specific individual, keeping always in mind that no two phobias are precisely the same; no two recoveries are achieved in like manner."

"Martin," Krystyna began, "when, in this introductory phase, do you convince the patient to sign a waiver releasing you from all liability?"

The smile dropped from Martin's face. He locked eyes with Krystyna. "Early on, Krystyna."

"And," Logan interjected a question of his own, "I suppose your fees are considered nominal?"

"What fees?"

Krystyna turned to Logan, her tone bitter and sarcastic. "Nothing new, Logan. Martin full well knows and appreciates the response he'll get when a patient hears the words . . . absolutely no charge!"

Toying with one end of his blonde mustache, Martin's smile deepened. "A true scientist works for the benefit of mankind; not for personal gain."

"And which of the two are you?" Logan asked angrily.

With effort, Martin elected to ignore Reed's question. "We organize support groups under which patients with similar or like phobias are placed. They meet here in one of several conference rooms, and at their respective homes. They speak on the phone with one another and I'm available to patients in crisis seven days and nights a week. We deal with the restlessness, the frustrations, the mental fragmentation. Recovery also involves a deeper understanding of the patient's motivational role in the healing process."

"Martin," Krystyna asked, "I'm curious to know if you discuss with your patients other possible treatments, other than your own?"

"Of course. I cover a broad spectrum of what's available to the average phobic seeking therapy."

"And what are those treatments?" Krystyna prompted.

"Hypnosis, systematic desensitization, muscle relaxation, visual imagery, just to mention a few."

"Aside from the obvious, how do your treatments differ?" Logan asked.

"Good question, Dr. Reed." Martin stated. "I've always been a strong proponent of implosive therapy with reinforced practices. That is to say, I do what is necessary to encourage patients to challenge their phobias directly, head on. But, I've also developed a way to ease this direct process, slow it down accordingly, little by little, acquainting the patient with their fear in an entirely intimate manner."

"How on earth?" Krystyna asked.

"Visually . . . of course." Martin's emerald eyes deepened their intensity; a passion smoldered there. "Fear makes people react in strange ways. I show the patient precisely how they look to the outside world when they are filled with fear. They observe their own bizarre behaviors and socially unacceptable patterns. They can, and do, observe themselves from afar. They are the actors in their own film, if you will; I, the director."

And the scenery much too real, Krystyna thought. "So, how do you manage that?" She asked.

There was a malicious turn of Martin's mouth. "Put simply; pictures. Pictures that induce altered states of consciousness."

Krystyna frowned. "Pictures alone cannot do what you are implying."

"But then, Krystyna, you are assuming we use ordinary pictures!" Martin answered. "There is nothing ordinary here. Our pictures will squeeze the fear right out of you!"

CHAPTER TWENTY NINE

Footsteps alerted the group of someone approaching; Stephanie was making her way to the black marbled podium. "Indeed." Stephanie added, "we've created a world within a world."

"Stephanie," Martin said, thankful to see that she had sobered up some. "I was just about to move our guests to the next room, RESEARCH AND DEVELOPMENT."

This room proved to be good sized, L-shaped, including a desk area with file cabinets, a dozen computers, and various electronic equipment lined one wide wall. Krystyna now noticed two other connecting doors with brass plaques signifying DARK ROOM and EQUIPMENT.

"I'd like to see." Krystyna said to Martin, pointing to these other rooms.

The DARK ROOM appeared to be typical, housing the necessary chemical compounds, processing solutions and developers, photographic plate holders, aluminum trays and sinks. Inside the windowless EQUIPMENT ROOM, there was a mixture of heavy duty steel tables, solid shelving, measuring flasks for chemicals, timers, a sophisticated camera with multiple lens, mirrors of all sizes, glass vials, and yet another computer.

Off to one corner was an object Krystyna immediately recognized. "Martin, what are you doing with a laser?"

"All in good time." Martin said, moving to the table, his hand caressing the laser reverently. "There is a window of opportunity that we have chosen to enhance; three dimensional photography. We've recorded on flexible plastic film the reflections of light waves in such a way that the observer senses interaction with the objects on the film. He or she can seemingly reach out and touch the enhanced object. He or she can walk into a scene and truly experience it!"

Martin only now took his hands away from the laser. "This procedure was initially developed in nineteen hundred and forty eight. A single laser light was split into two separate beams. The first beam bounced off the object photographed, and the second beam was allowed to collide with the reflected light of the original beam. The resultant pattern of light was then recorded on film as a three-dimensional picture. The clarity was so eerily convincing that early scientific efforts explored this further. Over the years, experimentation with this three-dimensional reality was conducted, but for the most part, in the privately funded sectors. Yet few had the insight to imagine the vast possibilities of this exciting field of photography. Few realized the potential."

Krystyna sought to digest the information. "What is this method called?"

Again, Martin ignored another question. "However," Martin continued, "some scientists realized that the human brain cannot always distinguish between what is actually seen, and what the brain believes it has seen. The image the brain receives from viewing a particular scene can and will impact on the body. The nature of the mind and body are actually one; feed the eye, the mind and body will respond."

Logan folded his arms across his chest. "And this has been scientifically proven?"

"Yes, without question." Martin smiled. "But, this alone is not my secret. There is another, far more important factor."

Gesturing to the door, making eye contact with Stephanie, Martin offered a suggestion. "Let's move to another area, shall we?"

"I'll set up in the COMPUTER ROOM." Stephanie said as she retreated out of sight.

Logan and Krystyna exchanged curious glances as they were led back into the long hallway, entering the middle room, PREPARATION.

Small by comparison, this room centered on two chairs arranged to face one another. Martin pointed to each of the four individual corners of the room where walls met with the ceiling, and a sophisticated camera was positioned. All cameras were linked to the COMPUTER ROOM, and an additional remote control device was within easy reach on a table nearest one of the chairs.

"Sit down, Krystyna." Martin instructed, claiming a seat himself and reaching for the remote control.

Reluctantly, Krystyna took her place, Logan standing to one side, arms folded across his chest.

"Not too close, Dr. Reed." Martin said. "I'll be taking Krystyna's picture and it won't do to have you in the frame. She must appear alone."

Logan took a cautious step back, then another without taking his dark somber eyes from Martin.

Martin directed his attention solely on Krystyna, holding the remote control casually in his hand. "Now, if you will, Krystyna, let's pretend you are a patient."

Krystyna could barely hear the soft click of a camera. It made her increasingly nervous.

"Just be yourself. This is a perfectly painless procedure."

Krystyna arched a brow, her expression relaying her doubt. "Quite unlike the outcome!"

"Rumors, Krystyna, unfounded gossip." Martin could see that Krystyna was unconvinced.

Martin took in a deep breath. "Let's pretend you entertain a fear of . . ." He glanced at Logan. "Heights, for example."

At this, Logan's tall frame stiffened.

The soft click of a camera could be heard.

Conducting a lengthy series of questions, Martin continued to snap photographs of Krystyna as she responded. Soon, Krystyna found she had lost track of the soft clicks of the camera. Her awareness of this took a back seat to the actual questions, and more specifically her answers, and with each answer she formed, a vivid picture of Samuel pierced her heart. Without recognizing this fact, Krystyna became truly involved and animated.

After a time, Martin suggested that Krystyna stand, taking a few moments to stretch her legs; pace back and forth if that suited her. The camera clicked again and again, catching a full spectrum of emotions in her body language, in her facial expressions, and in her choice of words.

Martin caught a flash of her innocent smile. He clicked the camera as she became angry, capturing on film the fear riddled words when Martin referred to standing on a tall building, looking down, peering over the dangerous edge.

Feeling weakened and vulnerable, Krystyna sat back down opposite Martin.

He leaned very close, a wicked gleam in his emerald eyes. "Now, let's see an expression of *real* fear."

"I thought that's precisely what I've been doing." Krystyna said.

"No Krystyna, you've given me only a subtle hint. I want to capture the real thing." Martin paused, leaning closer still. "Let's pretend something else entirely."

"What?" Krystyna asked.

"You're traveling in a car, heading south on the interstate . . ."

Instantly, Krystyna became rigid, her heart pounded.

Logan watched Krystyna carefully. She gave no signal to intervene.

Martin continued. "It's an ordinary day; California sunshine streaming in through the windshield, the car's engine is a steady drone . . ."

The first flush of panic seized Krystyna. The camera clicked.

"The oncoming traffic is drawing closer . . ."

"No!" Krystyna gripped the arms of the chair.

"One car in particular is traveling at an excessive speed, crossing the line, swerving."

"Stop it!" Krystyna screamed.

The camera clicked again.

Logan quickly stepped over to Martin. "I don't like this."

Ignoring Logan Reed, Martin pushed Krystyna to that necessary edge. "Your father is driving, your mother is in the passenger seat, they're talking, unaware that in just moments . . ."

208

The camera clicked, seizing for all time the very essence of Krystyna's fear. In her thoughts she could visualize her mother and father riding in their car that last fateful day. She could imagine the other car, speeding, finally losing control, careening up and over the lane barrier, tires screeching, metal grinding. The impact of the head-on crash was a single breathless moment away.

"Please stop," Krystyna cried, bringing her hands to cover her face.

"That's enough, Braddock!" Logan warned through clenched teeth.

Martin locked eyes with Logan. "Yes, I believe it is. Just enough."

"That was a nasty underhanded thing to do!" Krystyna said to Martin.

"Perhaps so, but very effective. It's results we're after here!" Martin answered, rising from the chair. "I'll return in a few minutes."

Staring at Martin's retreating back, Krystyna whispered, "I hate him." She trembled with pent-up anger, her hands clasped together tightly.

Logan knelt before Krystyna, lifting her chin so that he could see her eyes; there was pain, hard cruel anguish. "Say nothing more." He looked around the room and at each of the corners where the cameras were housed. "Give nothing away, Krystyna."

She pulled a tissue from her purse, dabbing at her wet eyes and blowing her nose. She took in a deep breath and let it out just as slowly. A faint smile surfaced. "I'll be okay. Martin simply knows which buttons to push."

"Braddock's in the right business then, isn't he?"

Later, Martin and Stephanie returned, holding their position in the opened doorway. "We've a few minutes before your computer generated sequences on film have been completed." Martin said. "Before you view them, I thought we could show you the remainder of SERENITY."

Part of their plan, Logan feigned an undying interest in computers, suggesting that Stephanie take him to the COMPUTER ROOM where she worked her own particular magic. Delighted, Stephanie led him away.

All traces of her tears wiped away, Krystyna turned to Martin, offering him an innocent smile. "Perhaps you'd like me to see your private office."

Martin's features visibly relaxed. "So, you've thought over my suggestion to meet with me later?"

"No, not quite." Krystyna answered, gazing down the hallway Logan and Stephanie had disappeared. "For now, I want to see the room you spend the most time."

"You do know me well, Krystyna." Martin laughed, a hint of his boyish charm lighting up his eyes. "I've not changed much, have I?"

"Oh, but you have Martin, and you frighten me."

Martin reached an arm around Krystyna's waist, guiding her to the east wing of the building. "I'm sorry about that, my angel, but these days, I frighten myself."

Krystyna looked hard at Martin. "Why?"

He stopped just outside another door. "You've already addressed the fact that something's gone wrong here at SERENITY. Well, you're absolutely right!"

"What then?"

Dropping his eyes, Martin's face nevertheless retained a guilt-ridden expression. "I have my suspicions."

Krystyna was appalled. "You're not sure?"

Martin pushed the door open. A porcelain lamp situated on a corner table illuminated the small office area. Entering, Krystyna quickly took notice of the furnishings, as always, seeking the one place Martin would choose to keep his infamous, tell-all, handwritten notes.

Martin's private office was simple and utilitarian compared to the rest of the rooms; two upholstered chairs were arranged before a chess set, a game in progress, the oak desktop covered with books, file folders, messages and unopened mail. A metal wastebasket was placed to one side of the desk and to the opposite side two glass shelves attached to the wall held a small sampling of books. None of Martin's diplomas had been displayed on the walls. There were no pictures either.

"No computer?" Krystyna asked as she remained standing.

"Stephanie takes care of that, thankfully."

Martin closed the door, leaning back against the wooden frame, folding his arms in front of him.

It made Krystyna very apprehensive to have Martin stare at her.

"Back to my earlier question, Martin. Why don't you know what's gone wrong with your therapy?"

"I'm . . . working on it."

"Shouldn't you postpone patient therapy in the meantime?"

"I'm certain it's something simple."

"You don't really care about your patients, Martin! Only your . . . creative therapy."

"That's unfair. I've given a good deal of my efforts to perfecting the therapy, and working out the bugs."

Krystyna shook her head. "My God, Martin, you're destroying lives, not saving them."

"It's only natural that some are to be sacrificed for the good of others, the vast majority who will be helped." Martin said, quickly moving away from the door.

Instinctively, Krystyna flinched.

He stopped in mid-step. "Am I really the monster you suggest?"

Krystyna eyed Martin cautiously. "I won't lie to you Martin. Yes, you are."

Martin grimaced. "That hurts, Krystyna."

Now, staring at an empty wall, his back to her, Martin's words were whispered. "My work isn't the same without you, Krystyna. I'm not the same man."

Martin whirled around to face Krystyna. "I need you."

"You've managed to survive without me for the past three years."

"Survived . . . barely."

"But the point remains; your work has continued despite my absence."

"Krystyna, I've lost my touch!" Absentmindedly, Martin groaned his despair. "I'm floundering."

"Then my advice to you is get back on track. Stop your work immediately. Close SERENITY. Fess up with the BOES; enlist their help. Find out what went wrong!"

"That is not a decision to be drawn solely by myself. There's Stephanie to be considered. She's worked long and hard, sacrificing when she's never before known a sacrifice. She's a big part of all this and . . ."

"And?" Krystyna asked.

"Never mind. It doesn't concern you."

"Martin, you can't continue this fiasco . . ." Krystyna began, halting her words as a faraway expression covered Martin's face.

"I've always known where you were." Martin whispered, a narcissistic twist to his mustache.

The full impact of his words stunned Krystyna. "Then why didn't you . . ."

"I was waiting for you to come back to me. Drop this nonsense about the divorce and return where you belong."

"What had you planned to do about Stephanie, if in fact, I did?"

"One word from you, my angel, and I'd send Stephanie back to New York where I found her! That's really where she's happiest."

"You've perhaps underestimated her, Martin."

Martin snickered. "Maybe, but I'd not give her a choice."

The moment had come, Krystyna thought. "All right, Martin, I'll meet with you at two o'clock this morning. I can slip out undetected while everyone else is asleep. Let's meet some place that's . . . secluded. How about the lookout, you know, the one at the top of the Falls?"

A bright smile appeared on Martin's handsome face. "I'll be there, my angel."

Playing her part, Krystyna forced a smile. Inside, something just grabbed at her gut, coiling and recoiling, spasms of a sinister foreboding.

Martin reached an arm around her slim shoulders.

"Now, would you mind if I read over your notes?" She asked.

"Why?" The arm Martin held around her shoulders, dropped instantly to his side. "I'm not certain that's wise."

"I merely want to help you find out what went wrong."

"Why?" Martin repeated, his tone cautious.

"Logan's brother, Samuel. I'm sure you know exactly who I'm referring to. I've seen the after effects of your treatments. It's not a pretty picture, Martin."

"You must believe me when I tell you it wasn't always that way. Patient's made remarkable recoveries in the beginning."

"Martin, I understand that. However, you must tell me more."

"It may be in your best interest not to know anything more." Martin paused, thinking. "But, I will tell you I believe the problem has to do with the laser."

"The laser?" Krystyna repeated, her thoughts spinning. "Has it malfunctioned?"

Martin was not smiling. "Think about it, Krystyna."

A mental image of the laser in the EQUIPMENT ROOM formed in Krystyna's mind. She knew the basics, little more. The laser was used to split the beams of light, enabling Martin to capture three-dimensional objects on film. And, at the tip of the laser was either a precisely machined piece of glass, high tech plastics, industrial grade rubies, or other gemstones.

Krystyna's thoughts were suddenly brought into a tight focus. And occasionally used were . . . diamonds.

CHAPTER THIRTY

Logan's knock at Martin's office door was well timed. Krystyna, having arrived at a partial conclusion about the diamonds, welcomed the intrusion.

The tour continued, Martin escorting Logan and Krystyna through the entire building and the numerous rooms, and they now stopped before the last door at the end of the main hallway.

The plaque above this door, polished brass with elaborate hand-crafted detailing, read: THE EMPTY ROOM.

"Why empty?" Krystyna asked Martin as they paused before the door.

Martin smiled. "It remains empty, vacant, barren, until the patient decides to fill the void with substantial will power to fight their fear. This is where emptiness comes alive, takes its first breath."

Entering the hollowed space, a circular room was revealed, iridescent white walls curving gently. If it weren't for the door, there appeared no beginning, no ending. A single, dark green leather chair was positioned at the exact center of the room and spotlighted with tiny fixtures hidden in the opaque ceiling. The thick carpeted floor was the same emerald shade of green as the chair, and Krystyna was instantly reminded of walking through a field of soft grass.

Logan looked at Krystyna. Earlier, they had agreed to accept the dangers of this room, recognizing the risks involved. They would do what needed to be done for Samuel, and all the other innocent victims. Yet, in this moment, Logan felt the sharp needle-twisting sting of regret.

"You mentioned computer generated sequences on film." Krystyna said.

"Yes, indeed." Martin answered.

"Would you mind explaining further?"

"I don't casually divulge mechanical details to my patients." Martin said, his words cold.

"But, we're not patients." Krystyna said.

Hesitating, weighing the pros and cons, Martin decided he would outline the basics. He knew Krystyna would undoubtedly be impressed, and it was increasingly important to Martin that he win back Krystyna's respect.

"Hidden within these walls," Martin gestured with his raised arm, "is a sophisticated sound system. Three hundred and sixty degrees of Ultra-Panavision movie screen surround the observer; the pictures seemingly without a point of origin, enabling a life-like three dimensionality. Even though this is a totally synthetic visual experience, it is the ultimate in psychological conditioning."

Absorbing the information, Krystyna exchanged glances with Logan. "So," she asked, "in essence, you've created a bizarre light show?"

Laughing out loud, Martin answered. "Not hardly! It would be easy to create dancing oscillating shapes." He dropped the smile. "My particular method is more true to life than you can possibly imagine. And never to be confused with a mere optical illusion."

"Virtual reality?" Logan questioned.

"No, Dr. Reed, nothing as commonplace as that. Technology of today has achieved great advances. We've developed new and exciting techniques in related areas such as electronics, aerodynamics, even art. And methods similar to mine are fast becoming useful diagnostic tools in medicine. Beyond that, this unique method of photography has enabled submarines a clearer sight under deep waters. It has proven useful in navigating through difficult areas, search and rescue missions, and as an aid in mapping out the bottom of the seabed. This method . . ."

Krystyna stomped her foot. "Martin, you have referred to your method, time and again, yet still refuse to tell us precisely what your method is."

"Have I?" Martin snickered. He continued, undaunted. "It's being used in lieu of microfilm. One day, it will be the center of our communications system worldwide. It will become a tool of modern society. It is limitless."

Krystyna's hands rested on her hips. "We still don't know what the method is called."

Martin looked at his watch. "You'll see for yourselves." He started for the door.

"Stop right there, Braddock." Logan said sharply. "I insist you stay where I can keep an eye on you."

Martin moved to close the door, stepping back into the circular room. He spoke aloud to a hidden microphone. "Stephanie, we're ready if you are."

A thin whispered voice came to them. "All set, Martin."

"I'm staying . . . for now." Martin said, walking toward the center of the room.

"Sixty seconds." Stephanie's voice announced.

Logan and Krystyna exchanged anxious expressions; neither one wanted to sit in the only chair, and sensing this, Martin chose to be seated. They were standing together now, halfway between Martin and the door.

"Thirty seconds." Stephanie's voice announced.

Martin twisted one end of his blonde mustache.

"Twenty seconds."

The intense power of control rushed through Martin and he savored the warm sensation.

"Ten seconds."

Welcome to the theater of the mind, Martin thought, as the music began.

The musical notes, soft, dancing, caught Krystyna's immediate attention. Martin had cleverly chosen her favorite classical opera. It stirred emotion in her, something he would have easily known, regardless of her tight control.

How much emotion this evoked, she thought, was up to her.

Krystyna had come into this room with a fierce determination. She would not allow Martin to manipulate her as he would like. No, if anything, Krystyna had become stronger willed.

The aria continued, the music expanding, throbbing. The room darkened ever so slowly, revealing shadowy silhouettes. As the light evaporated, a pale satiny sheen glistened on the walls, floor to ceiling, completing the circle. Gradually, the walls came to life, an emergence of colors leisurely forming and congealing. No true patterns as yet, merely elusive phantom shapes.

Suddenly, a swirling rainbow of colors was brought into tight focus, a clarity bringing to life a nature scene of perfect serenity.

Krystyna's immediate reaction was to step up to the wall and touch the kaleidoscopic field of flowers. They looked much too real. They looked much too welcoming.

Abruptly, Krystyna reminded herself to stay outside, remain uninvolved.

It was then that Krystyna smelled the undeniable sweet fragrance of roses! The strong musky scent filled the air. Sunshine, bright and balmy, now covered the blue sky of the background. The streaming rays slanted out and into the room; Krystyna could feel the radiating warmth upon her face, and along the front of her body and feet where the sunlight touched her.

It was incredible. It was inconceivable and at the same time, undeniable.

The walls of the room disappeared, vanishing. There was no longer a distinction between the room and the field of flowers.

If Krystyna didn't know better, she would have accepted that she had stepped forward, melding with the walls, physically entering the scene. It nearly felt that she had.

Krystyna forced herself to turn away, facing Martin. His eyes were dark smoldering emerald jewels, sparkling as they continued to stare back at her. She quickly looked over to Logan at her side. Alarm rushed through her as she found Logan deeply engrossed with the ever unfolding and changing scene before them. His expression told her he was not been prepared for these pictures of stark realism.

A lover of mother earth, it came only natural for Logan to appreciate and hold dear the sweet breeze of fresh clear air, the pine scented forest in the foreground, and the aromatic roses.

Feeling a strange compulsion, Logan allowed himself to experience the pictures as his brother Samuel had done. He could not have imagined a scene more real, and for a brief moment, he dreaded what he knew would come next as Samuel had told him.

Although subtle, the colorful collage of flowers and trees changed, first with shadows emerging and then with all boundaries erased. All but gone, the bright sunny sky had deepened dramatically, and was now marbled with dusky gray and deep velvety shades of livid blue and black. The scent of roses dissipated as the pine forest retreated into nothingness.

Everything turned coal black.

Brilliant twinkling stars illuminated the space and out of the corner of her eye, Krystyna saw the profile of Martin sitting in the chair. Logan was to her immediate left, nearest the door, or where she supposed the door was positioned. She no longer knew, having lost her sense of direction. There was only the scene; all consuming, enveloping, cloying.

A tall skyscraper, Samuel's skyscraper, peeked out from the starlit sky. Logan was unaware he had stepped forward toward the building, but somewhere in his mind he registered the hard crunch of his shoes against concrete. Logan next saw himself approach the entrance to the skyscraper. How can that be? Logan wondered, confused.

Logan felt, with embarrassment, the rigid expression of fear on his face, and he further recognized that, like Samuel, he sensed the silent hand pushing him forward. He also heard the silent voice, urging, pleading, insistent. However, Logan's fear was for Samuel, not for himself.

Certain that the scene programmed for them was a mere power play, Krystyna sought to remain grounded, ever cognizant of the fact that, it was not truly real, couldn't be, and yet . . . it was immensely difficult with the volatile proof of the pictures!

More than a motion picture, the scene before them was strangely hypnotic, and she could see Logan struggling to turn his eyes away.

Seated in the single chair, Martin watched his captive audience and not the screen, preferring to observe closely their fear when it was fresh, natural.

Logan watched himself approach the elevator of the skyscraper. Was that really him? He felt the muscles in his legs give and contract with the motions of walking. A sudden frigid chill coursed over him as the elevator door opened; he actually felt the "whoosh" of those very doors as they closed behind him. Somewhere in his mind, Logan heard Samuel's terrified scream.

Enough was enough, Logan thought. They had agreed to this, but he now found his instincts telling him this was all wrong!

In a split second Logan pulled out of the picture world, recognizing it had gone too far.

Somehow he found Braddock in the darkness, felt the soft flesh of the man's neck beneath his clenched fingers. "No more, Braddock!" Logan yelled.

Martin could not have anticipated Logan Reed's move; it had come unexpectedly, catching him quite unaware. Now, pinned in his chair, his breath being squeezed out of him, Martin struggled for release.

In the next moment, Logan lifted Braddock straight up and out of his chair, his strong hands secure at Braddock's throat, tossing him into the air.

Krystyna turned at the shuffling sounds, the mesmerizing momentum of the pictures halted, thankfully, just in time to see Logan throwing Martin directly into the wall. There was a wrenching, tearing and ripping sound as the picture screen gave way, Martin landing in a crumpled heap.

"End of tour!" Logan growled, standing over Martin, his breath coming in audible gasps.

The background music halted immediately, Stephanie's voice piercing from an overhead speaker. "Martin, is everything all right?"

Slowly, Martin brought himself to his feet, brushing at the debris from the torn screen and plasterboard off his clothing. "Totally uncalled for, Reed."

"What you've created here is monstrous." Logan said, turning to Krystyna briefly. "We want nothing of it."

Groping for his balance, Martin sought to explain. "You can't know the effects until . . ."

Logan grabbed Braddock again by the throat, their faces inches apart. "Until you awaken the next morning, battered and bruised!"

"Not true. Totally unfounded."

"Samuel did!"

The two men glared at one another.

CHAPTER THIRTY ONE

When Martin refused to answer her prompt, Stephanie became alarmed. She exited the COMPUTER ROOM, running down the hallway, crossing to another, and after noting the door was not locked, entered to find Martin and Logan about to tear each other apart.

The collar of Martin's shirt was now a ragged flap attached by a mere thread. His suit jacket and slacks were speckled with bits of debris. A nasty bruise was forming along one cheekbone and he massaged the abraded knuckles of his right hand.

Logan, however, Stephanie quickly noted, showed no signs of a physical encounter; his clothes unwrinkled, his dark hair unruffled. There was only the look of seething hatred in Logan's eyes as he glared at Martin.

There had indeed been a confrontation. This alone infuriated Stephanie because she knew Krystyna was the underlying reason behind the confrontation. Nevertheless, Stephanie was not consumed by jealousy. It was more complex than that. Stephanie merely regarded Krystyna as another setback; another in a long list of setbacks.

Would it never end? Stephanie wondered. Would she and Martin ever receive the recognition and reward from the scientific community that their work deserved? Invariably, something, or someone, kept getting in their way!

Stephanie walked over to Martin, the grace gone from her movements. There was a hard thin line to her mouth as she turned to Logan and Krystyna. "I want you both out, now!"

"I was just giving my fond farewells to Braddock." Logan said, his voice hoarse with anger.

"A few more parting words like that, and you would have torn my head off!" Martin growled, massaging his neck.

"You can feel fortunate those marks at your throat are not teeth marks. Unlike myself, my dog would have shown you no mercy."

Stephanie stomped her foot. "Out!"

"We're gone." Krystyna said quickly, stepping beside Logan.

Just as they reached the door, Martin called out. "One last meeting, Krystyna."

Stephanie's dark blue eyes were instantly suspicious. Martin leaned to whisper in her ear. "Monday morning, the attorney's office. Over at last."

Martin's comment did little to assure Stephanie. It was always one more meeting, one more patient, one more theory, Stephanie thought! Her life, it often felt, had been put on hold.

Stephanie was certain she could not tolerate any more delays. She needed forward motion, not stagnation! And for the second time this evening, Stephanie thought it was more than appropriate to call Martin's attention to his failed promises. Later, she decided, once they returned to the house, in private, and after another much needed glass of wine.

Logan was still shaking with anger when they returned to Krystyna's Jeep. He slammed his fist hard against the steering wheel. "Braddock is a bastard!"

"I know, Logan." Krystyna agreed. "He's lost all concept of right and wrong."

"I'm not so certain about that. He seems to know precisely what he's doing."

"No, Martin wants you to think that. I know differently."

Logan turned to face Krystyna. "Did Braddock ask you to meet with him?"

"Yes, just as we had hoped."

"Two o'clock?"

"At the Falls." Krystyna pushed up the sleeve of her jacket to check her watch. "It's nearly eleven now. That leaves us three hours before we come back to SERENITY."

"Unescorted this time. Logan added.

"Exactly."

They exchanged hesitant smiles.

Back at home, and seeing Stephanie was exceptionally edgy, Martin Braddock retreated to the solace of his den. Maybe Stephanie would leave him alone long enough to think! He needed to sort out a very tangled web of emotions. He checked his watch; it was a few minutes past midnight. He sipped at a freshly brewed cup of coffee. He needed to stay alert.

On the desk before Martin was a scratch pad. Absentmindedly, he scribbled some thoughts down on the paper, but his hand kept outlining the laser and its various components; the true heart of his method.

After a thorough process of elimination, Martin had ascertained the problem must be with the laser. The beam splitting capabilities checked out, as did the special film, the chemicals, the cameras. Everything else had been examined and reexamined.

Which continually brought him back, for the umpteenth time, to the laser. Twice, Martin had replaced the laser, thinking it had malfunctioned. That had been merely a waste of time and resources.

Martin felt the pressure of the problem weigh down heavily on him. He must find the problem in order to find the solution.

To have come this far, and now this, Martin thought in frustration!

Meticulously, he went over each and every step in the therapy process. As before, he drew no solid conclusion. Perhaps, the problem was as simple as human error, he proposed to himself. Martin doubted this as he and Stephanie conducted hundreds of dry runs and test trials in an effort to recreate the problem. Not once had the results been negative.

The trouble initially presented itself in a completely random manner. Not all the patients had been affected, detrimentally so, and those who were, failed to show any common denominators.

Worse than that, the trouble did not remain random for very long. Six, possibly seven months after SERENITY had opened her doors, hit and miss soon became the norm. The problem, once unpredictable and haphazard, evolved into daily recurrences. At that time patients had begun to complain about unpleasant side effects. This was soon followed by volatile displays of paranoia, nightmares, and a regression of previous progress.

Martin had been barraged with urgent calls from the majority of his patients.

Martin's world turned upside down.

He felt his lifeblood seeping away.

For the first time in Martin's life he had experienced raw panic. He chose, out of desperation, to swallow this panic, cover it up, and bury it where it could not be seen.

But inside, Martin knew the bittersweet taste of failure.

Martin sipped at the last of his coffee, dropping the pencil across his scribblings, rising from his desk. His throat felt raw; he winced. Also, the bruise across his cheekbone was now swollen and tender to the touch. Perhaps he needed some ice.

It was in the kitchen that Martin met up with Stephanie. She was pouring herself another glass of wine, still wearing the silk pantsuit she wore earlier at dinner. A scowl creased around her thin crimson lips.

"I wondered where you ran off to." Stephanie said, a slight slur to her words.

"Just trying to relax, Stephanie."

Stephanie eyed him closely. "You look like you've been pulled through the proverbial wringer."

"Rather like our patients, wouldn't you say?" Martin answered soberly.

Her smug smile surfaced. "Don't develop a conscience on me now, Martin."

"What are you trying to say?"

"You're carrying this poor patient bit too far!"

"Stephanie, in case you hadn't noticed, and in your drunken state I can see why, we've managed to screw up! Somehow, we lost control of the pictures and they've nearly destroyed innocent lives."

Stephanie's face was stone cold, lifeless. "Do we really *care*, Martin?"

Pouring himself another cup of coffee, Martin sought to control his increasing anger. "You tell me. What is it that Stephanie *cares* about?"

She slammed her clenched fist across the marbled countertop. "I've had it with the delays, the problems, the waiting game!"

"What waiting game?"

"Need I remind you again of the promises you made me, one of which was we'd spend a year at most in this isolated boring trench some have the ignorance to call a town!"

Martin raised his voice. "Yes, but that time frame did not allow for unforeseen problems."

"Problems have plagued you day and night. I've watched you worry yourself sick. It's time to give it up, Martin."

"I can't. I won't."

"Well, you should. There's no excitement here in WHISPERING FALLS, no culture, no opportunities to grasp, no rubbing elbows with influential friends." Stephanie set her wine glass on the counter, stepping over to Martin and then sliding her arms around him. Her eyes were dark, serious. "Let's leave this place. It's brought us bad luck."

Slowly, very slowly, something clicked in Martin's mind. There was a distinct possibility, plausible even, especially when the motive was known.

Bad luck; the Hope diamond.

Good luck; the Peace diamond.

Good God in Heaven, Martin screamed in the back of his mind, had Stephanie switched the diamonds? Were they switched inadvertently?

Or, worse yet, with purpose?

Martin decided Stephanie could have chosen to speed up the entire process by using the Hope diamond. This diamond, of course, was the only diamond he vehemently vowed would not be used. He had made this perfectly clear to Stephanie on many previous occasions when she had hinted at hurrying over the tedious procedures. After all, Martin remembered her once saying, fame and fortune awaited them.

Perhaps, Martin thought, Stephanie had grown tired of waiting in line.

It would be easy enough to prove, Martin finally conceded, pulling away from Stephanie's grasp, leaving the kitchen. He needed to check the exact contents of the diamond vault.

Martin rushed down the marbled steps, along the photograph gallery, Stephanie close on his heels, tugging sharply at his shirtsleeve.

He stopped abruptly several feet before the diamond vault. It stood open.

Martin looked to Stephanie. "What have you done?"

She pulled away. Martin now noticed the droplets of wine spilling down the front of her silk jacket. "I'm disappointed in you, Martin. I would have thought you'd have guessed by now."

Without thinking, Martin grabbed Stephanie by her blonde hair, thrusting her to the floor. A loud thump sounded when her right hip and leg hit the hard surface.

"Tell me what you've done!" Martin demanded.

Stephanie struggled to her feet, holding onto the wall for support. "I did it for us, Martin! For you! Dr. Martin Braddock, the distinguished scientist with the prize winning discovery of a lifetime."

Stephanie paused, suddenly frightened of Martin. She'd never seen that grisly look in his eyes. Yet, despite the terror he evoked, Stephanie must finally tell Martin the truth. She'd kept it from him long enough.

"Please understand, Martin." Stephanie stammered. "My actions were purely innocent."

His arm raised as if to strike her.

"I confess." She whispered. "I did it. I switched the diamonds."

CHAPTER THIRTY TWO

Now that Stephanie had confessed, confirming Martin's greatest fears, he at least knew the trouble had come through no fault of his own. "You fool!" Martin screamed. "You were directed to use only the Peace diamonds in the laser. We tested those extensively, and for reasons beyond us, they helped to create subliminal messages that attacked the phobias. True to its name, this diamond was the bearer of good luck. You knew that! We lived that. We were on the right track. Our method provided a visual reality that tricked the brain into thinking it was real! And yet, you took it upon yourself to use the Hope diamond, untested, without grounds or basis, knowing the evil misfortune associated with this particular diamond, superstition or not, and you did it behind my back!"

"Yes, I'm sorry," Stephanie said. "I had my reasons."

"What ever your reasons, they can't be good enough!"

Stephanie fought back tears. "I did it for us."

"You've betrayed me! I don't know if I can live with that."

Stunned, Stephanie held onto the wall.

Martin continued. "I'm closing SERENITY. You're leaving WHISPERING FALLS first thing Monday morning . . ."

Anger flared through Stephanie. "What about our plans to be married?"

"There are no such plans!"

"It's Krystyna, isn't it?"

"No, not entirely." Martin answered. "After what you've done . : ."

"Martin," Stephanie's voice was suddenly shrill. "It might interest you to know Krystyna has met with Michael Overby. She requested a list of your assets."

"You're grabbing at straws, Stephanie. I couldn't care less about that. Nevertheless, your knowledge of this proves to me, you and my attorney have a closer relationship than I would have thought."

Stephanie's smug smile evaporated. "I'm merely watching over your interests. As always." She had a running picture in her mind of the many sacrifices made, all in the name of science. It sickened her. She'd given too much, received too little in return. Martin had not even removed Krystyna as the primary benefactor in his will. It just wasn't fair!

Martin felt the force of fury push through him. The repercussions of Stephanie's actions were, one by one, coming to light. "I want the truth." Martin demanded. "Did you switch the diamonds tonight for Dr. Reed and Krystyna?"

"No, of course not." Stephanie answered, a hasty guilt-ridden thought surfaced of the computer program she had earlier devised, but had chosen not to use at the last minute. Now, she wished she had. That program, and the Hope diamond, would have kept Krystyna and Dr. Reed from interfering; a lethal dose in mental programming!

"Did you keep your records?" Martin snapped. "An accurate accounting of who . . ."

"Yes, I did. They're on disk."

"I want those records . . . immediately."

"Martin . . ."

"Did you use the Hope diamond on me?" Martin asked.

Stephanie's deep blue eyes widened and for a long moment she felt incapable of answering. Another face now stared back at her; the dark side of Martin. She opened her trembling lips, a throaty croak slipped out. Then, "Yes."

Martin's green eyes bulged, his face crimson with rage. "You've made me into a worse monster than I already was!" One strong hand reached and curled into Stephanie's blonde hair, grabbing fiercely, thrusting her to the floor. Her head met the marbled floor with a thunderous crunch, an inch long split in her scalp bleeding profusely upon impact.

Dazed, Stephanie found Martin hunched over her. "I don't know if I can wait until Monday to be rid of you!" Martin screamed.

"No," Stephanie cried, terrified at the total lack of mercy she saw in Martin's savagely twisted face.

He wanted to tear her apart, piece by piece! Instead, Martin decided to put his mark on her beautiful face; leave her with a life long haunting memory. Her exquisite beauty would no longer open any doors.

Martin leaned closer yet to Stephanie, bringing his wet lips to her flawless ivory skin, opening his mouth wide, burrowing his teeth deeply into her one cheek. He pulled hard, twisting the flesh, her blood spilling freely into his mouth.

He didn't hear her screams. He didn't feel her arms flailing wild against him.

Yet, somewhere deep in his consciousness, Martin registered the not terribly unpleasant taste of Stephanie's blood.

When he finally pulled away, he was pleased to see that she would bear the scar forever. He doubted any amount of plastic surgery could repair the damage.

However, Martin did not feel the satisfaction he needed.

He bent over her once again, her blood dripping from his lips, holding her head firmly to the side, clamping his teeth around her left ear. The flesh and cartilage tore away easily, ripping like cloth, Stephanie's ear nearly severed from her head, now dangling awkwardly.

Martin brought himself to his feet, standing over her as she cowered, whimpering, squirming in her own blood. "A little something to remember me by." Martin said, smiling.

He turned away from her, utterly calm, feeling much better. Ignoring Stephanie's screams, he retreated down the long photograph gallery, amazed at the satisfaction he felt, both sides of him, the monster and the man.

After showering, removing all traces of Stephanie's blood from his person, Martin descended the marbled stairs leading to the foyer. It was there on a chrome table that he found Stephanie's records and notes, including patient names, copied onto a computer disk. There was no sign of Stephanie herself. Perhaps, Martin thought, she had finally gone to bed. Better yet, maybe she had the good sense to leave.

He'd been a fool to believe anyone could take Krystyna's place.

Outside, Martin checked his watch. It was one-thirty. He had time enough to stop at SERENITY, put Stephanie's notes with those of his own, with plenty of time to spare in reaching the FALLS.

Krystyna would be waiting for him there.

Back at the Reed Ranch, Logan and Krystyna consumed large quantities of coffee. Orenda and Garrett were there, Samuel too, everyone conferring together on last minute details. Samuel would remain alone at the main house, the doors secured, shotgun in hand. He would be safe. Taima would go with Orenda and Garrett to the Falls. Logan had insisted his wolf-dog accompany his mother, knowing that no matter the outcome, Taima would protect both she and Garrett with her very life. Garrett's nine-millimeter automatic would further ensure their safety.

Orenda, dressed in a beaded gown similar to that worn tonight by Krystyna, would also wear Krystyna's wool jacket. Both women wore their long dark hair cascading down their shoulders and backs. In the darkness at the top of the Falls, Martin would assume he was meeting with Krystyna.

At the same time, precisely two o'clock, Logan and Krystyna should be inside SERENITY, hopefully locating Martin Braddock's notes. That was the plan.

At ten minutes past one, Logan and Krystyna climbed into Samuel's truck, the Reed Ranch insignia covered over, heading east for SERENITY. When they arrived the driving rain had calmed, but the windswept sky rolled fiercely, thick dark clouds spilling past the full moon, with an occasional glimmer of light filtering through.

Logan pulled the truck beneath a dense grove of fir trees about a hundred yards from the entrance of SERENITY. They were well hidden as they sat patiently, waiting for the black Mercedes to drive past SERENITY, heading for the FALLS.

They had only to wait a few minutes. After a short stop at SERENITY, it appeared Braddock had taken the bait.

Krystyna looked to Logan. "I guess this is it."

"I hope this works, Krystyna."

"It has to work, and we have to find Martin's notes."

"Yes, but we may have a problem breaking into SERENITY."

Krystyna smiled softly. "I've been giving this a great deal of thought. The security measures, I mean."

"You're concerned the security system will only register Braddock or Stephanie's voices?" Logan asked.

"I certainly hope that's not the case. I'm nearly convinced that since Martin has used his father's name, Harold, as a password to his house, why not use his mother's name too?"

"For SERENITY?"

"Yes."

"It makes sense." Logan concurred. "Didn't you say Braddock was very close to his mother and father?"

"Oh yes, and Martin was devastated when they passed away. He even built a memorial of sorts for them."

"All right then, what about the guard?" Logan asked.

"I'm not sure . . . but I've thought that over too. I'm nearly afraid to put my guesses into words, but we'll know soon enough."

Logan scratched his chin. "Maybe I should approach the guard from behind, knock him silly while his attention is directed on you?"

"If my guesses are right, we won't have to resort to that." Krystyna said.

"Okay. Let's go." Logan said, reaching an arm around Krystyna. "But, not before I tell you . . . that I love you." He kissed her gently.

Krystyna's smile was touched by a glimmer of moonlight. "And I love you, Logan Reed. Tomorrow . . ."

"No," Logan said abruptly, "leave tomorrow alone, for now. I can't bear the thought of it being closer to Monday."

Neither could Krystyna, now that she thought about it. How on earth could she just walk away?

They left the truck, Logan carrying the duffel bag which held a small assortment of tools, and carefully crept closer to SERENITY. As they neared the building, Krystyna was once again intimidated at the sight. She fought down her misgivings as she followed Logan. They blended with the trees, seeking the cover, until they were forced to walk in the cleared space down the long winding entrance.

Twenty feet from the small cubicle, the profile of the guard easily seen, Krystyna struggled to bring her thoughts together. There was something not quite right with the guard; they had agreed on this earlier. Now, she wondered if perhaps the guard was part and parcel of Martin's so-called method; a three-dimensional picture. It made sense to Krystyna, especially when she reconsidered all aspects of Martin's work; a picture that is not real but appears real.

Krystyna had a gut feeling and went with it, motioning for Logan to step before the guard, gaining his attention, as she stepped silently to the rear of the cubicle. She only hoped she was right. If so, Martin's secret was no longer a secret. If not . . . they may be stopped from entering.

Logan crossed over to the asphalt driveway, walking straight up the center, stopping directly before the guard.

A mechanical voice cut through the stillness. "May I help you?"

Krystyna heard Logan ask the guard question after question, the guard's monotone evident with every answer. She crept closer to the rear of the cubicle, finally crouching down, peeking in through the windows. She found the rear door, holding her breath as she slowly turned the knob. It was unlocked.

She pushed the door open just a few inches and paused, motioning to Logan. He continued with his questions, the guard continued with his answers.

The small cubicle was brightly lit, and although Krystyna was hesitant to enter, she did so, still crouching, trying to be quiet. The guard did not turn around, nor did he give any indication that he sensed her presence at his back. She held her breath for a long tense moment as the beads on her dress moved together, touching one another, rustling.

It had come down to this, Krystyna thought. She dearly hoped her assumptions were right. Her mind whirled with Martin's words, his fancy revelations, his elaborate electronics, his picture world.

She brought herself to a standing position. Two feet separated her from the guard. She stared at him; the crisp blue uniform, the neatly trimmed hairline at the nape of his neck, the hollowness of his words.

Here we go, Krystyna thought, whispering a hastened prayer.

She brought her hand up and near the guard's back, inch by inch, intending on tapping his shoulder. She was counting on the guard not catching her reflection in the windows.

Krystyna's hand wafted through the air, a clean sweep.

There was nothing there, not really!

Krystyna sighed with relief as she brought her hand through the space where the guard was sitting; again her hand passed right through him! Or rather, she thought, the illusion of a guard.

The guard was not real. Krystyna had guessed right. The guard was a three dimensional life-like picture.

Martin's secret was holograms.

There, but not there.

Hidden, but in plain sight.

CHAPTER THIRTY THREE

Stephanie lay in the fetal position, fighting down the panic rising bitterly in her dry throat. Waves of nausea came and went with the overpowering copper-like stench of spilled blood. Somehow, Stephanie inched up the wall, placing the good side of her face to the inviting coolness. She vacillated between anger and repulsion and physical pain. Had she not consumed a large amount of alcohol earlier, she would undoubtedly be in worse shape, Stephanie consented, able to more clearly sense the pain of her injuries.

Still, she writhed with the throbbing sensations, her heartbeat pounding in her ears, bewildered. The monster had stolen her beauty, and for that transgression, he would have to pay, she finally decided!

Stephanie allowed her anger to take control and to breed. She went where it took her. The anger churned inside her as she took a few tentative steps toward the kitchen. The anger became an ugly dark thing, growing with each twisting throb of pain, obliterating all other emotions, until she ached for sweet revenge.

Martin had begun the blood feud. Stephanie would now have her turn.

In those frail moments of a certain madness, Stephanie reached for the phone. In the dimmed lighting of the kitchen she caught her reflection in the glass of the double ovens. Instinctively, she brought a quivering hand to her face, turning to one side. A single soul-deep scream shattered the hard silence.

Stephanie then quieted considerably, internalizing, setting her priorities. She drew a long breath as she dialed the telephone number for Michael Overby. It seemed it took him nearly forever to answer. She counted the fresh blood droplets on the floor at her feet while he responded to her call, sleepy, yawning. "Hello."

"Come to the house, now!" Stephanie whispered.

"Stephanie? Is that you?"

"Who else are you in conspiracy with?"

Michael Overby swallowed hard, a sudden realization stinging him fully awake. An emergency, he quickly registered. "What's happened?"

"Everything's fallen apart, including me."

"Tell me . . ."

"No," Stephanie shouted. "Martin's gone to SERENITY and I need your help!"

"Now?"

"Yes, and don't argue with me. If you had taken care of Krystyna when I asked you, none of this would have happened!"

"Stephanie . . ."

"Just shut up and get over to the house. Bring plenty of bandages and peroxide."

"You're hurt?" Michael Overby asked, his voice shaky.

"Yes . . . and Michael, bring your gun."

"I'll be right there, but as far as the gun goes, you know how I feel about that. I've tried to tell you all along! I can't use a weapon against another human being; Krystyna Kramer or Martin Braddock."

"You don't have to, Michael. I will. And for that matter, Martin is no longer a human being. He's a crazed bloodsucking predator!"

An immediate picture formed ·in Overby's mind; it frightened him nearly as much as that look he'd seen in Stephanie's eyes the day at the FALLS. "It's only a twenty-two caliber." Overby said. "Not much rock."

"I don't care!" Stephanie screamed impatiently. "Five minutes; be here." She lowered her voice. "And yes, I'm keeping time."

With Michael Overby's help, Stephanie would wreak a little havoc in Martin's own little world, SERENITY, a fitting and proper place for Martin to receive his due.

Logan, astonished at the sight of Krystyna waving her arms through the illusion of the guard, quickly ran to the rear of the glass-walled cubicle and entered. "He's not real?"

"No, the guard is merely a hologram, a three-dimensional life-like picture."

"That's Braddock's secret method?"

"A big part of it, I suspect." Krystyna answered. "I also suspect he's using his diamonds in the laser when the photographic film is recorded. Undoubtedly adding in some way to the realism, I would guess."

"Good guess, Krystyna." Logan ran his fingers through his dark hair. "It would seem the guard was programmed to come to life, so to speak, with a motion sensor."

"It appears so. Did you notice the ring of lights come on just as the guard began talking?"

"Yes, must be on the same circuit."

"What do we do now, Logan?"

"Let's hope your theory about the verbal command will get us in the doors undetected and through the security measures."

"It's an outside chance, Logan, you know that."

"I know." He gestured to the duffel bag draped across his shoulder. "That's why we brought these tools; just in case."

"Let's find a way in, either way." Krystyna said.

Logan paused for a moment, scanning the electronic panel in the small cubicle. He pressed the switch labeled, FRONT GATE. The heavy iron gate slowly swung to an opened position. Outside, Logan and Krystyna ran through the gate, swiftly stepping to the far edge of the serpentine entrance, cloaked by the darkened shadows as they made their approach to SERENITY.

Pulling Krystyna with him into a group of heavily branched shrubs, Logan pointed to the double doors at the front entrance. "Let's stop for a moment, get our breath, make certain our movements have gone unnoticed."

"There can't be anyone here, Logan. There was no one else on the premises earlier during our tour, no janitor sweeping about, no receptionist filing correspondence. Only the guard and he's not real. No wonder we couldn't trace any employees to SERENITY; all the help were probably holograms too."

"You might be right, Krystyna. It does seems very quiet, and no lights, save for one in the foyer."

She leaned forward from their cover, craning her neck to look through the windows. A single light near the front entrance cast a gray wash over the gloomy interior. The other eyes of SERENITY were closed for the night.

"Okay, let's try the door." She said.

Logan followed, turning on his heels, watching behind them for any trace of movement in the murky shadows. When he caught up with Krystyna, she was calling out, "Marie."

Nothing happened.

Krystyna tried again. "Marie."

Logan touched Krystyna lightly on the shoulder. "Maybe the verbal command to open the doors isn't Braddock's mother's name, after all."

"It must be." Krystyna said, whispering again, "Marie."

The front doors remained locked.

Feeling a bit silly, Krystyna whispered other family member's names, with the same result. The doors were locked securely.

"I'm sorry, Logan. I guess I was wrong about the verbal command."

"It's okay." He said, drawing Krystyna back into the shelter of the shadows. "Let's find a back or side entrance. We'll force our way."

Krystyna nodded, following Logan as they weaved their way along one side of the structure, and to the rear. Incredulously, there appeared to be no other entrance or exit. The minutes slipped away as they struggled to find a rear door. Finally, a streamer of moonlight caught the doorknob; a sliver of metal peeked out through the haze.

Taking several tools from the duffel bag, Logan worked on the locking mechanism, groaning with his efforts, pushing and pulling until at last the door gave way with a loud thundering screech. They both crouched to the ground, watching and waiting. Amazingly, no alarm sounded. All was quiet.

Logan replaced his tools, setting the duffel bag among the overflowing shrubs. Once inside, they dashed for the first room they spotted, INTRODUCTION, and waited for the sounds of footsteps, an alarm, anything.

Again, the stillness confirmed that they were indeed alone in SERENITY.

This was far from a comforting thought for Krystyna. But, she conceded, they would leave just as soon as they had Martin's notes safe in their hands.

Krystyna checked her watch. "It's almost two o'clock already."

"Don't worry, Krystyna. Martin will wait for you at the FALLS until you show. He'll anticipate that you're late; you've already explained to him your need to slip out undetected. He'll merely think it took you longer than you could have guessed. He'll wait until he sees you."

"You mean, until Martin sees Orenda portraying me, winding a hopeless trail through the trees."

"Exactly. Enough time for us to find the notes."

"We must do just that, Logan." Krystyna said, stepping tentatively out into the hallway, flashlight in hand. "Now, if we only knew where to look."

Michael Overby was appalled at the task before him, bandaging, however ineptly, Stephanie's scalp laceration, her torn ear, and covering as best he could, the jagged opening in her cheek. He cringed as he imagined Braddock's mouth clenching down in the soft pliable flesh with Stephanie sprawled helplessly. He shuddered again. He shouldn't be here, he knew that, but he failed to have the courage to say no. It was easier to go along with Stephanie's plan, follow her orders. Just like before.

The money Stephanie promised him sounded better than ever. With that kind of dollars, Michael Overby could forget this night ever existed. He could vanish from sight, and would, just as soon as he helped her one last time.

Overby was a small town attorney, living the quiet life, and he liked it that way, but now that he had reconsidered the unending madness of Braddock, he would soon find a new town to call home. Preferably some dot on the map where peace and harmony lived.

"Ouch!" Stephanie shouted. "Watch what you're doing."

"I'm sorry, Stephanie." Overby said, his hands shaking. "There, that's the best I can do for now. You need to go to the hospital."

Stephanie cast him an indignant frown. "There's no time for that. Later."

All business now, she put her hand out to him. "The gun?"

His hands brushed over the pockets in his jacket, looking for the small pearl-handled gun. He felt immediately queasy when his hand struck the metal. It felt lethal although covered in a benign cloth pouch.

Stephanie, tapping her foot incessantly, waited for him to pass her the gun. As he did so, his stomach churned, burning, sour. Overby watched Stephanie check the revolver to see if it was loaded. It was, and her smooth movements told him she was no stranger to guns.

He nodded, reaching for his overcoat. "I'll be going now, Stephanie."

He watched her out of the corner of his eye. Overby wanted to leave before she could change his mind for him.

"Yes, I expect you will." Stephanie said, a sinister twist to her mouth. "Sweet serenity awaits us!"

"Us?" He stammered.

"Yes." Stephanie turned, sending Michael Overby that caustic and malicious expression, the same one he wrestled with in his nightmares. He had a lot of nightmares, and each had a name. He named this particular nightmare, BLOODLUST. He'd seen that lust in Stephanie's eyes, down deep, just a sliver of a hint if you dared to look close. And, he had. Bad thing.

For a breathless moment, Overby wondered who the monster was, after all?

His vote, the gruesome face before him.

CHAPTER THIRTY FOUR

Garrett drove Krystyna's Jeep another quarter mile beyond the parking area at the top of the FALLS, pulling the Jeep finally to the rear of an abandoned home. A rusted, partially denuded Camaro sat lopsided along a doorless garage. Plastered across the cracked windshield of the Camaro was half of a "SWEET SERENITY" bumper sticker, fluorescent hot pink, and it glowed in the path of their headlights.

A bit nervous himself, Garrett glanced over to Orenda, turning the ignition off. Her smile was tentative, yet sorrow lingered in her mahogany eyes. She's putting herself at great risk, Garrett thought, cringing inwardly, yet there was a silent courage in those eyes too, an undeniable grace.

Taima, wolf instincts pumping like wildfire, was exceptionally attuned to the human family around her, sensing their emotional turmoil. She recognized their need on this most unusual excursion taking place in the dead of night. She sat in the back seat listening, absorbing, anticipating an urgent command.

According to Garrett's watch it was twenty minutes before two in the morning. Right on schedule, he thought, arriving well ahead of Martin Braddock. They would retreat into the woods, maintaining a parallel course with the road, mindful of the rain slickened forest floor, and head for the thick shrubbery which would keep them a safe distance from the graveled parking area.

Once Braddock arrived there, he'd be easily spotted parked under the few overhead lights. Orenda and Garrett would watch Braddock as he waited for Krystyna. He'd have a wait, to be sure, Garrett mused.

However, if Braddock became impatient, leaving his vehicle, they would move to heavier cover. Tonight, the rule of thumb was, if Braddock moved, they moved.

Michael Overby had to think quickly, something which had never quite been a natural asset to him. He felt his mind fumbling. The best he could come up with was a dastardly, cowardly thing, but it would get him out of a bad situation gone berserk! He decided to do it, worry about it later.

Michael Overby felt overly warm, his thick overcoat bundled around him in his eagerness to leave. He left it on, standing impatiently while Stephanie poured herself several straight shots of tequila. She downed them, one after another, without a blink of an eye. Nothing seemed capable of penetrating her steadfast hunger for revenge.

However, it was her anger that truly frightened Michael Overby. Something about it . . . squeezed into corners of his mind; corners he didn't know he had, into his thoughts, paralyzing him, just as in the nightmares.

The worst nightmare was that Michael Overby was a weak man, who was now considerably weaker. This saddened him greatly. He could no longer deny the truth. The treatments, orchestrated by Stephanie, had not worked for his problems. He was worse off, if anything. He was a panic-prone coward without respect, even for himself.

To get Overby's attention, Stephanie tossed the empty glass from her hand. It flew across the kitchen where it smashed against the wall, the splintering of the glass prompted Overby to flinch, his body drawing up in a spasm.

"Brush the glass from your coat, Michael. We're ready to leave now." Stephanie said, almost casually.

"I'll follow you in my car." He said, forgetting to breathe, clutching his hands together.

Stephanie offered him a smug smile. She was well aware of Overby's intentions. Let him sneak away, she thought, he'd only be in the way. She'd be better off without him. Had him pegged right, though, she thought again. God, she detested weaklings!

Stephanie retreated through the kitchen and to the garage where her car was parked. Moments later, the garage door opened and she backed out into the driveway. Michael Overby's brown Oldsmobile was nowhere in sight, nor could the slightest tinge of his red taillights be seen in the distance. The weasel had indeed run away.

She glanced at the clock in the middle of the dashboard. It was twenty minutes after two. She turned the wheel, pointing the car for SERENITY. Martin Braddock would surely be there, and alone. One last little thing to tidy up, and Stephanie would be on her way.

She glanced in the rearview mirror, the large gauze bandage a startling sight. Raw anguish started to rise. She'd become ugly, disfigured for life. She took a deep breath, using her determination to push that anguish back down and away. She didn't need any distractions right now.

Her hand reached out to stroke the leather of her handbag. In the bag were stashed the entire contents of Martin's diamond vault. With this amount of capital, Stephanie could, and did, expect a miracle; several of them! She'd be beautiful again. Those doors would not close in her face.

And, Stephanie thought, Martin will be left feeling . . . particularly sorry.

Michael Overby did not bother to stop at the cluttered cottage he had called home for the past couple years. Most of what he truly needed, he'd send for later. But then, he wondered, who in town would send them to him? There was hardly anyone left. His small circle of friends, a total of two, a drinking buddy and his secretary, were among the first group to leave WHISPERING FALLS. Smart they were, Michael Overby thought.

He stepped hard on the gas pedal, continuing down the mountainside. The farther he got away from WHISPERING FALLS, the less intense his head ached, his breathing came easier, and a long denied freedom tasted sweet on his lips.

Logan and Krystyna, flashlights in hands, were frustrated in their fruitless attempt to locate Martin Braddock's all-important notes. Both had discarded their jackets, a fine film of sweat on their faces and arms, their skin strangely luminescent in the mixture of lighting; tendrils of moonlight, tiny rounded fixtures recessed into the marbled floors of the hallways, two flashlights, and one overhead light in the foyer.

Of the sixteen rooms, Krystyna had counted them earlier on their tour, they had rummaged through a total of seven, the most obvious rooms first. They had just begun their search of the eighth room when hopelessness seized Krystyna. It was a needle in a haystack, all over again.

She plunked herself down in a nearby chair, lifting her long hair up and away from her neck, fanning her face with a file folder. "This is useless, Logan!"

He felt a sharp twinge of regret at Krystyna's remark. He had just been thinking the same thing. Still, the notes were here, somewhere. Had to be. "Think, Krystyna. Again, put yourself in Braddock's mind . . ."

"Do I have to?" Krystyna said, grinning now.

Logan turned to her with an equally capricious smile. "Forget him then. Where would you hide the notes?"

Krystyna dropped her arm, allowing her dark hair to fall back down to her shoulders. She stopped fanning herself with the file folder. "The EMPTY ROOM, of course."

"In the walls, you mean?" Logan asked.

"No, yes, I don't know." Krystyna stood up from the chair. "It's next on our list to search."

"What's to search? A single leather chair?"

"Let's look, just the same." Krystyna suggested.

Without putting things back in drawers or file cabinets, Logan and Krystyna stepped out into the long dark hallway, continuing another fifty or sixty feet, and entered THE EMPTY ROOM. The room was just as they had left it, not six hours before. A large gap in the curved walls showed evidence to Braddock being flung through the air, crashing into and tearing the fine screen fabric covering those curved picture walls.

Logan stepped over to the gap in the wall, aiming his flashlight into the space. There were the standard insulation products, electrical wiring, two by sixes, a few of which were broken into pieces, sheetrock, and of course the finely textured screen on the wall. Nothing seemed out of the ordinary. He hadn't expected to find anything. Logan didn't think it feasible Braddock would have hidden his notes in the walls, but he felt better checking, nevertheless. And, Logan thought, so would Krystyna.

Standing in the center of the room, Krystyna was staring at the overturned green leather chair, the only chair in the circular room. She bent over, got down on her knees, reaching her hand well under the seat of the chair.

When Krystyna turned back to Logan, it seemed she was grasping something in her hand, her gray eyes suddenly alive with excitement.

"What is it, Krystyna?"

The excited expression dropped quickly from her face. "It isn't anything, now." Krystyna brought herself up to stand. "But, something was here."

Logan watched Krystyna raise an object in her hand, bringing it closer for him to see, while he adjusted the beam of his flashlight.

"This small box," she said, the box covering the palm of one slender hand, "is a treasured keepsake of Martin, given to him by his mother. He always saved special things in it."

Krystyna looked at Logan, a grim sadness in her eyes. "The box is empty. We're too late!"

It was at that moment Logan heard muffled footsteps and immediately turned toward the opened door. The silhouette of a tall figure stared back at them from the shadowed entrance to the room. Behind the ghostly apparition thin rays of moonlight drizzled down, the light finally coming to rest on an object held by the figure. The object looked to be a pearl handled pistol, glinting eerily in the moonlight, Logan quickly assessed. Small caliber, probably a twenty-two, typically not big trouble, but up close . . .

Dr. Martin Braddock eased the black Mercedes into the graveled parking area at the outlook of the FALLS. He felt a surge of disappointment that Krystyna's Jeep was not there, but he felt content to wait, confident that Krystyna would meet with him. She had agreed and would keep her word.

His angel! His only light in an otherwise dark world!

Orenda was the first to see the headlights of Braddock's Mercedes as they careened off the dense background of evergreen trees. From their viewpoint, she could hear the hard crunch of tires upon gravel, the engine of the vehicle halting. The car door did not open.

Wordlessly, Orenda reached for Garrett's arm.

Heavy clouds rushed over their heads, bands of moonlight changing forms as they quickly drifted across the marbled sky. Taima hunkered down, turned her nose to the air. She moved her amber eyes to the car not fifty feet from them, sniffing at the air once again, her powerful body turning rigid.

Orenda knelt down and patted Taima, offering her assurance. "Taima, be still." She whispered to the dog. "The time to wait and watch has come."

Logan realized their situation was not good, backed into a circular room with no exit, the ghostly figure standing in the doorway holding a pistol at both he and Krystyna. Without a word the figure gestured with the gun for Logan to step forward. Another gesture, more steps forward.

When Krystyna started to follow, the figure held up the other hand, motioning that she was to remain where she was.

Retreating, the figure slipped into the darkened hallway, the pistol pointing to Logan, and then to the hallway. He was to follow the figure. Logan offered no challenge at this point, stepping out of the room.

A second later Logan heard the door close behind him, the locking mechanism engaged, clicking with a loud thump.

Immediately, Logan felt something tighten in his chest. Krystyna was now alone in the circular room.

Logan's eyes blurred momentarily when the barrel of the pistol was viciously rammed into the middle of his spine, forcing him forward, the figure quickly stepping away, just out of his reach.

His mind raced. The figure could not be Braddock; he'd been sent up a lost trail! There was an outside chance the figure was Michael Overby, Braddock's attorney, but Logan counted him out, based on Krystyna's assumptions of the man.

That left only Stephanie.

Logan tilted his head ever so slightly, managing to glimpse a dark colored scarf draped over the head and shoulders of the figure, effectively covering most of the face as well. The rest was a blur.

"Where are you taking me?" Logan asked the figure.

There was no answer.

Rounding a corner, Logan stopped abruptly. "I'll not go further!"

Something hard smacked into the back of his head, the searing crunch bellowing and rumbling in his ears. The object he'd been hit with was jabbed into his left side now, the power of the blow taking Logan's breath from him. It was not the pistol, he thought, wincing with the pain, pressing down with his arm along the injured rib cage.

Another driving blow came from the object, it was feeling more and more like a baseball bat to Logan, the ribs on the right the target of choice this time, forcing Logan to his knees. He got up, perhaps a second too soon, but he kept walking forward. When his pace slowed, another onslaught came with the cruel object.

In the distance he could hear Krystyna screaming his name, could hear her faint pounding at the locked door. And hearing Krystyna's screams, the shadowy figure tried to suppress a peal of scornful laughter, unsuccessfully.

Logan whirled around to the figure behind him. Indeed, a lock of blonde hair peeked out from the scarf secured over the head and shoulders, confirming the figure was Stephanie.

In her right hand, the small pistol glimmered in the darkness. Logan then took particular notice of the object with which she had struck him; a shotgun, sleek and deadly, held poised and comfortable in Stephanie's left hand.

CHAPTER THIRTY FIVE

"I'm equally proficient with both the pistol and the shotgun, Dr. Reed!" Stephanie threw back the scarf, unaware that fresh blood was seeping through the gauze bandages over her face and around her ear.

"Here you see an angry woman with a loaded shotgun! I strongly advise you to follow my instructions . . . to the letter."

Logan eyed Stephanie closely. "What's happened to you?"

Scowling, Stephanie thrust out her chin. "None of your concern." She slipped the pistol into a front pocket of her long raincoat, bringing both hands to steady the shotgun. "Now, turn back around. We're headed for the COMPUTER ROOM."

They were far enough away now that Logan could no longer hear Krystyna's screams. Slowly, Logan took a few steps along the darkened hallway, speaking over his shoulder. "I'm not sure why you're doing this . . ."

The barrel of the shotgun smacked into the back of Logan's head, knocking him unconscious with the single vicious blow, his body crumbling.

Stephanie did not approach Logan immediately. She waited a long minute before stepping over to him, looking down at his expressionless face.

Her frustrations shook at her resolve. She was exasperated. First, she entered SERENITY, intent on settling the score with Martin, only to find that he wasn't there! Second, she happened upon Krystyna and Dr. Reed, two meddlesome troublemakers, sneaking about where they shouldn't!

Perhaps, Stephanie thought, they needed to be taught a lesson. After that, Stephanie would deal with Martin. He'd be here later, of that she was certain. The man just couldn't stay away; he'd always come back for the sake of his work, if for no other reason.

Stephanie groaned her displeasure as she set the shotgun aside, bending over Dr. Reed as he lay prone, hooking her arms under his, and dragging his large frame across the marbled floor.

It was slow going, Stephanie's injuries hindering her progress, but she finally pulled him into the COMPUTER ROOM.

Using a heavy steel file cabinet to support his back, she braced Dr. Reed up and into a seated position on the floor with his legs stretched out before him. From her pocket she extracted a roll of three inch reinforced plastic tape, halting for a second, thinking this was intended for Martin, binding Logan's feet tightly together at the ankles. Next, she placed his arms along his sides, winding and wrapping the tape around his torso and the file cabinet.

When she was done, she tugged sharply at the makeshift restraint. The tips of Logan's fingers peeked out from beneath the wide strips of tape. It would hold, Stephanie thought, long enough for Dr. Reed to witness a tragedy.

She wasted no time now, going to the main computer terminal, calling up the program she had earlier designed for Krystyna. Martin knew nothing of this program, tailored to a grisly perfection with a secreted switch of the diamonds. It was created in the lonely hope of lashing out at the one woman Martin would always love! It was to be Stephanie's brand of revenge.

Stephanie engaged the hidden camera located in the EMPTY ROOM. Krystyna's small frame slowly sparked to life on a wide bank of monitors. She appeared to be pacing back and forth, her arms folded together and pressed closely to her body. Indeed, Krystyna looked angry, cold gray eyes scanning the curved picture walls.

This is perfect, Stephanie thought, moving one of the monitors over to where Logan was effectively bound to the file cabinet. She positioned the monitor carefully, finally stepping back and smiling at her work.

When Logan awoke, the first sight he'd see would be Krystyna as she experienced the dark reality of the phobic mind. Krystyna would have no choice but to interact with the pictures on the walls. She would step into the shoes of the many predecessors before her, reliving the workaholic's unending nightmare, another patient's intense fear of germs, yet another's terror of needles, the gruesome dread of heights, the intimidation felt by another who was deathly afraid of thunder and lightning.

They were all there, each patient's worst scenario, the hideous screams woven together, including Krystyna's own screams as she was made to envision the crash scene that claimed the life of her mother, and nearly her father. A fine-tuned blend of bloodcurdling cries for help, and escape.

But, Stephanie thought, there would be no escape for Krystyna.

Logan began to moan, his eyelids fluttering open. Instinctively, he tried to raise an arm to the swollen knot on his head, but soon found he could not move. Panic swept through him, and in seconds he was fully cognizant of his surroundings and the bleak situation. An unsettling desperation settled in as he viewed the monitor positioned before him. Krystyna was there on the screen, a tiny figure, enveloped in a meadow of wildflowers.

Logan could hear the music that was being fed into the EMPTY ROOM. He then saw Krystyna's features relax as she stepped cautiously toward the pictures.

Frantic, Logan called out to Stephanie. "Stop the pictures, right now!"

"The best is yet to come." Stephanie said, her mouth twisting unevenly, the injured side of her face slack and drooping. "I only wish that Martin were also here to witness this tragedy!"

However, Stephanie wasn't entirely disappointed. There was little doubt Martin would recognize what she'd done to Krystyna. Stephanie would save the recorded tape and play it for Martin when he returned to SERENITY. Undoubtedly, this would infuriate Martin, and hurt him worse than anything else.

A very fitting revenge, Stephanie thought.

Martin glanced at his watch, the illuminated face reading half past two. Krystyna was late, yet he remained hopeful. A momentary panic caught him as he wondered if she had already arrived, parking elsewhere, and was waiting for him at the outlook over the falls. Deciding he should wait for her, Martin opened the door to the Mercedes, and climbed out. She would see his car and know where he was.

The rushing waters greeted him, a cascading crescendo, as Martin walked across the graveled parking area, stepping onto the well-worn path. He'd only taken a few steps, when suddenly he stopped, certain that he'd heard a rustling in the shrubbery. Craning his head around, looking back to the parking area, he stood very still, hands in the pockets of his raincoat, staring into the veiled darkness.

Orenda and Garrett were alerted to the fact that Dr. Martin Braddock had stepped from the Mercedes, and was walking to the outlook area. They moved through the dense cover of trees and shrubs, maintaining a safe distance between themselves and the scientist. The ground was slippery from the heavy rain that had fallen earlier in the evening, and at times they clung to one another for support, Garrett dragging his wooden leg stiffly behind him.

Garrett was doing his best to be quiet, yet in order to keep Braddock in their sights, they were forced to circumvent a steep crevasse in the rocky terrain. That was when Garrett slipped on the wet earth, both feet coming up from under him, landing on his rather generous bottom. He continued to slide down the muddy incline, first colliding with the slender trunk of a small hemlock, then sliding down again.

Orenda turned to Garrett, who was no longer at her side. She heard the rustling sounds of Garrett's descent down the side of the crevasse. Quickly, she turned to see if Martin Braddock had also heard the noise. Her stomach churned as she saw that he had.

Orenda quickly decided to stay where she was, hunched beside Taima in the thick shrubbery.

Time slowly passed.

During the last few minutes, Krystyna had undergone a complete circle in her emotions. She'd been frightened at the sight of the figure suddenly intruding, forcing Logan to accompany the figure, and later locking the only door to the room. After her fear, anxiety was added to the mixture, to be followed by hopelessness, frustration, and bitter resentment. Krystyna lived a lifetime in just a few moment's time, or so it seemed to her.

Her mind raced, questioning the reason she had been left alone in the EMPTY ROOM. Was she the next target? She had no answer and she could not immediately identify the ghostly figure. She doubted it was Martin. He always commented that his own face was mask enough.

Who else, then? Krystyna found she didn't have to think long and hard. It was ever apparent Stephanie Roberts had a vicious plan up her own sleeve. As if to sanctify this notion for Krystyna, a soft aria began, the musical instruments delivering crisp clean notes of a classic.

Instantly, Krystyna felt the ice-cold fingers of panic gripping her. The music always came first, then the field of wildflowers, then . . .

She had to get out!

Martin Braddock finally decided the noise was probably an animal foraging about in the forest. Nothing to worry about. He turned around, stepping once again toward the outcropping of large stones overlooking the waterfalls. A fine mist covered his face, startling him with a pinpricking sensation; a sensation that led Martin to a refined clarity of mind. He breathed in deeply as he reached the wrought iron railing, drinking in the clean night air, hope filling his heart.

Martin smiled in the moonlight, leaning against the railing, emerald eyes intent along the pathway he'd just walked. Very soon, he thought, Krystyna would be here. She'll make everything all right. He felt better than he had in years!

He felt for the large manila envelope in his coat pocket. It contained not only his and Stephanie's notes, but also a copy of his last will and testament. Martin would show Krystyna just how profound his love for her was. He had proof in his pocket.

Martin Braddock was also glad he had left a little surprise for Stephanie should she decide to return one last time to SERENITY. A bubble of laughter rose in his throat. All Stephanie had to do was turn her computer on . . . and the rest would take care of itself.

Everything was coming together as he had planned.

"Krystyna," Martin whispered aloud, emotion choking him. "My angel, come to me . . . now!"

The overpowering aroma of roses and other flowers too, filled the room. Krystyna's body stiffened. She looked closely at the walls. They were filled with a picturesque scene of a lazy meadow, branches of flowering trees spilled out and into the room. A climbing rose branch swept past Krystyna's arm, a tender breeze catching the branch and lifting it about, causing a sharp thorn to scratch her skin. Beads of blood pushed quickly to the surface.

Immediately, she recognized the need for escape. However, Krystyna had already found the door to be locked securely and no amount of maneuvering would open it. Frantically, her eyes scoured the EMPTY ROOM for a tool. There was none.

The sunlight in the scene began to fade. Darkness would return in the form of madness, Krystyna thought recklessly, desperate now to escape what would soon appear on the screen surrounding her. She knew it was holograms, three-dimensional pictures, but that alone did not allay her fears.

This was evil, pure and simple, and Krystyna wanted no part of it!

She grabbed her flashlight and stepped up to the gaping hole in the wall, peering inside. It was difficult for her to concentrate, the music picking up in tempo, cadence, and strength. As if they were truly alive, the rumbling sounds of the music controlled her heartbeat, faster and faster, until she thought she would explode.

Krystyna fought the impressions, forcing into her mind's eye the face of Logan. She held his face steady, reminding herself of the love they shared. She knew she must do something and do it now.

She reached her arm into the hole in the wall, her fingers meeting with insulation, wiring, other items, until her hand grasped and held steady a broken section of a two by six. It was caught between another two by six, and an unseen object. She pulled at the broken piece of wood; it was wedged in tight. Krystyna tugged again to free the piece of wood, and huffing and puffing, she could hear the slow crackle as the wood separated and fractured. At long last, Krystyna extracted the section of two by six.

She knew what had to be done to escape; the door was hopeless, the circular room nothing less than a cage. She would force her way through the picture wall, and onto the other side. After all, Krystyna thought, wasn't it just another interior wall behind all that stuffing?

Krystyna prayed that would be the case.

Just as she was about to pass through the wall, the jagged end of the two by six aimed and ready, the hidden camera caught her actions. Anyone watching would have seen Krystyna step into the scene covering the picture wall, the sky now darkened overhead, the music morose and painfully shrill to her ears.

CHAPTER THIRTY SIX

By the time Orenda caught up with Garrett, he had slid down the rain slickened crevasse a good hundred yards.

Now, after instructing Taima to stay in place, Orenda rushed down the steep incline, her feet slipping on the treacherous muddy underbrush, grabbing wildly at tree limbs to help slow her descent.

Several minor scrapes and cuts later, finally reaching the bottom of the crevasse, Orenda called out to Garrett in a hushed, breathless voice. "Garrett, where are you?"

"Over here . . . I'm here," Garrett responded, having managed to catch his breath in the interim.

Orenda reached for him in the darkness; slender threads of moonlight were now dissolved and blackened by thick overhead trees and the steep rocky bank.

"Are you hurt?" She asked, feeling the woolen fabric of his jacket beneath her fingertips. It was so dark she could barely see the features of his face.

"I'm not sure."

"Take a few moments, Garrett."

He did as Orenda suggested, gradually moving his arms, stretching his back. The left side of his rib cage felt bruised.

"Well, nothing feels broken," he said, "but I'm afraid my artificial leg took quite a beating as I slid down the crevasse."

Silently, tentatively, he brought himself up to stand, testing his overall strength and coordination. Nothing that a little tune-up wouldn't fix, Garrett finally decided. "Come on, Orenda. We've left Braddock up there at the lookout all by himself. Some watchdogs we are!"

"I'm sure he's still there."

"Well, I hope you're right. It wouldn't do us any good to lose track of that madman on a night like this!"

Orenda shivered at his side.

Garrett put an arm around her slim shoulders. "How much time do you think we lost due to my clumsy fall down the crevasse?"

Orenda directed her small flashlight over the crystal face of her watch. It was longer than she would have imagined. "A good fifteen minutes."

"We've got to hurry, then." Garrett urged. "Anything could have happened in that amount of time."

Stephanie concentrated on the computer monitor. She could easily see Krystyna cautiously approaching the picture scene, feeling and exploring the wall with her hands, reluctantly stepping into the field of wildflowers. All at once the scene surrounded Krystyna's entire body, absorbing her, pale ivory skin disintegrating.

It was now done, Stephanie thought smugly, wringing a sadistic pleasure from her perverted deeds. She reveled in the power of her control over others. She glanced over to Logan. He continued to stare at the monitor, the blood drawn from his face, struggling with the tape that held him prisoner.

In desperation, Logan rocked back and forth, trying to turn the file cabinet on its side, in the hope of either breaking the thick bands of tape, or optimally, stretching the reinforcements just enough to get his hands free. Unfortunately, it wasn't working.

Amused, Stephanie watched Logan's futile attempts for a moment. "You can't budge that file cabinet, Dr. Reed. Give up, just as Krystyna has done." Her eyes were drawn again to the monitor.

Logan glanced at the screen. It appeared that Krystyna entered the picture world and had not returned to the room. Something cold twisted inside of him as he pulled his eyes away. Was Krystyna where Samuel had been taken? Would she survive, unscathed? He could not bear to answer his questions. Just then something caught his eye . . . movement . . . perhaps footsteps. Was it, he wondered, another figure approaching?

Logan turned to the right, as much as his bindings would allow, and stared at the opened entrance to the COMPUTER ROOM, beyond where Stephanie was positioned at her terminal. He held his breath, expecting the worst.

Logan's expression changed dramatically, his eyes widened with fresh alarm. Stephanie turned to Logan, her tone sharp and intolerant. "Dr. Reed, do not play games with me! We're the only ones here."

"Don't count on it, Stephanie." A voice announced.

Stephanie's eyes now widened, a cold sensation creeping across her skin. The voice speaking was behind her, the tone . . . so much like Martin. She whirled around. In the flash of a second, Stephanie's world crumbled at her feet. Martin Braddock stood in the doorway, a dark brooding scowl upon his gnarled features. It was a malicious face, colored and carved with rage.

A buzzer sounded, loudly, impatiently. Startled, Stephanie was immediately torn between Martin and the computer terminal. The buzzer was actually an alarm. It meant that something was very wrong with the program she had arranged for Krystyna. Stephanie's fingers flew across the keyboard. Nothing helped. The buzzer continued to scream. She tried again. There was no response.

The computer-generated sequences on film had been tampered with, Stephanie's access codes erased, the program severely altered! Angry, she slammed her fist against the ineffective keyboard. The buzzer stopped with a screech.

The figure of Braddock advanced, Stephanie leaping from her chair before the computer, scrambling to the farthest corner she could find. Cowering, she felt her heartbeat throbbing and ricocheting throughout her weakened limbs, her torn ear a searing blaze of fire.

Martin Braddock twisted the one end of his blonde mustache, fiendish emerald eyes locked on Stephanie. "I stopped by earlier, decided to remain a step ahead of you, Stephanie. I see you've tried running your program, and have found that it no longer works. That's my doing."

Martin slowly closed in on Stephanie, the hunter stalking his prey. "Just part of the pay back, Stephanie. And," he smiled, "there's more!"

Cringing, huddled in a corner, Stephanie knew all her plans had backfired. "It's enough, Martin . . . please." She whispered.

Watching the interaction between Braddock and Stephanie, Logan began to think it quite odd that Braddock had not once turned to look in his direction. A mere fifteen feet away, Logan could hardly have been missed, sprawled across the floor and braced up against the file cabinet. Logan decided, however, to remain silent, without drawing any unwanted attention to himself, while he continued to pull and tug at the bands of tape.

Braddock threw his head back with a peal of unnerving laughter. "I thought you might see it that way, Stephanie. Nevertheless, you need to understand that I cannot forgive you for switching the diamonds just to hurry the process along. Well aware of the consequences, you saw the damage, one patient after another, and still you persisted in playing your little game. And, at a time when we were onto something spectacular!"

"I'm so sorry, Martin." Stephanie murmured, her lower lip quivering.

"Stephanie, my last sentiments to you are these; I forgive you nothing! Take your personal belongings and get out! Consider this my final and ultimate warning."

Martin paused. "I have but one, small, very insignificant transgression to confess. Perhaps you'd care to hear it before you go?"

Overwhelmed, Stephanie could only nod her head slightly.

Martin smiled a generous, toothy grin. "I lied to you, Stephanie. I switched the diamonds myself . . . but only once."

"You did?" Stephanie asked, confused.

"Yes. The switch was made when I was experimenting on *you*." Martin answered evenly.

The dawning of meaning slowly penetrated Stephanie. A long, heartrending scream ripped from her throat.

Krystyna used the section of two by six as a battering ram, breaking and splintering through the existing hole in the wall, enlarging the gap considerably, forcing her way through the sheetrock, and into the INTRODUCTION ROOM on the other side. She could hear the music change behind her, eternally grateful to have escaped when she did, and quickly finding the dimly lit hallway.

Once there, she came to an abrupt halt. Somewhere in the distance the trail of Martin's voice reached her. It couldn't be, Krystyna thought! He's at the FALLS, waiting for me.

Or was he? Had he come back? Was Martin, Krystyna wondered, the one responsible for locking her in the picture world and leading Logan away?

She could waste no time. She must find Logan.

A scream pierced through the stillness, and it seemed to be coming from the same direction as that of Martin's voice. Krystyna hurried along the darkened hallway, stopping near the entrance to the COMPUTER ROOM. She could hear a scuffling sound and detected the groaning of a metal object. Taking a deep breath, Krystyna inched along the hallway, listening, waiting. A small shaft of light reached out from the room, accompanied by more scuffling sounds. Finally, Krystyna peeked inside, quickly drawing her body back into the gloomy corridor.

Martin was there! Krystyna felt a tremendous wave of fear threaten her, yet she leaned forward again, stealing another glance. This time she spotted Logan, bound with something resembling tape, and crouched in a far corner was Stephanie.

Before Krystyna could decide what to do, Stephanie screamed again. The bloodcurdling cry echoed over the vast spaces, spilling into every dark corner. Krystyna peeked through the doorway to find that Martin was moving closer yet toward Stephanie. Quickly, Krystyna stepped behind Martin, camouflaged by his tall frame, becoming his shadow.

Nearly as she had done so, Krystyna realized this was a grave mistake.

Stephanie stood up from her cowering position in the corner, locking eyes with Martin. "You're no better than I," Stephanie growled as she withdrew a small handgun from her coat pocket, pointing it at Martin. "This little trinket just might convince you to reevaluate your position! If that doesn't convince you, I have a shotgun as well. After what you've done to me . . ."

Frozen in place behind Martin, Krystyna's mind raced. As yet, she had not drawn Logan's attention, shielded from sight as she was, and amazingly, as far as she could guess, Martin was no more the wiser. It startled Krystyna when Martin spoke again. Something in his voice was . . . peculiar.

"That's all I have to say, Stephanie. Nothing further is open for debate." Martin said.

Stephanie wrapped both hands around the sleek pistol, arms extended, elbows locked, the gun aimed directly at Martin. There was a dangerous glimmer of revenge in her eyes. A single finger was poised on the trigger.

At that moment, Krystyna chose to dive behind a desk rather than risk being shot. Her timing was fortunate. She turned away just in time to hear the blast, the bullet slicing through Martin and into an adjacent wall.

Without hesitation, Stephanie fired the gun repeatedly into the chest and head of Martin Braddock. For her efforts, the image of Martin all but disappeared. Only the faint illusion of his wicked gleaming eyes persisted, and the fading sounds of his maniacal laughter.

Stunned, but nonetheless outraged, Stephanie had little choice but to accept that Martin had left her a message delivered by his proxy; a hologram made in his own image! A surrogate performance, he'd not had the courage to tell her these things himself! Too bad, Stephanie thought, Martin would be dead by now.

From the corner of his eye, Logan spotted Krystyna as she leaped for cover behind a desk just as the first shot rang out. Thank heavens, she was all right. Now, the immediate problem was that Stephanie had also seen Krystyna! Logan quickly turned to catch the smug smile on Stephanie's face.

Undoubtedly, Stephanie's smile conveyed that killing Krystyna would be the next best thing to killing Martin.

"You coward, Braddock!" Stephanie screamed, throwing her head back, causing a fresh stream of blood to ooze through the gauze bandages. "You couldn't even tell me, face to face."

Turning sharply on her heel, Stephanie growled at Logan. "And now, for you, Dr. Reed, and your friend, Krystyna, who thought I didn't notice her hiding over there behind the desk."

Stephanie pointed the gun at Logan's head, stepping closer to him. "Come out now, Krystyna."

"No! Krystyna, don't do it." Logan yelled in return.

Krystyna hesitated but for a split second, standing up to reveal her position, slowly crossing around to the front of the desk. "Leave Logan Reed out of this. He's got nothing to do with it."

"He's a witness. That's bad enough." Stephanie said.

"Just like Martin, wasn't it?" Krystyna asked, her smile bright and knowing. "Quite convincing . . . Martin's hologram."

Uncertainty flashed in Stephanie's blue eyes. "How do you know about the holograms?"

"I've just seen one for myself. Regardless, I figured that out earlier. I've also deducted that you're in a great deal of trouble already, Stephanie. You need to stop and think about . . ."

"Think!" Stephanie screamed. "I'm beyond thinking, beyond feeling. See for yourself. Look at what Martin's done!" She reached one hand to the gauze bandages covering most of her face and the one ear, tearing the bandages away, exposing the gruesome bite marks.

Krystyna felt herself shiver, groaning involuntarily. Indeed, it was a repulsive hideous sight. A sense of pity overwhelmed Krystyna. "I'm sorry, Stephanie . . . "

"Sorry doesn't cut it, Krystyna." A sour twist curved at Stephanie's mouth. "Someone has to pay. It may as well be you."

"You think by hurting me, you'll be getting even with Martin." Krystyna asked, her heart clutching sharply at her chest.

267

"It's close enough. Nothing else would hurt Martin more."

"You're entirely wrong. That's not nearly low enough. Surely, you can dream up something better." Krystyna said, stalling for time, hoping for a miracle. "But, I must warn you that Martin is returning to SERENITY. It's likely he'll be here at any moment."

"Don't feed me that crap, Krystyna. Martin has already put in his so-called appearance. He won't return in the flesh."

"You can't know that." Logan interjected as a heightened sense of helplessness drilled through him. "Stephanie, Braddock wanted Krystyna to meet with him this morning. When he realizes that she's changed her mind, Braddock is certain to return here. I have my doubts you're safe in that event. We can only hope you'll listen to reason . . ."

"To hell with reason!" Stephanie shouted, the motions of moving her mouth and jaw now causing her excruciating pain. Deep down she recognized a desperate need for medical attention and yet . . . the wheels were already in motion. She wasn't certain she had the strength to stop the momentum. It was just easier to carry on, like before. See it through, until the bitter end.

Krystyna was watching Stephanie very carefully, witnessing the wave of pain creasing and contorting Stephanie's face. During this window of opportunity, hands behind her back, Krystyna's fingers frantically searched across the desktop, hoping to find anything that could be used as a weapon. She felt a stapler, papers, pencils, small boxes of useless items having no weight, no substance. Finally, Krystyna seized one of several bottles of developer used in the process of the films. Knowing that the developer contained a mixture of toxic and destructive chemicals, Krystyna reasoned these chemicals thrown into a fresh wound would almost certainly induce immediate and intense pain! Perhaps, Krystyna hoped, enough pain to cause Stephanie to drop the gun from her fingers.

She needed more time, however. The top of the developer bottle was sealed tight. Krystyna must get Stephanie talking, divert her attention.

She looked over to Logan, risking the eye contact. Fear now drilled through Krystyna, and her greatest fear was of losing Logan. To lose him now would be a monumental travesty.

It was all or nothing.

Perhaps serenity would come . . . but only at a dear price.

CHAPTER THIRTY SEVEN

"What was that sound?" Krystyna asked, looking to the doorway, her voice an anxious whisper.

"That was your imagination, nothing more!" Stephanie snapped. "Now move over to Dr. Reed."

"Stephanie," Krystyna said, raising her voice. "I thought I heard footsteps." Hands behind her back, Krystyna's fingers continued to struggle with the tamper-proof opening of the developer bottle.

"Krystyna wasn't the only one to hear them." Logan said. "They were coming down the hallway, heading this way."

Stephanie shifted her eyes to the door for a very brief moment.

"It's Martin! I knew he'd return." Krystyna cried out, forcing her voice to shriek, her fingernails breaking as the plastic ring around the bottle refused to break.

"No, you're wrong." Stephanie insisted, keeping her back to the entrance.

"I heard him, too." Logan groaned, rocking the file cabinet with a renewed effort. "And I don't want to be here when Braddock returns!"

Logan's eyes went wide. "Wait! Listen to that . . ."

"Listen to what?" Stephanie urged.

"Footsteps." Logan answered, his eyes drawn to the doorway. He wriggled in place, pulling and tugging at his bindings as never before. "Cut me loose, for God's sake!"

Krystyna looked exceedingly anxious as she glanced over to Logan, adding, "We can't let him find the notes . . ."

Stephanie's eyes lit up.

"Yes, Martin entrusted his beloved notes to me." Krystyna answered Stephanie's unspoken question with this fabrication, fingers prying recklessly at the bottle's neck. The wretched thing wouldn't tear open!

"I want them! Hand them over immediately." Stephanie demanded.

"They're not here, Stephanie." Logan said in a steady voice. "Unbind me, and I'll take you to where they're hidden. But, hurry, what ever you do!"

Finally, Krystyna felt the plastic ring give way at the neck of the bottle of developer. She unscrewed the mouth of the bottle, setting the top aside. Now, all she needed was just the right moment. She brought one hand to the bodice of her dress, signaling a cue to Logan as she caressed the turquoise beads.

"Too late!" Logan cried out in alarm. "Braddock's here!"

Turning toward the doorway, Stephanie aimed the small pistol with a single hand. Her other hand searched recklessly in a coat pocket for the butt of the sawed-off shotgun.

Instantly, using the momentum of forward motion, Krystyna grabbed Stephanie's hand that held the pistol, forcing her body around, wrenching the hand and arm up and away. The twenty-two bounced to the floor. At the same moment, Krystyna brought the bottle of developer closer to Stephanie's face. Krystyna had needed a clear shot and this was it.

With speed and accuracy, Krystyna splashed the liquid chemicals straight into Stephanie's face, immediately dropping the bottle, freeing her hands. She stepped back, her eyes determined, inflexible, and ready to fight.

Krystyna found she need not press the issue further. There would be no counterattack. Eyes screwed shut, Stephanie screamed, her cries high-pitched, wailing and sobbing, hands clawing helplessly at her face. Stephanie then fell to the floor, writhing in tremendous pain, shrieking obscenities, her body contorting in agonizing spasms.

Krystyna bent over Stephanie and wrangled the shotgun from her coat pocket. Next, she retrieved the small twenty-two where it had fallen a few feet away on the floor.

"Quick," Logan called out to Krystyna. "Find something to cut this tape."

Pulling several desk drawers open, Krystyna found a hefty pair of scissors, and in less than two minutes she had freed Logan from his restraints. A cursory look at the gash in his head stopped Krystyna cold. It was bad.

Logan brushed Krystyna's hand impatiently away from his head. He stood up slowly, the muscles in his cramped legs tight and uncooperative. He looked over to Stephanie. "We're leaving now. You dare to follow and I'll finish what both Martin and Krystyna started!"

Stephanie gave no indication that she heard Logan's parting comments. She lay on the floor in the fetal position, moaning, fingers clawing at the festering bloody wounds.

Turning for a last look, Krystyna saw the pathetic picture of Stephanie. There was no sorrow in her heart for the woman now, having overheard comments earlier confirming Stephanie was primarily responsible for the ruination of many lives. Her impatience had led her to act with abandon. The remainder of the guilt, however, was indeed Martin's to bear.

Glancing at his watch, Logan found that it was nearly three o'clock. "We must leave immediately."

Nodding, Krystyna followed him, Stephanie's screams of misery slowly but steadily fading in the distance.

At the rear entrance, Krystyna turned to Logan. "Are you sure you're all right?"

"Yes. It looks worse than it is."

They exited the building, pausing before they crossed the rain-splattered parking lot. Depositing both the twenty-two and the shotgun in his duffel bag, Logan spoke over his shoulder to Krystyna in a hushed voice. "I only wish we could have found Braddock's notes."

"Yes, I know."

"At least Stephanie confirmed she doesn't have the notes in her possession. Braddock must have them with him. Maybe he does plan on giving them to you, after all. I don't know. Somehow, we'll convince the BOES board members with what information we do have, namely the taped recordings."

Doubting that would be enough, Krystyna nevertheless felt hopeful. "They'll have to suffice. It's all we have."

"For now," Logan said, "we must reach the FALLS before anything else goes wrong."

When Garrett and Orenda reached the top of the crevasse, a low whisper brought Taima running to them; there was an urgent growl deep in her throat conveying that something was amiss.

Huddled together deep in the shadows, Orenda heard the soft crunch of footsteps along the graveled path. A moment later, Martin Braddock made his way to his Mercedes, bringing his key to the door.

It looked as though he had given up on Krystyna and was about to leave. Orenda could not let that happen.

She leaned close to Garrett, whispering in his ear. "Stay here."

Before Garrett could voice his objections, Orenda left their hiding place in the thick shrubbery, maneuvering through the velvet gloom, drawing nearer the parking lot. She reached for the small tape recorder in her coat pocket, felt in the darkness for the ON button, holding a finger on its location. She tugged at one of Taima's ears, urging the dog to follow her.

Martin Braddock had his car door open, ready to sit behind the wheel, when she pressed the ON button of the recorder.

Instantly, Krystyna's prerecorded voice called out, the volume turned up. "Martin . . . I'm over here."

Snapping his head around, Martin Braddock quickly closed the door of the Mercedes. He turned his head, peering out to the vast ebony cloaked forest. "Krystyna?"

Orenda pressed the button again. "I'm over here . . . follow me."

Now, Orenda tossed a good-sized pebble through the air. It landed with a thump, rustling through the branches of a tree. Martin Braddock turned toward the sound, stepping forward, his movements eager, impassioned.

"Stop where you are, Krystyna! Let me catch up to you." He said.

Another pebble was thrown in the opposite direction of the first.

Puzzled, Martin Braddock whirled around. This time he did not speak. He stood still, listening, cautious.

Orenda pressed the button of the recorder once again. "Come to me, Martin."

"Keep talking, Krystyna. I'll find you." Martin called out anxiously, stepping toward the trail of Krystyna's voice.

It was time to move her position, Orenda decided. Taima moved with Orenda, step for step, her amber eyes surveying the darkness, very well aware that a hunt was taking place, even more aware that the stranger calling out to them was not to be trusted.

The cat and mouse game had begun, Orenda thought, tossing out another pebble. Sooner, rather than later, she suspected, this would not work. Braddock would smell trouble.

She moved from place to place, hiding in the shadows, Taima within arms distance at all times, hunkering down amongst the underbrush. She did not have long to wait.

Frustrated, Braddock threw his hands up in the air. "Krystyna, I can hear you but I can't see you. You're playing some kind of game with me, and I don't like it. Either come out now, or I'm leaving."

He slowly approached the Mercedes, eyes scanning the edges of the graveled parking area where it met with the merging wall of evergreen trees.

"Last chance, Krystyna." Martin said, reaching once again for his keys.

Orenda had been afraid of this moment, but now that it was here, she knew what had to be done. If only Logan and Krystyna would hurry . . .

Slipping out from under a heavily branched hemlock tree, Orenda stepped onto the graveled area, her shoes crunching on the rocks. As she had anticipated, the noise caught Martin Braddock's immediate attention.

He spotted Orenda, her silhouette in the moonlight revealing her ankle-length beaded dress, Krystyna's jacket, and long flowing hair.

"Krystyna!" Martin cried out.

Orenda darted back into the trees, circling to the left, Taima at her heels, keeping her eye on the one and only light in the immediate area to keep her bearings. She hunched down again once she heard Braddock's steps on the gravel.

"I saw you, Krystyna." Martin called out. "I know you're there!"

She watched him turn back toward his car, mumbling his frustrations under his breath.

Orenda moved to the edge of the trees, slipping out of the cover, just as she had done before, twisting her feet in the gravel to call attention to herself, allowing Martin Braddock another glimpse of her.

It was working thus far, Orenda decided. Braddock thought she was Krystyna. However, he was displaying all the signs of being disgusted with the game. How long could this go on? Something had to give.

When she was certain Braddock had spotted her, Orenda darted back into the trees, circling again to the left. She glanced over her shoulder, and stopped immediately. Taima was no longer at her side. The dog had followed her to the graveled edge of the parking lot, apparently not able to restrain herself, and was now poised for a confrontation.

Martin Braddock saw the dog a moment after he caught a second glimpse of Krystyna. Agitated, he returned to the car, muttering to himself, retrieving his keys and this time opening up the trunk. He slipped the raincoat from his shoulders, tossing it up over the car.

Now he reached inside the trunk, feeling for an object with his hands, his eyes never leaving the deeply shrouded edge of the parking lot. When he slammed the trunk lid down, he raised a long dark object in his hand.

Horrified, Orenda saw that the object was a tire iron. She looked quickly back to Taima. The dog had seen the man retrieve something, and the man was now brandishing the object in the air.

A verbal threat sounded from the man.

Instantly, the dog recognized the man's voice. Taima inched forward, teeth bared, sensing a battle moments away.

After leaving the truck along the edge of the road, Logan and Krystyna ran on foot heading for the parking area at the top of the FALLS. They quickly spotted the black Mercedes, the trunk lid left open, a raincoat haphazardly thrown across the top. Martin Braddock was standing to one side waving a tire iron.

Blending with the shrubbery, they leaned back into the murky shadows, assessing the situation. Neither Orenda nor Garrett could be seen, yet Taima stood out in the open, alone, her growl menacing, glowing amber eyes fixed on Martin Braddock.

A move borne of desperation, Orenda decided she must entice Braddock with yet another glimpse, leading him toward the lookout. She stepped well away from cover, ran toward the pathway, nearly in full view. Braddock called out to her just as she disappeared once again from his sight.

"Krystyna, stop this nonsense!" Martin yelled. "Stay where you are."

Taima's watchful eyes followed Orenda, and now followed the man in pursuit of Orenda. The dog knew that her duties belonged with the woman, and she followed their course, slipping into the deep forest, easily able to outrun them both.

Krystyna had seen Martin turn his head, speak to someone, turn again, breaking into a run down the graveled path leading to the rocky overlook. She exchanged glances with Logan. "We're too late!"

"No." Logan said. "We can catch up if we hurry . . ."

Running side by side now, Krystyna quickly estimated that Martin was a good five or six hundred feet ahead of them. "I don't see your mother, or Garrett . . ."

"There's Garrett." Logan breathed.

Krystyna looked to the left and saw that Garrett was limping along, slowly making his way across the parking lot. He raised the gun in his hand, pointing to the air. Garrett could see where Logan and Krystyna were headed, but realized they would reach the lookout far ahead of him.

Still running, Krystyna could see another light emanating from the overlook, the illumination weaving eerily through the dense trees, highlighting the graveled pathway before them. She knew from her previous visit that the overlook was merely an outcropping of massive rocks and stone cliffs, partially enclosed with a wrought iron railing, the cascading waterfalls directly below.

Turning to Logan, Krystyna pointed with a finger, disbelieving of her eyes.

There at the overlook, her back to the wrought iron railing, Orenda stood like a statue, perfectly still, out in the open. Martin, running along the graveled path, was fast approaching her. He carried a tire iron in one hand as he cried out, "Krystyna, wait!"

Less than fifty feet now separated them from Martin and Orenda. It was then that all action seemed to move at a leisurely crawl. It felt more like a dream, Krystyna thought, perhaps more like a movie, frame by frame, born of a slow burning madness.

Krystyna turned to Logan. There was a seething hatred in his eyes, the vision of his beloved mother in harms way, and he quickly sprinted forward.

Twenty feet from the overlook, time stood still for Krystyna. Martin had reached an arm out to Orenda, only to attempt pulling back, now painfully aware that she was not Krystyna. Martin whirled around, spotting Logan and Krystyna fast approaching, confusion twisting his face.

Suddenly, Martin tried to raise a protective arm to his face, his mouth slack with fright, half-open, ready to scream.

The scream was interrupted as Taima leaped from the underbrush, making a mad dash for Martin, and in particular the arm that still held the ominous tire iron. The dog's powerful haunches lifted her body into the air, driving her muscular wolf-like body at the man. The dog's coarse fur brushed against Orenda as the dog pushed the man's body well away from her, crushing him against the wrought iron railing, the accelerated momentum forcing the man over the railing, and down beyond the edge.

CHAPTER THIRTY EIGHT

Martin Braddock's tortured scream echoed across the canyon, bounced off the rock-faced cliffs, becoming one with the avalanche of cascading waters.

Rushing to his mother's side, Logan peered over the edge of the lookout, and down to the jagged boulders below. He was certain Braddock could not have survived the fall. No voice called out to them for help, nor was there a succession of death defying screams. The white foam of the waves, clearly seen against the blackened rock formations, failed to provide Logan an outline of a lifeless body as it lay battered and beaten. Down river . . . by now, Logan thought.

Orenda spoke to her son. "Go to Krystyna. I think she needs you."

Logan turned around, his heart instantly twisting sharply in his chest. Krystyna, moving slowly toward the lookout, was in shock, her eyes hard, her expression dazed. He stepped over to her, reaching out, taking her in his arms, carefully drawing her away from the wrought iron railing.

"Krystyna . . ." He said. "Look at me."

Tears glistened in Krystyna's eyes. She felt numb, old, ancient, tired . . .

"It happened so fast." Logan said. "An accident none of us were prepared for."

Krystyna could merely shiver.

Limping along, Garrett approached their group, Orenda whispering in his ear the tragedy that just took place. Astonished, Garrett swore under his breath, quickly finding a large rock to sit upon. His oval face turned pale under the moonlight, the nine-millimeter handgun slipping without notice from his trembling fingers to the wet ground.

Logan held Krystyna by the shoulders, trying to penetrate her blank stare.

An agonizing silence followed.

Overwhelmed, Krystyna was digging deeply into an already crucially tapped reservoir of strength. She finally asked. "Is Martin . . . dead?"

"Yes."

Krystyna closed her eyes. Still, everything moved in slow motion for her.

"He couldn't have survived?"

"No." Logan answered.

Opening her eyes, Krystyna breathed a long sigh. "I would never have wished this on him. Never . . ."

"None of us would." Logan said soberly.

"I came for my divorce." Krystyna said, emotion flooding her heart. "I could not have known that I would end up a . . . widow."

Orenda approached Krystyna. "Krystyna," Orenda said, her voice soft and comforting. "Sometimes we receive what we most desire, yet not entirely in the manner we expected. Regardless, it's not for us to question what fate offers us."

The two women exchanged a thoughtful glance.

"You're absolutely right." Krystyna whispered. "I'm sorry Martin has lost his life, but that's all I'm sorry about."

Krystyna felt Taima nuzzling at her fingertips, the dog's motions urgent, a silent bond of love radiating from amber eyes as they stared up at her. She bent to the dog, and hugged her desperately, an incredible mountain of guilt giving way, tenacious regrets and tender memories mingling with her tears.

Minutes later, it was decided that Garrett and Orenda would go into town, locate the first available phone, and contact the county sheriff's office to report the accident. They estimated it would take the officers nearly an hour to arrive from the neighboring county; plenty of time for Garrett and Orenda to return to the lookout at the FALLS. As a group they would wait at the scene for the authorities.

It went nearly as Logan had hoped. Two uniformed officers arrived, taking verbal statements from everyone; a formal written accounting would be taken later that day at the sheriff's headquarters. Closely surveying the parking lot, including

Braddock's Mercedes, the officers scrutinized the overlook with a fine-toothed comb. They took photographs of the tire iron that lay in the mud-splattered gravel, precisely where Braddock had dropped it before going over the railing. They systematically measured distances from point-A, all the way through point-Z. They were exceedingly thorough, a shimmering pre-dawn light aiding their search.

However, no body was immediately found.

Regarding SERENITY and the covert activities professed to have taken place there, one of the officers thought this trouble appeared to be strictly a civil matter, and hardly under their jurisdiction. First and foremost, the officer went on to explain, the accident was their only concern.

They were also advised there would be a search and rescue effort at first light in an attempt to recover the body of Martin Braddock.

In conclusion, the taller of the two officers turned to Krystyna. "Mrs. Braddock, I have something intended for you." He said, placing a large manila envelope in her hands. "This envelope was found in the pocket of your husband's raincoat. Since he was meeting with you, we've assumed he meant to give this to you. See right here? Your name is on the envelope."

Instantly, Krystyna recognized Martin's handwriting. Her fingers shook as she accepted the envelope. "What's in the envelope?"

"We've searched the contents. It appears Dr. Braddock wanted you to have a copy of his will, actually . . . this appears to be the original. And, he has included, for reasons that might make sense to you, a zillion handwritten notes. They made little sense to us. Also, there's a computer disk."

Krystyna and Logan made eye contact.

"Thank you." Krystyna said in a soft whisper.

There was little else to be done, all pertinent questions answered fully, the situation well under control, and the two officers were confident the investigation would be wrapped up in a matter of hours.

Later, the sun rose up over the snow-capped mountains, a great golden globe rising in a clear blue sky. The storm had passed. Samuel was the only one who had managed a few hours of sleep. The others, after showering and changing into clean clothes, sat in Orenda's kitchen, sipping coffee after a hearty breakfast. Everyone's eyes moved to the phone as it rang.

Orenda looked to Krystyna, motioning for her to answer the call.

Krystyna's hand trembled slightly as she picked up the receiver. "Hello." Her eyes grew wide as she paused, listening. "Yes, Jonathan, we're here waiting for your arrival."

She listened again for a long moment. "I understand."

She replaced the receiver, turning to the others. "That was, as we expected, Dr. Jonathan McCabe, the BOES board member. He and an associate, Dr. Kelly, have arrived in WHISPERING FALLS."

"I noticed," Logan said, "that you failed to mention Braddock's accident."

"I thought it best to wait until they arrive, tell them in person."

Logan nodded, catching the faraway look in Krystyna's eyes. "What's wrong, Krystyna?"

Thoughts coming together, Krystyna realized she had indeed heard a faint voice whispering to her that first visit to the FALLS; it had come from deep down inside her own heart. "I've decided . . ."

The doorbell rang announcing the arrival of the two BOES board members. Once the introductions were completed, the group assembled together in the living room, Krystyna explaining in great detail the events leading up to her desperate calls for their help. She then went on to describe the drastic incidents which had occurred over the last twenty-four hours. As expected, both Dr. McCabe and Dr. Kelly were shocked to find that Martin Braddock was dead. More than that, they were

282

horrified to learn of his experimentation and the use of holograms in his treatment of phobias. They were intensely concerned about the emotional and physical well-being of the patients who had been treated at SERENITY.

Dr. Jonathan McCabe, a silver-haired middle-aged gentleman, reached for Krystyna's hand. "I'm terribly sorry about Martin. A tragedy, I'm reluctant to say, that would have happened sooner or later. Martin was hell-bent on a reckless road the day I met him, close to twenty years ago. Nevertheless, I must confess to you the use of holograms instills some rather exciting prospects."

"How do you mean?" Krystyna asked with some reluctance.

"True, holograms are a rarefied industry. But, several major cities in the mid-west are presently undergoing experimentation with sophisticated holograms. Interactive movies, you might say. Empirically, they are being used to project the image of a state trooper's vehicle, situated along a heavily used road, pretending to monitor the speed of passing cars. Of course, it's not real, but the hologram of the state trooper's vehicle looks real. I'm told this experiment has been highly effective, as you might well imagine. The dollar savings in equipment and manpower alone could be monumental, staggering. That's merely one example. And, Martin told you the truth when he explained the government has worked with holograms for the express purpose of brainwashing. They've already had years to refine this immensely persuasive method, labeling it political warfare. However," Dr. McCabe groaned, "you didn't hear that from me."

Dr. Theodore Kelly leaned forward from his chair, his eyes clear and bright under thick gray brows. "Krystyna, you mentioned that Dr. Braddock left you his notes?"

"Yes." Krystyna glanced over to Logan. She then reached to a nearby table where she had placed the manila envelope Martin had intended for her. She extracted all the items from the envelope, placing them in her lap.

"You'll need this," Krystyna handed Dr. Kelly the computer disk. "It's a fair assumption that it contains all of Stephanie Roberts files."

"And these," Krystyna's fingers clung fiercely to a single crumpled corner of paper. She was hesitant to let go. "You must understand that Martin truly wanted to help mankind. Please, I urge you; find it in your hearts to make some good come of Martin's work."

Finally, Krystyna let go of the notes. A sense of relief showered over her. Now, the people who mattered could take charge of cleaning up after Martin's madness. They would know what to do, and how to do it. They would trace the patients who had been treated at SERENITY, with an offer of free counseling and aid. Wounds would heal, hearts would be mended, a new hope envisioned. It was a good thing, Krystyna thought.

Clearing his throat, Dr. Jonathan McCabe stated, "Krystyna, I've always known that one day you would call me. It was inevitable; Martin, a maverick scientist, a deceitful Jekyll and Hyde, a creature of the night."

Thumbing through the notes, Dr. Kelly laid a hand on Dr. McCabe's arm. "Maybe so, but the man was brilliant, Jonathan. Pieces missing here and there, yes, yet he's touched on something very profound here."

Dr. Kelly reached for his briefcase, extracting a laptop computer. He loaded the computer disk, and once he opened the first file, he was lost in the dizzying information, oblivious to the others.

"We'll check back with him later." Dr. McCabe said, nodding to Dr. Kelly. "Krystyna," he continued, "Dr. Kelly and I have been authorized to establish a recovery program here in WHISPERING FALLS for the patients whom Martin treated. Maybe I should say the patients that Stephanie Roberts maltreated. At any rate, we are ready to proceed with . . ."

"I can help you there." Krystyna said, handing Dr. McCabe the remaining object from the envelope. "Here's Martin's last will and testament. I suppose we could say it's appropriate now.

I'd like you to read it over, but for the sake of time, I'll simply tell you that he named me the primary beneficiary of his estate. It's impressive, as I'm sure you'd expect, knowing Martin. Then again, you also know me."

Krystyna smiled softly. "I've decided that SERENITY will close her doors. There you will find the facilities and land needed for your recovery program. She's all yours, you and the BOARD OF ETHIC SCIENCES."

Logan grinned from his position at the fireplace.

"I'd like to think," Krystyna continued, "that Martin's home would make a suitable lodging, perhaps with some modifications, for staff doctors and other employees who will be working on the project. It's close location to SERENITY is a plus. I'll donate what ever you need to return to those patients what was taken from them. I know you can trace the patients; you have ways . . . ."

"You bet we do." Dr. McCabe said. "Ways which will include tracing the infamous Stephanie Roberts, another exploiter of human weaknesses."

Krystyna smiled. "We can hope the patients returning will again call WHISPERING FALLS their home." Her eyes misted over. "People were happy here, once."

Dr. Jonathan McCabe was clearly surprised at Krystyna's generous offer. "I'm amazed and confused, but I could never turn down a helping hand. Thank you, Krystyna."

"I want to help, Jonathan. And I will. You will too, starting with young Samuel Reed."

Orenda and Garrett exchanged smiles from the loveseat. Logan, his thoughts whirling, stared at Krystyna.

"You see, Jonathan, I've taken quite a liking to this little town. It's become more like home than . . . well . . . I feel that I belong here. I want to rebuild, repair the damage, give back instead of take."

"Besides that," Krystyna continued, her smile soft, "I have . . . family here." She looked to Logan. "I'm hoping also . . . a husband, and one day, children."

A mixed blessing, Krystyna thought, her coming to WHISPERING FALLS. First bitter, then sweet.

THE END

About the Author

After working twenty years in the medical profession, Louetta Oney's pursuit of publication began in earnest. Understandably, as a medical transcriptionist, she tired of typing other people's words. It became far more important that she write her own. *Bittersweet Serenity* is her third book, and she is currently writing a fourth, another mystery.